WHAT DOES IT
PROFIT A MAN?

WHAT DOES IT PROFIT A MAN?

Jon Bulgari

Published by JB Publications

© Copyright Jon Bulgari 2020

WHAT DOES IT PROFIT A MAN?

All rights reserved.

This story is a work of fiction the Beales Family is real as are the details of Family origin and Name, the Author has had no contact with any of the Italian or American Family since 1950. Most of the WW2 incidents did occur with the exception of the realization of great wealth unfortunately. The role of the Russian President is fictional, the incident with Bernie Ecclestone is accurate as remembered by the Author. The incident in Piandelagotti with Dino Lucarotti is fictional. Any other resemblance to actual persons living or dead, or actual events is purely coincidental.

Condition of sale

ISBN 979-8-570-94180-9

Book formatted by www.bookformatting.co.uk.

Contents

Dedication

Dedicated to Camillo, Tommy, Lina, Karen, Nikki and all my Family especially my long suffering wife Carol without who I would never have typed the first word. A special thank you to Forte Dei Marmi in Versilia which should be on everybody's Bucket List with only a few of the Restaurants mentioned.

1

Tommy Beales closed his eyes and waited to wake up from his exploratory operation, he thought about his beloved wife Lina who passed away from Dementia in a care home a year ago. They had been childhood Sweethearts years before the War, as second Cousins in an Italian Immigrant family in England. Robert their first `born had died in a car accident on the week of his eighteenth birthday in the car Tommy had given him as a present. It was Tommy`s car an Austin Healey 3000 drop top in pale blue with wire wheels, Tommy had been to Italy and back in it several times and knew it was a sound car.

Robert was going to say goodbye to his girlfriend as he was due to report on Monday to the Army base at Aldershot to start his National Service. He said to Tommy the night before "love the car Dad but it is too fast for me, Tommy laughed and said "use a lighter right foot, the acceleration can get you out of trouble sometimes but you don't have to use it"

Robert suffered from hay fever, the thinking at the time was that he went into a right hand bend too quickly, possibly had a sneezing fit, over adjusted the steering, hit and mounted the verge, then a tree, rolling over on the canvas roof with the car catching fire. There was no anti roll bar in those days. A motor cyclist going the same way stopped and tried to get Robert out, but he mercifully was unconscious and the flames were too fierce with the possibility of an explosion, so the man had to abandon his brave attempt.

For years after Lina would not drive in a car, she said she

could see Robert coming the other way towards her. She refused to drive with Max, her youngest son, as he drove like an out of control racing driver, much too fast for her liking.

Mixed memories came flooding back to Tommy in dream like sequences War time situations when he was in France, one time when they were bivouacked in the north in a Normandy village. He as the officer in command stayed with the Mayor and his family. The Mayor had a beautiful daughter Camille eighteen who took a shine to Tommy and after a full French festive feast of a dinner, to celebrate the Liberation and two fine bottles of local wine, they went for a walk before retiring for the night.

Tommy had just put his light out when his door opened quietly and Camille got into his bed. For Tommy this was hospitality beyond his wildest dreams, his first bath in months and the amazing meal was more than he could have hoped for, but thinking tomorrow could be his last day alive gave an urgency to surrender to a warm girls tenderness, in such comfortable surroundings. They made love for hours climaxing several times, never speaking a word until Camille left as dawn broke, leaving Tommy fast asleep. Tommy`s convoy stayed another day and were ordered out next morning back to the nearest depot then up to the front line again.

He replayed an incident just after the war when he was setting up the coffee bar for Camillo his Father in Law in Bournemouth, he had it refurbished in American style and the Yanks who were stationed nearby loved it, so it was packed all day and open till 1am in the morning. When all the pubs emptied out,that was the place to be, there was quite a large Polish ex pat group in the town and they liked a drink at the week end, they could be a problem.

It was a Saturday night, Tommy could see it as he relived it again, he was serving behind the counter with his manager Charlie an ex Paratrooper with a 52 inch chest who worked out, he had arms like tree trunks, when three of the Poles came in drunk and abusive despite already being barred, Tommy was out from behind the bar as they came in Charlie followed. Tommy told them they were barred and they were to leave, they tried to push past swearing and cursing about how the English had abandoned them to the Russians and Churchill had broken his promises to them, the biggest one took a swing at Tommy, he easily avoided it and returned with a quick and solid left uppercut which came from behind Tommy`s left knee with his full weight behind it. The Pole went head over heels out of the door landing on his back bleeding from his head, where he had hit it on the kerb outside. An ambulance arrived and took him off while Tommy was with the police.

This morphed into the time Tommy was in Lerici on the Italian Riviera where he had bought a coastal seaside apartment and they were filming "Some Girls Do" a James Bond spoof film with Richard Johnson, an English heart throb actor of the time. Tommy got on well with Richard and was shot as an extra in the beach bar scenes, with some of the top totty of the day.

Before he could enjoy any more dreams, he heard "hello Mr. Beales, how are you feeling? the operation is over it went very well, you are in recovery rest up, the Specialist will be in to see you shortly"

"Tommy how are you feeling you will be a bit groggy till the anaesthetic wears off you have a drip in for any pain relief you require, though it should be minimal. It went well and gave me the answers we needed, I need you to get over to Italy get some R & R plenty of seafood and homemade Pasta, fresh air, then we can look at taking the final step at the end of the Summer in Lausanne, we will keep you monitored every month till then. You will be able to go home in a couple of days."

"Thank you, Geoffrey talk to you soon."

The mobile tinkled gently on the bedside table Max looked at the message "Don`t be late tomorrow, 7pm. sharp."

He turned back to the girl stroked her arched back, from the nape of her neck to the base of her spine, he gently tugged her long thick mousy blonde hair, tied up in a plait, Greek style which touched the base of her spine, he admired cupped and tweaked her toned butt cheeks and tanned body, his middle digit deftly slid past her dark pink sphincter, lingering on her vulva as she parted her long legs, turning over to him checking to see if he was still erect, as her nails floatied over his pubic area, as he took his hand off her soft baby down blonde landing strip.

"Like a butterflies kiss" he sighed "sorry you can`t stay, you were good today but I have a meeting in an hour" he said.

"Better than your other favourites?"

"Maybe, Charlize."

"Give me a clue."

"If I told you that you might not work so hard next time. What really turns me on is when I know you`re doing something for me you might not like doing, but you do it as though you do, that is a skill and a turn on."

"How do you know whether I like it or not?"

"My intuition, I back it every time, it`s never let me down yet, girls aren't the only ones with feelings, don't believe everything in the girly mags, some of us guys have it as well" he gave her a playful slap on one of her toned and muscled cheeks she didn't flinch.

"Why do you use Agency girls? you could get any number of permanent mistresses, I thought that`s how it was in Italy."

"Not so much now, but I like to be with a beautiful woman, take what I want and work to ensure she enjoys herself, then drive away. A mistress I would have to consider her mood, keep her happy, wonder who else she is fucking. Agency girls I can change as and when I want, never wonder what else they`re doing. Its rude to say but it`s almost like a cold that comes and goes, the need to try someone new, enjoy it then forget about it, till the next time. At my time of life, I need to take my pleasures where I can. Some men have other needs, more than a wife is willing to provide or even that a husband could dare to ask, from one. It doesn`t make it right it`s in the genes a flaw, no doubt.

Men are hunters no? No one is permanent, only my wife the

mother of my children. I've been happily married for thirty five years with two amazing girls and a lot of freedom, it's a good life. I remember someone saying once "if it floats, flies, drives or fucks renting is best "that was just after his multi million pound divorce settlement, which goes to prove its easier to make money than lifelong relationships that work. My Dad always used to say son don't get involved with anyone or anything you cannot walk away from in five minutes, except in business."

"Were your parents happily married?"

"My Dad was, my Mum idolized him, would never hear any criticism, but she could give him hell then he would walk on eggshells for the rest of the day, or go golfing. He visited girlfriends, or picked them up for drinks when he wanted their company, she knew about some of it but he came home every night to her. Like a good Italian wife she kept the home going for the family. Why do you do, what you do?"

"It's a long story, I studied, got my Law Degree and Masters, worked at a top London Firm fell in love with my married boss, then he got careless, his wife found hotel receipts in his wallet kicked him out, sued him for half of his assets, I was out of a job and none of the firms we dealt with would touch me."

"Did you love him?"

"I got over him after a month, then a friend introduced me to the Agency I did a couple of meets, which went better than I expected, I realized that it could give me the money I wanted and more, but gave me the freedom to make my own choices. I now see no more than half a dozen regular wealthy clients who have my private number, I top up from the Agency if I need a holiday or I'm changing my car and I am content at present."

"Have you been in love since?"

"I fell in love with a boy from a very wealthy Arab family, very good looking, we were getting engaged, a big party was planned so I could be introduced to the entire family, I spent the day at the hairdressers and beauticians, bought a stunning designer dress in Chelsea put my best jewellery on. My man picked me up and we went to their luxury house in Knightsbridge, fifty or sixty guests. It all went swimmingly well until his Mum introduced me to one of his Uncles, who I immediately recognised as an infrequent client of mine with a foot fetish. He avoided me for the rest of the evening, but all contact with my boyfriend stopped immediately, he was sent back to Quatar I never heard from him again. So, I learned business is business, keep privacy separate and in some cultures family is everything."

"I`m glad it worked out for you in the end, a hard lesson to learn when you are young Charlize. I need to leave in an hour, we can share a bath, I have a meeting downstairs then I have to be in Bournemouth by 10pm. You can take your time, let yourself out. I`m only here for today, I will call the Agency, next time we can make it an overnighter, if you`re free, or maybe a trip to Paris or Berlin."

"I`ll make sure I am Max, I look forward to it"

Max ran a bath had a relaxing massage for ten minutes with a couple of glasses of Dom Perignon then went down to the bar for a cocktail, before dinner. The Carlton Tower had just reopened after a refurb with its Casino, he wandered in but it was too early, only two Roulette tables open, which was his game. When he first married, he had worked at the Palm Beach in Mayfair and got interested in the game and worked out his own "system" which usually gave him a good return. He smiled as he remembered his first shift as a dealer.

He was put on Blackjack and his first punter was a wealthy American who motioned to the Pit Boss he wanted a closed table, so no one else could play at his table, he was a known big hitter, so the table was duly closed to other punters. Max shuffled the four packs, placed them in the shoe, the punter placed an aptly named Joker card facing the wrong way in the shoe, which would create the need for another shuffle when it was drawn, he dealt the punter a card to all five boxes, the punter flicked over two £100 chips from the small rack he had got from the cashiers desk, which would be £1000 in today`s money, Max dealt the second card, another £200 flicked across to Max. Max dealt his third card to each of the punters boxes, two went bust as Max had nineteen the punter had drawn a twenty one and two blackjacks. The punter made no comment, pointed to three boxes and placed £200 at the edge of each box, Max dealt the first card to each box, an ace and two queens, the punter doubled up, Max dealt the second cards, three blackjacks. As he paid him out he said, well done sir! he went to deal another first card, the punter beckoned him closer and said "son a word of advice, just deal and never say well done, to any customer, you have no idea what I've lost on the other tables, before I came to yours", gesturing for the Pit Boss he said "I want another dealer."

Max apologised as the Pit Boss told him to take a break.

Next morning Max pulled up at the offices of Camillo Corporate Holdings in Canary Wharf in his Ferrari Red California Corsa at 7.50am, Jimmy the Concierge, who had known him as a boy quipped "Nice to see you Mr. Max, early today? the meeting doesn't start for another ten minutes, you are covering for Mr. Michael today, how is your Dad? on the mend I hope?"

"Hi Jimmy I could hardly be late in this little lady, could I? look after her for me. Dad is doing really well I am seeing him later in Bournemouth l will give him your regards"

The meeting convened at 8.00am sharp, on the 20th floor in the main Boardroom the minutes were all discussed as the various Divisions presented their progress for the quarter, targets achieved, with any new business. The purchase of the new Craft Beer Companies had gone smoothly and essential cost cuttings with consolidation would be achieved by the third quarter, with additional anticipated annual profits of £15M. The profits from last year's purchase of the worldwide Hairdressing and Beauty Salons Franchise group had performed above expected growth figures, and was deemed a successful acquisition, with the Far East division gaining an increased 8% net profit year on year. The Debt Management Division in the UK was doing better than forecast, with the purchase of two smaller companies, one specialising in Marine Acquisition involved in luxury yachts, the other in Private Aircraft repossessions.

The company Accountants had booked an early lunch at The River Cafe in Hammersmith as they knew it was one of Max's favourites. He felt this could be the highlight of the trip, many of the best chefs in the UK had started out there and gone on to make a success of their own Restaurants, the décor was like an Airport lounge in Milan, all glass and stainless steel with an enormous Wood Oven at one end, in full public view.

The Chefs all working away behind the main counter, running the full length, with always one of the owners on the pass scrutinising every meal before it went out, just like in Italy. The staff all trained to the highest standard, knowing every item, in each of the perfectly presented dishes. The produce flown in weekly from their own suppliers mainly in Tuscany, the cold meats infinitely superior to anything in a supermarket in England, Max's favourite tranche of Turbot in the Wood Oven and the speciality Desserts all homemade, every bit as good as his favourite restaurants in the old homeland.

A quick call to Alexis telling her what a great lunch she had missed "Are the girls back yet? I thought they might have been back for the meet at Dads, I'm on my way down to Sandbanks now"

"How did the board meeting go?"

"Same old, same old, good reports on the girls from everyone, are they back yet?"

"No darling you know them, probably tomorrow, Karena left a message saying there was a delay at JFK and she's staying at the Airport Hotel for the night, back tomorrow, Nikki won't be back till Sunday, she went to New York to meet up with Karena and Roberto when she left Melbourne, apparently they're looking into something serious that's come up. Drive carefully see you soon, call me on the way back, ciao Caro, Baci a Papa."

On leaving River Cafe at 2.30 pm he decided to kill an hour at The Sportsman off the Edgware Road another of his favourite watering holes, the roulette wheel was kind to him as usual, Alexis, Nikki and Karena`s birthdays rarely let him down and he left after an hour £4k ahead of the game thinking life truly was not so bad after all.

As he opened the Corsa Red V8 lady up on the Great West Road he loved the surge in the base of his spine as the 4.3 litres kicked in at the blip of the throttle, past the Old Fullers Brewery out of Hammersmith, dancing effortlessly round the too numerous roundabouts and heading for the M3 and the south coast, he wondered what Dad had on his mind this time.

He pulled into the services at Winchester for a quick loo stop and a bottle of chilled water. It started to rain as he came out of the services, he quickly tapped the button to close the metal roof put on his seat belt and slid onto the approach road to the M3 saw the monster Tank Transporters and Army lorries in convoy on the inside lane with the petrol tanker in the middle lane overtaking he could have let them all pass but that`s why he liked his boys toys, when he saw an opportunity to leave the rest behind why go at 70mph in convoy, when you can leave them all watching you fade into the distance.

In the instant he floored it to get through the gap and jump all three vehicles he had not seen the motorcyclist on the outside of the tanker he swerved right a fraction avoiding the motorcyclist, heard the bang at 100 mph as he corrected his swerve, realizing he had blown a rear tyre, his rear offside, his correction too little too late made him clip the motorbike. Spinning a full 90 degrees, he hit the central safety barrier careering across the carriageway, going airborne as he mounted the motorbike, rolling with his front end embedded in the tracks of the Challenger Tank on its transporter, which slewed to a halt on the hard shoulder, at which point the car fell on its roof as the chaos of crashing vehicles ensued behind.

Max`s last thought was, I am going to be late.

Tommy Beales got the call from his Head of Security, Able

Truman a former Mossad operative now responsible for all the UK families security, it was 6.30 pm. Tonia had just pulled up outside in her Maserati SUV, Michael was just getting out of the Company Helicopter a Sikorsky S-76 C one of the top rated copters in the world, comfortably seating 16 and used by the Royal Family, so 100% reliable.

"Sir Able here some bad news, I will be with you in five minutes I am overseeing the family meet tonight as usual, I have two operatives covering the perimeters of the house now, Mr. Max has had a road accident in his vehicle on the way to you, its serious"

"How serious? is he alive?"

"At this moment yes sir."

"Where is he now?"

"He's been air lifted to Southampton University Hospital one of two major Trauma Hospitals in the South of England."

"Get here ASAP you're qualified on the Sikorsky, Michaels just flown in, get your two operatives to stay covering the house and send more to the Hospital now."

"Already dispatched sir, pulling in now."

"Michael, Tonia, the meeting will have to wait till I get back later, Max is in hospital in Southampton, a road accident, I'm flying there now with Able to get a handle on the situation, then I'll be back, stay put till you hear from me, two of Ables men are here keeping an eye on the outside, open up to no one."

"We need to come Papa."

"That's a definite no, till I know it's safe, once I have found out what happened, maybe you can go tomorrow, let's go Able."

"Sir, I have logged us in with Eastleigh Airport, we are only ten minutes to the Hospital from there."

As Tommy buckled up his first question was "How sure are you it was a road accident?"

"99.9% sir, army vehicles were involved no civilians directly, a motorcyclist was killed peripheral damage, that is from the traffic police attending."

"Have you spoken to the Surgeon?"

"No sir they have put Mr. Max into a coma, to stabilise him till morning, when they hope to do tests then."

"Traffic Superintendent said he was lucky the Army were there, just back from Afghanistan, battle trained medics in the convoy, went into overdrive probably saved his life, they had done a great job before the Air Ambulance arrived."

"Ten minutes ETA Eastleigh Airport sir."

"Thanks Brian."

"Able I've never asked you before, I know your CV inside out, service to Israel etc, but tell me how come a good Jewish boy has an English Christian name, not spelt Abel the Hebrew way, your surname, was it after the American President?"

"That's easy sir, my parents named me Abel which in Hebrew means worthless or vapour. Worthless made me achieve more to prove myself, vapour my teachers said suited me as I vanished so easily from classes I did not want to attend, they said I should have been named Ninja, but Able had a better meaning as I grew up, so I just changed it myself, the Family name Truman originally came from a village in Latvia, Russia called Trumany so when the family emigrated they dropped the last letter?"

"Well you certainly grew into Able, I will vouch for that."

"Thank you sir, on the approach in now."

Professor John Lindsay Senior Neurological Trauma Surgeon at Southampton Trauma Hospital came back into his office past Able, outside on the door "Mr. Beales sorry to keep you, I have just left your son who is holding his own at the moment."

"Mr. Lindsay I need a snapshot of where he is right now, to process what needs to happen from now on going forward, I understand he is in the best hands as we speak, you need to do your tests tomorrow for your analysis of what is doable, but I need to know how soon he can be moved to the best facility worldwide, you understand, money is no object whatever is needed, he must have from tomorrow."

"As I said Mr. Beales he is in the best possible place at this time, he is in intensive care, we have induced a coma till he stabilises, to nominate the obvious physical problems, he has a shattered right clavicle, the seat belt snapped it like a matchstick, his right arm likewise, his left leg broken ankle, chipped from being trapped between the brake pedal and accelerator on impact.

We can see from the injury to the left of his head, that he expected to impact something in front of him, as he contorted his head to the left while grappling onto the steering wheel to the last seconds, the metal strut on the head rest went deep inside his left ear, as far as we can see at this stage destroying his inner ear.

On the right side the entire roof of his car collapsed, either on impact or when it fell to the road after the collision, the right side of his head has received major trauma, he is severely concussed and we have stopped the bleeding from both ears, we hope to be able to do more tests in the morning, to find out more, but at this time moving him anywhere would be the greatest folly possible. If you would like to see him now please come this way."

"Certainly thank you."

"When will you have answers if you are able to do tests in the morning?"

"Within a day or two depending on what we find as we move on Mr. Beales."

"Thank you sincerely Professor, my friend and our family Surgeon at Royal London and Barts will contact you in the morning, if there is anything you need contact me directly, I will ensure you have it by next day or earlier, thank you again until tomorrow."

2

"Tonia is everything good there with you? no problems? when are the girls due back?"

"We are fine Papa how is Massimo? have you spoken to Alexis she is in pieces she has not told the girls, they are flying back early tomorrow."

"We are on the way back, Max will be fine, he has been a lucky boy again, the Surgeon will know more tomorrow, tell Michael to cancel all meetings for tomorrow you both need to stay over tonight, I will be with you in half an hour."

"Able can you get a female operative to Alexis`s for a week or so, anything she needs call me, I will speak with her when we are home."

"Done sir, seeing as there is no contra indication from outside sources, I recommend downgrading alerts to amber, if you agree."

"For tomorrow yes, we will speak then, there are issues coming up shortly whereby your expertise will be key, we need to be away for a couple of days to Russia."

Tommy put a call through to Sir Geoffrey on his private number "Geoffrey it is Tommy here I need a favour, it`s my boy Max again, he has nearly totalled himself in a car wreck on the M3 tonight, it made South Today News, you may have seen it, he is in Southampton Trauma Hospital, Surgeon is Professor John Lindsay, can you liaise with him tomorrow, anything he needs etc etc. I need the boy back ASAP, now is a bad time for him to be out of it, I would appreciate your thoughts tomorrow, as soon as you are up to speed."

"I know John well, he is a top man very experienced in Trauma Operations, he has written many Theses which are in use in Hospitals worldwide, now. Your boy is in good hands Tommy, I will speak with you tomorrow, I have not seen you at any of the Charity do`s this year are you still active?"

"I lost Lena last year, so I do not do the charity rounds anymore, not too clever myself to be fair, she used to love the auctions, it was more about seeing who paid more or not enough for her contributions, as it happens."

"Sorry to hear about Lena, Tommy I knew she had been unwell, I will call you tomorrow without fail."

Tommy got out of the Sikorsky at the rear of the Helipad the security lights were all on, Albie his live in butler was waiting and saw him into the large open lounge living area, overlooking Poole Bay with Brownsea Island to the front,Tonia and Michael leapt up as he entered.

"How is he Dad?" asked Michael, Tonia was crying and managed to reiterate the same.

"He should be fine, his Surgeon assured me" Tommy repeated what Able had found out from the traffic Police, then he told them Sir Geoffrey would call him tomorrow with the latest update after tests.

"Albie would you get me a bottle of the Cannonau from the cellar, one of the latest vintages, young and light unlike myself, something else for you, Michael and Tonia? bring a well chilled Cristal up please Albie, it helps me to sleep, then take the rest of the night off, I will have breakfast at 7am in the morning please, on the veranda if it`s warm."

"Certainly sir."

"Michael, Tonia, I have to get down to the reason I asked you to come down today its important, on more than one level and now with Max......anyway, hopefully we will get answers on that situation tomorrow, I need you to take in what I am saying, then questions at the end, va bene?"

"Sounds serious Dad, you`re not getting married?"

"No Michael it`s more serious than that."

"Last week, I had my annual check up in Geneva, I had endured a few waterwork problems which I put down to my age last year, then some migraine type headaches and vision problems, like everyone my age I have been told to cut back on food, drink, everything, the usual. They did CT & MRI scans with a dozen blood tests. I had to stay over for results next day, so they gave it to me there and then, they want to start a new course of Radiotherapy & Chemo with a new drug, but for now that`s out of the question.

I have a Stage 4 Brain Tumor, which is 9 cm now and is inoperable, I have been lucky in one way, as the symptoms have for me been attributed to old age, by my own self diagnosis of course."

"Pappa Noo!" Tonia screamed, Michael went white " its treatable though Dad no?"

"They have put me on opiates for pain management, the prognosis is not good."

"How long Dad?"

"Six months maybe, if I am lucky."

"But you don`t look ill Papa."

"I have been lucky in that respect darling, they want me at the clinic tomorrow for more tests and to see more specialists, but with Max and the other problems that will have to wait, we have more important issues to deal with."

"Nothing is more important than your health Papa, tell him Michael."

"There is no time for dwelling on possibilities, Michael, now is not the time for me to be ill, our position within the Gruppo Camillo Banking Finance Organisation is being challenged. While I was in Geneva last week, I met with the other three shareholders, Roman sent his Chief Finance Officer, its most unlike him to send someone else, ostensibly our Russian friend wants to realise his Holdings in our Banks, as he believes he no longer needs to belong to the Organisation.

Reading between the lines I think the Russian Government is leaning on Roman, they want what he has, it`s his turn for the thumbscrew treatment. Over the last few years the Oligarchs have either been forced to make bigger contributions to the State Central Funding Office or had to get out before they are brought to court on false embezzlement or tax fraud claims.

The American Shareholders are uneasy but still want us to keep it all together to continue as before."

"And Italy?"

"They are 100% with us for continuance, no surprise there, the way their top five banks have performed over the recent years."

"What are the terms of severance if a shareholder wants out?"

"There is nothing written down, it was never deemed necessary, always the majority ruled since founding the Organisation, we all agreed if someone wanted to leave they could walk away, but they would leave all contributions to the Main Fund in tact with their original investment, as a minimum. They would have no further access to it, no one has ever questioned this it has always worked for and benefited all Shareholders."

"I have never known all the ins and outs of how our business got started or became so big as it is today, is now a good time to enlighten me?"

"Tonia mia belleza, your Mamma Adelina, rest her memory, was never involved in the business and the Heads of each Family have always been male probably a throw back to the old traditions."

"Times have changed now Papa, I even drive my own car now you know."

"Do not be so smart, I know you are, so here is a potted version of what happened to enable us to grow our business to where we are today."

"Top the drinks up Michael."

"Should you Dad?"

"It`s a bit late to worry about a drink now son. The family as

you know came from Piandelagotti in Emilia Romagna, N〔
Italy at the foot of the Dolomites, it was one of a series ol
villages, but now it's a thriving popular ski resort for cross
country skiing, we still have family there, they are the biggest
employers in the area, engineering contractors, now with licences
for snow clearance in winter which will keep them busy up there,
with rock falls on the roads as well.

It is a two and half hour drive from our Villa in Forte up
tortuous mountain roads, you barely get out of third gear. Single
track in places, with constant rock falls on the whole route. In
winter you could literally drive out to a village restaurant for
lunch and be unable to get home, because the road is blocked by
rockfalls, but it's a good living for the family, as they work for
the Commune on licence to clear the roads.

Originally the family with four sons, were scraping an
existence, when times were really bad between the wars in Italy
and all Europe, the brothers decided to emigrate. In 1919 your
Grandfather Camillo came to Scotland originally, before moving
to the south coast, Giuseppe went to Rome, Lodovico had a boy
Roberto, Stefano a Son called Gianni, they went to Chicago,
keeping in touch as best they could with Giuseppe in Rome being
the main point of contact.

Camillo as you know was Adelina's father, my parents were
cousins of Camillo and also emigrated from La Spezia, in Liguria
to England, at the same time. Your Mamma and I were third
cousins we fell in love and got married, with a special
dispensation from the Bishop as we were Catholics, nowadays
you can marry your first cousin.

Robert was our first born, then Michael followed by Max,
finally you Tonia, the image of your Mamma. We now have two
beautiful twins Karena and Nicoletta courtesy of Max and Alexis,
who are going great guns in the business.

I had a sister two years younger than me, but she died from
injuries from an abusive alcoholic husband, a year after they
married, you never knew her. Giuseppe in Rome had two sons

Mario and Piero who had no children, they never married. Mario was a Forensic Accountant, Piero was mad about cars and joined Alfa Romeo as a designer he was into racing cars, he left them and went with a friend to start a new Racing Team, called Ferrari, I bought some shares and still hold them for sentimental reasons.

Roberto had one boy Enrico who as you know is in The Federal Reserve in the States working with Roberto. He also has one girl Mia. Gianni had a daughter Aria and Giorgio who died in the War, he had two girls he never saw, Alessandra and Arabella they have a Trust Fund set up for them by all of us for them and their Mum.

I joined the Army when War was declared to see the world, your Grand Father Camillo was old school a hard task master, he could not read or write, signed all paperwork with an X. I worked for him in his businesses, Cafes and Fish and Chip bars, cash was king, then he bought property with undeclared money, his first house cost £700.

By 1960 he owned six houses, all rented out, three of them he let for free to girl friends, your Nonna Amneris never knew. When he died I administered his estate and went to get them out, but he had signed them over to his mistresses legally. He also bought a couple of Villas in La Spezia and an apartment block in Migliarina nearby, renting them out with a family cousin looking after them.

I had to work 7 days a week, hardly had a couple of hours to see your Mamma. I had to get away, so I signed up and took the Kings Shilling. As I was over 6ft the recruiting Sergeant said I could join the Guards, I said my hearing was not too good so he put me down for the Royal Army Service Corps.

When I turned up at Catterick Barracks in Yorkshire for basic training I was told to report to the duty Officer he said "What's all this Bulgarelli bollocks, don't you know we are at war with Italy boy? you'll have to change that, now! what name do you want to be called Smith or Jones?"

"Beales sir please, sir."

"Where did that come from?"

"I`m from Bournemouth sir, it`s a big department store in the town sir."

"Beales it is, not Marks or Spencers? that would never do for a good Catholic Italian boy eh? Sergeant put the change in on Service documents todays date."

"I`ll cut to the chase with my war effort I went from private in 1939 up through the ranks, lucky to get out at Dunkirk as a Sergeant, sent to Mons Officer Training College passed out as a Second Lieutenant, ending up as an acting Major in 1944 demobbed in `45. As we were making ready for the final push for Berlin, it was a race to get there first, between us the Yanks and the Russians to get control of the Capital.

Our American cousins were in the war of course, two brothers Mario in Rome, Piero was a design engineer for Ferrari he was excused military service as he was needed for the war production, he was used as a design engineer on military vehicles. Roberto was excused service in the war, with chest problems, he was working at The Federal Reserve in New York. Gianni was a Captain in U.S. Intelligence, Giorgio was killed in `45 when he ended up on the Swiss German border at Lake Constance, a month before the war ended, stepped outside his bivouack for a pee in the night, crossed the taped line for the cleared area and trod on a landmine.

We had kept in touch during the advance since Normandy, agreed one way or another we would meet up, before we returned home. We made it to the outskirts of Berlin then we were ordered to stop, we could not believe it, the Politicians were giving away our gains to the Russians, to appease Stalin. Churchill wanted to go on but the Yanks wanted to go home, we could not go on alone, France only wanted peace at any cost. We set up our demarcation lines, dug in and waited for the Russians to arrive, a Cavalry Division first, part motorised but still big on horses.

I was now an acting Major in Transport in the RASC and had

19

made it all the way to Berlin, losing a lot of good guys on the way. It was a crazy time, we ran the Red Ball Express from Normandy to Germany keeping the front lines supplied. Every Corp in action needed us, we were designated to different area, sometimes on a daily basis a lot of opportunities came up, for quick operators in the chaos, to make money.

We would enter villages as the Germans were leaving the other end, take over Chateaux, Banks, Churches, anywhere with cover for a few hours sleep, before going back for a reload then up to the front again. Squaddies would go into Chateau see a painting on a wall, could have been worth a lot of money, cut round the edge with a bayonet roll it up into their backpacks, making it worthless. One of my Sergeants was a stamp collector, he made straight for any office, ransacked any bureaux, checked underneath tables for hidden compartments etc, looking for stamp collections, he would go through them and would send any valuable ones home, to his wife in the normal army postal service. All post was checked and censored for sensitive information, but they never picked up on the stamps, he made a lot of money from what he found, after the war.

I became very friendly with a Russian Cavalry Colonel, Roman Orlov my opposite number, who encamped right up next to our demarcation line, but made no attempt to go further. We downed lots of their Vodka, they loved our cigarettes, theirs were unusable. Roman and I would go riding on their amazing stallions in the woods and we would go wild boar hunting in jeeps I provided, mounted with Bren guns, which seemed a more fair fight to me, the larger old males would ram a jeep head on even with a couple of rounds in them. At nightfall we ended up at his tent downing bottles of vodka, if the Russians were without some equipment they were never short of vodka, enough of that and the infantry would charge anything.

The final assault on the city itself went ahead, wave after wave of infantry and tanks followed the days and nights of heavy guns and aerial bombardment, nothing could hold out against the fire storm that enveloped the city. How anyone survived was a miracle, living underground like rats, eating literally shoe leather, cannibalism was not uncommon bits of rotting horse flesh, anything.

It was April 25 1945, Hitlers birthday it would soon be over, with Hitler dead in ten days.

We waited on the edge of Berlin for the final surrender to come, Roman and I would go out on recce patrols together. One day we came on a small Auto Union German staff car abandoned, with the engine still warm, it had no Regimental Insignia which was odd, Roman was on horseback with two guards I was driving one of my jeeps from the motor pool, with my own sharpshooter along for the ride. Shots rang out, my guard died instantly, both of Orlovs men were down, he managed to get off two shots and got both of the Nazi officers bodyguards.

The officer with the Deaths Head Insignia in his cap stood stock still, with his hands in the air "Kamerad, Soldaty don't shoot"

Orlov smashed the side of his head with his carbine, dismounted and was about to put a bullet into his head when I stopped him. There was a small woodsman's hut in the clearing, we dragged the officer inside, with his briefcase from the staff car. With Roman desperate to take his head off with his hunting knife, he started talking as he realized it was his last chance to live. His English was near perfect, he had been at a meeting in Hitlers bunker with Himmler and Goering, alone that morning, he was a trusted member of Himmlers personal bodyguard and had been given letters still unopened, to deliver to Albert Speer, the Nazi Armaments Minister, North of Berlin. Himmler and Goering had flown out on the last plane out of Berlin, before the final assault.

Both had sworn oaths to fight to the death to Hitler, but immediately Himmler contacted the Americans offering to surrender all German forces. Speer also contacted the Americans, stay with it this is where it gets interesting.

Goering and Himmler had worked with Speer on the massive requirements for weapons grade steel, aluminium and iron, tungsten and other essentials for the war effort which had to be imported mainly through Spain, which was neutral.

Switzerland being neutral was the designated country of entry for these goods into the Reich, dollars or sterling and gold were the preferred payment methods. Goering and Himmler set up private accounts in the two main Swiss Banks in Geneva, where they siphoned off payments to their private accounts, for the entire period of the war. Speer as Armaments Minister had sole authority for purchases and payments to and from Switzerland, for the Reich. Goering particularly was a prolific collector of art and gold, as well as jewellery, or anything transferable into Swiss Francs for his future. Himmler came a close second.

These private accounts were highly secret and available only to high net worth individuals. Set up at an original meeting with the Bank Directors. The Banks were forced to take both Nazi leaders onto their main Boards as Shareholders, in the Banks. They had little option as Switzerland was surrounded by the German Army on all sides and the Swiss feared occupation at any time, though this did not suit Hitlers plans at the time. The letters, in German of course to Goering and Himmler`s families explained about the accounts and how they could access them, in case they did not reach their families again. They both committed suicide in Allied custody later.

The Bank accounts were set up with a 16 digit numerical code with the last number rotating to the first number each month and a six letter code at the beginning and end which had to be changed completely, every month without fail, either with any two Shareholders providing the same codes by Telegraphic Transfer or three Shareholders. The third Shareholder had yet to be nominated in person with a validated National Passport and again with the same codes. Statements were produced but kept in strongboxes in subterranean vaults. Artworks were transferred to Bank branches in Lugano, the Italian Swiss Canton where they were stored in caves beneath the Alp foothills, in perfectly controlled temperatures, to preserve the items.

Any three Shareholders attending the Banks only had to produce the codes to have access to the strongboxes. Money could be transferred or withdrawn telegraphically only by using the entire codes, if the codes were not changed by the end of each month the accounts would revert to the Banks control. Whoever had the entire codes had total control over the accounts and were de facto deemed to be Directors of the two main banks in Switzerland.

The officer a Major in the Deaths Head Division, an elite personal Bodyguard Regiment loyal to Himmler had been ordered to telegraph new codes to the Banks before the monthly time limit expired, he was trying to reach a secure usable telegraph system, as no secure systems were still working in Berlin. He had no knowledge what the codes were for, what was in the family letters and sealed instructions to be delivered to Albert Speer, the entire codes were in his briefcase, at this point Orlov despatched him with a single shot to his right eye."

"Shall we get a bite to eat, or do you want me to continue?"

"Go on Dad, I am hearing new stuff myself, I thought I knew the history."

"Hang in there Michael, Roman and I knew this was our moment to make the war work for us, we had been through a firestorm of hell, lost good friends and seen enough horror to last several lifetimes, on a much bigger scale than any of the Mafia battles in the old country. We saw an opportunity to change our lives forever, I knew what we needed to do, we had ten days to comply with the time limit at the Banks.

Roman had orders to return to Moscow in ten days as his Regiment was being pulled back to Poland in two days time. His Divisional Commander was taking him as his Attache to a planning meeting in Geneva with British American and Russian top brass, the great Russian General Zhukov, the only General to never have lost a battle, headed up the Russian group. He was the only military commander Stalin trusted, he had won the battle of Kursk in `43 where over 6000 tanks fought the finest Panzer Tigers to a standstill. It broke the capability of the German Panzer Commanders and was a major turning point in the war, Zhukov went on to organize the final assault on Berlin, he was promoted to Field Marshal after winning the final battle for Berlin in 1945. Orlov had been at Kursk he had served with distinction, being commended to the High Command personally by Zhukov.

I had a two day compassionate leave to meet my other cousin at Lake Constance, to bury the remains of cousin Giorgio.

Mario was coming up from Rome, Piero could not come but we were going to meet as promised, when the war ended after all.

Roman and I took the code details, changed the new letters for the code and we agreed to meet at the Hotel D`Angleterre on the shores of Lake Geneva, where I had arranged to meet my cousins, we would then visit the Banks in Switzerland."

"Dad, surely the smart move would have been to remove Orlov, then just meet your cousins."

"Mike you never met him, he was not a man to take on, awake, or asleep, I once saw him jump off the back of the jeep we were in and finish off a badly wounded wild boar, with his hunting knife, when I said, why not use another ten rounds from the Bren? he said he deserved a better death, he fought well, he charged the jeep head on, Cavalrymen respect strength in an enemy.

Also, more importantly I owed him my life on several occasions, luckily you have not been in that situation when you owe the rest of your life to someone who was there at the one split moment taking a decision to stop your immediate death, but that`s for another day.

I needed to speak with our cousin Roberto in the States at the Federal Reserve, for urgent advice, this was a mind changing situation, full of potential, at the same time a potential for disaster, if it was handled badly, I believed the odds for success were in our favour, but we had to move quickly.

I need to move this epic on now, we've got a busy day tomorrow. We met up in Geneva, Mario from Rome was now in the State Finance Police, working on a Government task force vetting any Fascists who were thought to have salted away stolen assets, the State now needed to help rebuild the economy, the war in Italy was done. Gianni from the US in Military Intelligence and Giorgio was the brother we were having a Service for that evening.

I outlined my idea to Mario and Gianni both, in detail, they were 100% on board, I explained what was involved and agreed we would see the Chairmen of both Banks the day after, as I had set up appointments before we arrived in Geneva.

Its estimated today that Swiss Banks hold over $6.5 Trillion in assets or 25% of all cross border Global Assets. Even today with all the Governments trying to collaborate to stop money laundering and getting a unified banking code to stop it, the Swiss still remain one of the most secretive banking systems in the world, they actually invented the idea of Banking Secrecy and wrote it into Swiss Statute. They make all the right noises about Global Compliance, then ignore most of what's agreed. Michael you are the top man in our Global Hedge Fund business, only last month the two biggest Swiss Banks were fined several hundred millions of dollars for knowingly laundering funds from clients associated with terrorist connections. We severed our connections with both Banks years ago "It's business, we had no knowledge or proof the funds came from any illicit source, having done our due diligence" was the cry from them and so it goes on till the next time they are caught at it again.

The Chairmen of both Banks were surprised to see us, as they knew we in no way resembled Himmler or Goering, but to their credit they were completely unflappable, as I put my proposal to them. Firstly we demanded our Passports be registered as the new Shareholders and Directors, myself Gianni and Orlov changing the identification codes there and then. My well rehearsed speech to both Chairmen went down like a lead balloon, but they realized with the three of us all in different Military dress uniforms and Mario with his Italian State Finance Police identification we were serious about what we were saying.

I put it to them that we all worked for a Special Allied Intelligence Task Force, tracking hidden Assets of the German High Command.

We as the bearers of the codes were the acting beneficial owners of the Accounts concerned and Directors of both Banks concerned. We would continue to operate the Accounts as part of our ongoing investigations to establish if any outside sources were involved that we needed to be aware of. I asked for updated current details of all holdings in each Bank. They had anticipated this request and had a variety of folders on a separate table in the room.

In a most matter of fact manner the Chairmen went through the folders in detail explaining that these Secret Accounts were not included in the main Fiscal Revenue and Accounts of the Banks as they had Offshore Special Treaty Status and as such did not require disclosure to the Swiss Revenue Authority, briefly both accounts in the first Bank had a total of cash reserves in Swiss Francs, US Dollars and Sterling a little over £15Million, with Gold in Bullion form to the value of £8Million, cut and uncut Diamonds to the value of another £6Million also Artwork stored in Lugano with an assessed value of around £15-£20Million all of this at the exchange rate at that time not todays value. The second Bank had total cash reserves of £12Million and Assets of £10Million in Gold Bullion and Diamonds.

I notified the Chairmen that we would be transferring some of the Reserves, but for their cooperation they would receive shares in the Bank which received the deposits. Orlov in perfect English explained should there be any problems with transfers the various Governmental Departments of the four Nations would immediately be appraised of the full details of the Accounts and how they had been so well endowed, with Swiss connivance, they would most likely end up at the Hague as war criminals, or worse.

At this time we all thought it was simply theft by the Nazi hierarchy, from the looted occupied countries, to feather their own nests, a year or so later, we learned a lot of the Gold came from the victims in the concentration camps.

The Chairmen of both banks realized their best option was to maintain the status quo and their freedom, also to comply with my proposal was to their benefit and they duly completed the identification details as requested, the only comment being "We are business people gentlemen we hope to have a good working relationship with you all, for the future."

"One final item, Herr Director we require four separate amounts of Swiss Francs each to the value of 40,000 cash as we are only here for two more days."

"Gentlemen a pleasure to meet you all, the Chief Cashiers desk in the main banking hall will have the envelopes ready for you by the time you reach his section at the far end of the main entrance, I look forward to hearing from you shortly with advice for any transfer instructions."

On leaving the bank we agreed to meet after the service for Giorgio in my hotel room at 9pm, to go through the days events and make sure we were all in agreement with my ongoing plan, to make the most of our current situation, as quickly as possible.

The service for Giorgio was at The Notre Dame Church near the station in Geneva, it was a small private Mass.

Unlike Italy, Switzerland is mainly Protestant, but there are many beautiful Catholic Churches as well. Orlov being Russian Orthodox attended and was glad to be able to have some private time in front of a Crucifix, without artillery going off or the threat of imminent attack. We left and headed to my hotel, the D`Angleterre where I had organised a luxury supper for us all in my room, hot and cold buffet with champagne and seriously iced vodka, with strict instructions we were not to be disturbed, only for the supply of more drinks if we rang reception.

The room was a large double with a sofa, drinks cabinet and

small ensuite with bath, shower and toilet in, they had put a round table laid up for four with the buffet next to the table. I opened three bottles of Louis Roederer Cristal Brut by which time Roman was on his second tumbler of Mamont Vodka which he informed us came from the oldest distillery in Siberia. Unusually, it was made from Malt with a crisp and clean taste, served nearly frozen as it had a really warm after taste, strictly senior officer tipple only.

After proper introductions all round I wanted Roman to take the floor to my Cousins and give them a brief history of his journey to date, so they could understand where he was coming whereby he had a very different culture to our own in Western Europe."

"Friends I start by calling you that, Tommy and I have become brothers in a short time living together, close to death on several occasions, each saving one anothers lives on more than one occasion. For myself I am a Cossack from the Don region, after the Bolshevik Revolution there were Red Cossacks and White Cossacks, the Whites supported the Tsars and were mainly from wealthy landowning families and were virtually wiped out by Stalin in a de Cossackization programme, my family moved to Moscow and joined the Reds. As soon as I was able, I joined the Red Army, a motorized Regiment but we still had horses and with my love of them from my family life on the farm, where Cossack babies are put on horse back before they can walk, I quickly got on in my Regiment and was promoted. I had to work twice as hard as the others, as the Commissars appointed to every military unit kept a special eye on me, as I was a Cossack, part of a minority ethnic group not especially sympathetic to the Bolshevik ideology.

They were there to instil party principles and policies and to ensure we all toed the party line, what you would call brainwashing. I excelled in my military studies, learned to speak English and waited for the war to come, which we all knew would not be long. When it was declared I was a Sergeant in a Reserve

Regiment outside Moscow. Our frontline troops were no match for the Panzer hordes that attacked from Poland capturing and destroying Soviet Divisions in an unstoppable onslaught, our Armies retreated destroying everything behind them, as with Napoleon, in the last attack on our Motherland.

Stalin replaced General after General, changing his plans with no coherent strategy and without any clear strategy that made sense. I was sent to a one month Officer training course in preparation for an offensive my Regiment was taking part in. The Commissars were shooting as many Officers and men as the Germans were. Stalin told the Army to fight to the last man, in completely untenable positions, promotions were made quickly, to fill the gaps in all the front lines. My Regiment was sent to the front and we were quickly outgunned with our inferior mechanized Divisions, I lost good men and comrades and was lucky to survive a fall back to regroup, as winter started to come in, at Stalingrad our second largest City.

Hitler wanted to capture it at all costs, firstly because of its strategic value, but also of equal importance, it bore the name of his most hated enemy. We were being supplied by the Americans with heavy Armour, coming from England by sea, without these supplies we would not have survived. By now Stalin had sacrificed millions of troops and the Germans had annihilated millions of civilians as well. Stalin had been building up Reserve Armies behind Moscow, with a new Commander in Chief Marshal Georghi Zhukov, a former Cavalryman with a whole new way of thinking, having studied the tactics of the top German Commanders, Rommel in North Africa and Guderian their best Tank Commander in the West.

Hitler helped us at Stalingrad, as he refused to allow the Sixth Army under Von Paulus to escape encirclement, when they were fought to a standstill, with no supplies reaching them, the Luftwaffe could not get through to the troops, in the remains of that great City, they had no food left and were virtually counting their last ammunition. Hitler had just appointed him Field

Marshal, urging him to fight to the last man assuring Von Paulus he would send reinforcements to relieve him. Though they could not now break out through the impossible depth of our winter snow, as well as being encircled with our surrounding, now well equipped Armies.

I was in the 65th Army led by General Chuikov ready for the final assault when Von Paulus arranged a ceasefire, with unconditional surrender of all his forces, on January 31st `43. General Schreck surrendered the Northern Sector in February `43, we took over 24 Generals and 100,000 prisoners, an entire Army Group, the largest ever surrender of a German Army in history, the starving remnants of the mighty Wermacht Army group of 400,000 men, who had fought for five months in -30 degrees in the winter months, it was the beginning of the end for the Wehrmacht their all conquering invincibility was destroyed.

I was in the great Battle of Kursk commanding 6 tank squadrons before ending up north of Berlin, at our designated latitude in the Battle Plan. That is where I met Tommy and we became comrades and friends. The rest as you like to say, is history, back to you Tommy."

"Thanks Roman, coming back to the present, I have thought this through day and night for the last ten days and having run the basics through with Roberto, with the Bank Accounts now available to us, we can go on to set ourselves and families up for generations to come. We are going to need all our collective family skills. After I put my idea to you, we must agree we are all in, or we can all go our separate ways, with a mountain of money each, with no need to consider this idea again, there is not much time to decide.

As I said we have all the skills within our families to get what we will need, Roberto in the States is calling me tonight, at midnight our time, with what we will need to take my idea forward, so Roman we need to have clear heads when he calls."

"Tommy when we went into the Kursk Salient against 3000

Panzers I had had two bottles of Vodka in the final briefing and my attack plan worked as I proposed. My Squadrons had the highest kill rate on the day, with least losses in our centre of fire."

"I know you Roman, but hopefully there won`t be any guns crashing in your ears to keep you concentrated on what`s going on, this time."

"Net problem brat, he said, pretending to blow me a kiss, it`s not as rude as it sounds it translates to "no problem Brother."

Mario, because you are in the Italian Finance Police you will have access to and knowledge of upcoming moves, which could damage what I propose we do, likewise Roberto, in the Federal Reserve in the States will have priceless knowledge on upcoming moves, for business and investments worldwide. Gianni, your move into your new job in Banking in the US with Lehman Brothers when your demob arrives, is perfect timing for my project.

What I propose is that we split the Swiss Assets four ways British, American, Italian and Russian. We need to remove the majority of the Reserves to Banks of our own individual choosing, under our own individual control. We keep 5% where it is in the oldest Banks in Switzerland, as it gives us a proven track record with impeccable banking affiliations. It will be more difficult to convert Artwork for example, as its original ownership will be traceable so could not go to the open market, but when the dust has settled there will be private buyers who will want them at any price, for their own private pleasure, not for public display.

Mario could eventually unearth some of the unsaleable Artworks, during his ongoing investigations for the Italian Financial Police, he may even get a promotion. Diamonds cut and uncut will also be apportioned to the individual accounts, they will increase in value and should stay in individual banks under individual control and could be used as collateral for loans."

"Sorry Tom this is all sounding great, but my Bank in New York isn`t used to me depositing millions of dollars, from an unknown source out of my suitcase."

" Gianni I get it this is where my call to Roberto will give us what we need, bear with me I will come back to this in a minute.

I suggest keeping 5% in the Swiss Banks in the Organizations Account to keep the Chairmen onside, for their own personal, at least until their demise, it's not in their interest to divulge our agreement or keep any record of it. Under their own Banking Secrecy Laws they would never live long enough to come out of jail for breaching confidentiality on Accounts past or present. We select one main bank, we all agree on, then deposit 50% of the remaining funds into it, with each of us as Directors and Shareholders of the Fund.

This Fund can be accessed for business loans only, proposed by any Director repayable within an agreed term, at nominal interest rate say 5% granted by majority vote of the other Directors, one veto means no loan. So your planned purchase needs to be sound and remember you all have a veto. Capital and Interest repayments into the Fund must be made quarterly in full. Your profits will come from your operating revenues, your repayments must be made on time, or come from your own reserves if your investment fails.

Coming back to your comment Gianni, my call to Roberto was to get his advice on the safest home for our golden egg, something he has a lot more knowledge of than any of us, it's called Offshore Banking.

Any of you can take your share now of £1M each in cash, or one third share if you join my venture for major growth and profit. You need to decide before we leave in two days time, because we need to move quickly and get the funds into secure accounts of our choosing. You can live anywhere in the world happily for the rest of your days, but we are all still young men and we can build something together that we can create an amazing future for our families, for years to come, with chances our parents never dreamed of, we can link up or go it alone, the choice is yours Roman and I are both in."

The phone rang at exactly 00.01am.

"Reception sir, a call for you from New York."

"Put it through please, can we get some more ice, thank you."

Roberto explained various options about possible Offshore Banks with the contacts he knew, who were actively looking for investors in their Countries, he was able to get some time off, to introduce us to key people in the business. I asked him to be ready to set up some meetings in New York in a months time. I had received papers notifying me of my posting back to England, as I had already decided I didn`t want to stay in the Army any longer. I had been offered promotion to full Major, if I signed up for a permanent commission and another 25 years, but I declined as, I had other plans.

I thanked Roberto and told him I would call him in a few days, to go through what we agreed later that night.

"Tom let us hear more on this idea of earning more money from a fortune that is already in our hands."

"Mario we know what some of our countrymen from the old country have created in the U.S. the Sicilians, from Castellamare have built an empire across the States built on bootlegging crime, gambling, racketeering, prostitution and drugs.

The FBI under Hoover tried to take them off the streets after their turf wars, especially in New York with the Five Families. The Families then got together to calm things down and formed the Commission to make their enterprises legit or at least more business like, with less blood on the streets. The Government offered the Capos, bosses, immunity from jail when war broke out, if they contributed to the War effort with their contacts back home, which they did, but now it`s over they will go after them all.

I am suggesting we go much further than the Families, without the blood and without the illegal enterprises. We are all clean with no criminal records, War veterans with virtually unlimited funds between all of us, in Offshore Accounts with virtually our own Banks and the ability to create our own personas.

The opportunities now in rebuilding all the broken countries England, Germany, Italy, France and the other European occupied countries with Japan and South East Asia are staggering. Roberto has the heads up on the U.S. who are now investing some $40M in a Loan Scheme called The Marshall Plan to help rebuild the remains of the European and South East Asian countries without which the landscape and infrastructure would stay devastated for years to come. They will make a profit on this of course. Where they were starting to get back up from the Great Depression the war had taken many millions, in funding the men and munitions built up by the Government, the public had also helped raise millions in War Bonds.

For people like us with Capital who can move quickly, with the right connections, that will be our opportunity. We have funds to set up businesses in any country worldwide, with our funds in Offshore Registered Companies and Trusts, untraceable deposits, money creates wealth and its ours for the taking, when the opportunities show. We need to set up profitable investment funds in our respective countries, for now Roman it may be safer to keep yours in Switzerland until you can find a home for your money in Moscow, if they ever allow Capitalism to take root there. Mario you and Piero will know who you want to use in Rome or Milan, or maybe keep the Banks in Lugano on side as it's on the Italian border. Gianni, I'm coming over to see Roberto soon, I will decide where I'm going to get involved after I've spoken to his contacts, he mentioned Panama as being a prime mover looking for investors."

"Tommy, what exactly are these Offshore countries and how do they work?"

"It's new to me as well Roman, but take my word for now, they exist and have done since Roman times. The Romans would reward certain areas in their Empire by making them tax free zones, to tie them to Rome by Treaty, or to reward them as Allies in battle.

Getting to where we today. After the First World War,

Switzerland of course was neutral. The countries involved needed to rebuild, so raised taxes in all their countries. As the Swiss did not need to do this, they kept their tax low, attracting investment from all over the World on special terms. That was the start of modern Offshore Banking.

3

Businesses in highly taxed countries registered their Companies structure in say Switzerland or Liechtenstein and then paid the lower tax rate of the Swiss Company, on earnings made in higher based taxation countries they operated in, it was called a double taxation strategy which was enabled by a Treaty between both countries, the rich got richer.

Mario, you must have come across this in your work for the Finance Department?

"Yes Tom, in some of my dealings with foreign banking."

"Why did you not say?"

"You didn`t ask and I did not want to stop your flow anyway."

"Coming back to where I interrupted myself, Roberto works in the Federal Reserve, he will be able to see what the US government plans are for rebuilding projects in Europe and South East Asia, he will be able to find out who the preferred contractors will be and so on.

Fortune will favour the fast movers and we are in a position to get it done. The main contracting companies will all be quoted on the various stock exchanges, so we can buy Shareholdings in the major players, small at first, until we either get more inside information on any strategic moves or before any announcements are made on major projects in any of the countries we operate in.

The point of us doing this together is we are in different countries, but with one aim to enrich us all to the benefit of us all. As the main fund grows, so we can all fund different projects in our own countries, or around the world, but with a central link governed by all of us, all equal in the main fund. We can also link individually with each other, if your project is vetoed by the Board. We need to remain anonymous and not attract media attention, especially to our connection with each other, this is a major benefit of the Offshore Banks, anonymity.

Gianni said count me in, Mario said yes, but wanted Piero on board. He was a Design Engineer with Alfa Romeo who were getting ready to launch a new assault on the Grand Prix World, as the races had been suspended since 1939. 1 was sure Roberto would agree and we needed him to get organized for our set up as discussed.

The logistics meant all the families relocating, as existing neighbours and friends could present problems with our individual lifestyle changes, no one had any problem with this.

We agreed to travel to the Banks in Lugano next morning, to tie up the Italian Banks, Roman had to attend his first meeting with the Zhukov contingent next morning, so he could not come. I had arranged with the Concierge to send a couple of ladies of the night from a local agency to Romans room at mid night, they would be waiting for him, I told him there were a couple of "hot water bottles" in his bed, as the Concierge called them, for any guests with a sensitive nature. We agreed to meet Roman again next night at mine as we were due to go our separate ways the day after. Suffice to say it went well in Lugano and we were set up as the new Account holders and Shareholders in both Banks. It was starting to come alive.

"Tonia, Michael it`s 2am, we`ve got an early start tomorrow, let`s call it done for now, we can pick it up tomorrow night, you need to be down for 8am breakfast, I need to make some calls, then off to Southampton Hospital, for updates on Max, we can all go in the Sikorsky unless you`d both rather drive."

"No Papa we`ll come with you, if you`re coming straight back, I need to see Alexis and bring her up to speed."

"Certo Carissima, a domani, see you both prompt at 8am."

Professor Lindsay greeted Tommy, Michael and Tonia in his office, an assistant went for coffee for them all "Mr Beales I'll get straight to it, Max is stable, out of intensive care, I am waiting for latest results from CT and MRI scans, which should be with me in about half an hour. If all is well we can bring him out of his induced coma and he should be able to talk to you, later today.

Before you ask, he cannot be moved at this early stage, until I have the all clear on the brain scans, he was severely concussed on impact, there are some metal fragments in his skull that must remain, until we have a clearer picture, I would not extricate them at this stage, we need to be sure there is no neurological damage that requires immediate intervention now."

"What are you anticipating Professor?"

"I am proceeding on the side of caution, the area with the fragments is a complex part of the brain, sometimes it is of greater benefit not to do the obvious and remove all objects, as it can create bigger problems, I would ask you to wait until I have the scan results in front of me, within the hour, when we can take a more considered decision on moving forward."

"We are in your hands Professor, we will wait in the canteen."

"I will send someone for you."

Tonia called Alexis with a positive update and Tom assured her Able would pick her up next morning, to see Max in Southampton, when he would be sitting up, desperate to get home to see her and the kids.

"Hello Mr. Beales."

" Tom, please Professor."

"Of course, Tom, I have been through the scans with my Consultant Radiologist and it is not as good as I had hoped, the scans have shown up the areas of remaining fragments and in laymen terms they present no immediate threat to Max`s well being or recovery, but they have shown up an Aneurysm and Tumor growing at the base of the brain."

"What can be done? how critical is it? is it life threatening?"

"He's not going to die Professor? please, you must be able to save him, your initial response was so positive, first thing today."

"Tonia and Michael, briefly, yes it is critical and its fortunate he came in as a result from the accident, the Aneurysm having gone undetected, could have burst at any time and would require immediate open brain surgery, we can with your permission tackle the situation today."

"Exactly what is the procedure Professor? what is the prognosis after the operation? and what after effects are likely? how soon before full recovery can happen?"

"The answers to all of these questions come at a later date Tom, I will explain what I need to do immediately today, as follows. The Tumor at the base of the brain I can remove with an Endonasal Endoscopy which is minimally invasive and removed through the nose and sinuses with a telescopic device with camera and lights I have had 90% success rate with the procedure."

"How can we be sure Max will not be part of the other 10% Professor?"

"Tonia, there is never certainty in operating in most critical situations, which this is, I can only say, for this procedure the majority of the unfortunate 10%, had other pre-existing conditions, which while they opted to go ahead, precluded the result we wanted."

"You mentioned a secondary problem, the Aneurysm Professor."

"Yes Tom, the brain Aneurysm may have been there a while and has not ruptured, I propose to tackle it first, by inserting a catheter into an artery in the groin area, as it has not ruptured the repair should be a straightforward procedure, had it ruptured we would need to do a Craniotomy which is open brain surgery and more invasive, with all the attendant higher risks, I am sorry I haven't got better news for you, but you will appreciate with the extent of Max's injuries and his current status we are fortunate to have him still with us. I will leave you for ten minutes to discuss what you want to happen and I reiterate we need to act as quickly as possible for Max`s sake, I am going to call Sir Geoffrey as promised, I will get him to call you on my line on my desk, please pick it up as it rings."

"He sems very positive Dad."

"Yes Michael, let`s hear from Geoffrey on his take before I decide."

"Oh God poor Alexis, expecting to see Massimo sitting up and chatting to the nurses, I need to stay with her for a bit."

"Good call Sis, what`s your thinking Dad?"

"I need Geoffrey`s affirmation to decide."

The phone rang "Tom, Geoffrey here I`ve just come off the line with John, he needs to act quickly, with your approval on the Aneurysm, then deal with the Tumor, I`m sure you`ve had his thoughts on where he is with what he needs to do."

"Yes Geoffrey, thanks, what I need from you is your best advice on the likely outcome for my boy, after Lindsay has done his best."

"Tom, I have known you a long time, so I speak to you as I know you would like it straight from the balance sheet, biologically the prognosis with John at the helm means Max is in sound hands and on a positive note John will get him through what`s needed, right now. The only caveat being as long as there are no major life threatening, other hidden problems to deal with, that appear during the route John takes at the time of the actual surgery. I say to you as a friend who understands the balance of chance in life and death, if it was my child I would have to go with Johns knowledge and skill and some prayers, to help him and Max for the next few hours. You will know what is best for you both, God Bless Tom, let me know, when you have the time."

"Thanks Geoffrey, I appreciate the candour, we will talk soon."

"John, thanks for the use of your office, I have one other question, can you say with any certainty what Max`s psychological state will be like after surgery?"

"An impossible question Tom, in cases like this there will be minor changes in some instances, possibly major in others, almost a different persona is one possible outcome but at this stage its Max`s life that is in the balance. What transpires after recovery is beyond my personal remit, suffice to say I`m sure you will see he gets the best help that is available in the world."

"John, please go ahead and do your best for my boy is there a private room we can use?"

"Tom, you can stay in my office as I will be operating, I will come to you as soon as I have completed the surgery."

"Thank you John, God speed."

"Able, once Max is back in his room I want two of your best on his door 24/7 till we move him, only hospital Staff or Police to get in, no Press. No comment to any outsiders.

I`m flying to St. Petersburg on Monday morning to see my old friend Roman, I`ll need you and one other to come, we go on the Company Jet with Panamanian Diplomatic Passports, no need for Visas entry and exit times already arranged, I`ll confirm details tomorrow."

"On it, sir."

"Michael we need to put a statement out for press release saying Max`s accident was beyond his control, the culprit was the exploding rear tyre, he is doing as well as can be expected, our family share the grief of the motorcyclists family, at his untimely demise etc. etc. and Max is expected to make a full recovery, in time. Please respect family privacy at this time, that`s it for now."

"Sure Dad I`ll text our Press office now."

"Papa I know you have so much going on at present, my best friend Lara is coming with The Mariinsky Ballet from their Theatre in Petersburg. She`s on her final season she`s 40 this year and she had an operation on her ankles last year, she can no longer do the practice sessions without drugs, they`ve offered her a technical teaching role if she wants it, she`s coming to stay, when their tour comes to London next month, to see a Consultant to the Ballet Performers at the Royal Ballet, I`m hoping I can persuade her to make her move here permanent and get her to move in with me, I could have hitched a ride and surprised her."

"We looked at a project there with Roman some years ago, one of the Theatres was going under and they needed £30M to renovate it, now I think there are 80 or more Theatres in the City they take their culture very seriously, for them it was a labour of love, too much of a long term commitment for us to get involved, I think Roman took some shares in it."

"We didn`t think the same about Disney Paris though eh Papa?"

"It was long term, you`re right Tonia, but 24/7, 365 day cash returns, is a different culture Carissima. I`m going there on business, besides Max needs you here and Alexis with the girls as well, I`ll be back next day I hope."

"Why are you having to go to Russia now Dad? surely Roman could have come to London for a jolly and catch up with you, especially as you don`t need the travelling now, with Maxi as things are right now."

"There will be a reason Mike? he couldn`t discuss it, as I wasn`t on a secure line at the time we spoke. I`m going to call David at Oxfords to see if they`ve got a table for a quick lunch, we won`t get anything till much later tonight. Able bring the car round please, we`ll only be an hour, Mr. Lindsay won`t be finished for at least another couple of hours, give his Secretary your mobile number ask her to call if anything changes, we can be back in 10 minutes, we can`t take his office up all day."

They had been back in Mr. Lindsays office for an hour when the door opened slowly and he came in out of his operating gown and back in civvies.

"Tom, Tonia, Michael your brother has come through it and is stable at present, everything went as I hoped with no hidden nasties to add to the table. The actual surgery and anaesthesia went well, he is now still under and in intensive care for the next 24 hours, you can see him as soon as he is transferred from theatre to a private suite, where he will have 24 hour monitoring I will be at the hospital until 8 or 9 tonight any retro change in his condition will come straight to me when I have left, of course I will attend if necessary during the night. Understand that with the trauma and surgery he has gone through he is heavily bandaged at present to ensure his sutures remain in place so he is not his normal handsome self, hopefully for not too long, I would ask if possible to let him rest. I don`t expect him to come round till the morning, we will keep him sedated overnight. I will be here at 8am in the morning after I have the latest results, I will discuss the next move with you Tom.

Early days but it went as planned, so far so good, get some rest tonight all of you I will send a Sister in as soon as Max is made comfortable in his room, for now I must see my other patients."

"Thank you John for everything, I look forward to speaking with you tomorrow."

Twenty minutes later they were all round the end of Maxi`s bed, he had tubes going in and out of his arms, his head and face were heavily bandaged with a breathing mask over his nose, he was hooked up to various monitors all bleeping away, it was good to just be in the room with him.

The sister checked everything was correct and said "Stay as long as you need, no problem, we will be monitoring him closely through the night, if you need any tea or coffee the machine is at the end of the hallway, there is no problem for your business colleague to have a chair outside the door of the room overnight", they stayed for an hour.

Tonia phoned Alexis and brought her up to speed, Able drove them back to Sandbanks checked security, then left for the evening.

Albie had prepared a cold buffet before he went off, laid up in the cold servery in the kitchen, Cannonau and Crystal at the ready, he left a note saying he had packed an overnight case for Toms departure next day.

"Right boys and girls it`s been a long day but positive results so far, hopefully we`ll get a better picture once Max comes round call me tomorrow if that happens, I'll be back tomorrow night most likely. I want to just briefly run through where we left off last nights family storyline in case anything happens and I never get to finish it with you both."

"If you think that something bad may happen, why are you even thinking of going Dad?"

"Always cover the worst scenarios then if it does not happen it's a real bonus and it gives you an extra spring in your step Mike."

"When we were in Lugano to see the banks we ended up in a Casino for a meal and l had a lucky run on my numbers, with my remaining Swiss Francs I ended up transferring 10,000Sf to my Midland Bank as it was then, now HSBC in Bournemouth, I messaged your Mum to treat herself and the family as I would be home within a few months, with some good news.

I came back to England in early '46 and was demobbed in my free grey suit they gave me, with some back pay and a thank you letter from the Head of the Armed Forces, saying I could use the honorary title of Captain for the rest of my life, I had other ideas. I went to Oxford street where the latest menswear shops were all the rage, I got an off the peg suit from Cecil Gee with all the accessories shirts, ties, shoes and even socks it felt good after five years in khaki battle fatigues, I wanted to go home in style.

Coming home was a strange feeling, after what we had seen and done, seeing how everywhere was different to how I remembered, seeing the damage from bombing on the train journey but arriving and seeing your Mamma more beautiful than ever was fantastic. Camillo was glad to see me back, to get straight back to work next day in the business, but I had to put him straight, which I had no problem in doing as I was now my own man. I explained to them both in detail what had happened with our good fortune, looking ahead to what I could see we could achieve, with the opportunities that we could open up for ourselves in the world. I knew I had to get to New York as soon as possible to set things up for us with Roberto and Gianni.

I took your Mum with me on one of the first flights out of London on a BOAC Comet Jet to New York, JFK airport as it is now known, which then took about fifteen hours with refuelling at Shannon in Ireland incredibly exciting. I remember it cost about £300 for a ticket, that's about £7000 today, when you think only 30 years later the flight time went down to three hours on Concorde, but after the fatal French crash, they abandoned the planes they lost their Licences to fly them and finally wrapped them up in 2003.

On the flight we talked non stop for most of the journey, I had asked Camillo to scout the Estate Agents in Bournemouth and Poole for a suitable property for us all to live in, with room to expand for a family and animals, close to the water, cash only.

We had a suite booked in The Plaza Hotel, Fifth Avenue, Central Park South, Gianni and Roberto were coming over for lunch and dinner next day, with their wives to take Mum shopping, she could not believe the shop windows we passed in the taxi from the airport.

Next morning the cousins and wives arrived, I had asked the girls to take Mum shopping charging it all to us at the Plaza, if they got back for lunch fine, otherwise we would meet them back in the bar for drinks around 7pm.

Roberto had set up a meeting with the Chairman of a large Bank in Panama who was actively in the States looking for big Investors, with Share Options available in the Bank itself, part of the benefit package was a Panamanian Passport, with permanent Residency for Investors and their families.

The meeting was set for 1pm, lunch at the Plaza in a separate VIP side room off the main Restaurant.

Roberto also had several interesting projects to consider Stateside that were going to tender shortly, with an up to the minute breakdown of the top 50 companies on the Wall Street Exchange, that he estimated were sound investment vehicles to get on board with, while prices were still low, waiting for growth to kick in. He would work on their current positions, assess the likeliest half a dozen, in their different categories, seeing how undervalued they were, factoring the likelihood of the growth effect if they succeeded in getting any of the large Government Contracts on offer.

He had just been appointed to the panel of the Treasury Department for Internal Affairs part of whose responsibility was to oversee any new awards of Government Spending, for the new drive to get American Growth on the move again, the Presidents promise to the people of America.

This is where it gets a bit messy, bear in mind I wanted to focus everybodys mind on the benefits to come, but to make it as simple as possible while combining us together in the overall enterprise.

Basically the families in the US, USSR, UK and Italy would each receive £6.5M in any international currency to a Bank of their choice. The Gold and Diamonds would remain in the largest of the Swiss Banks in separate Secret Accounts as collateral for future investments.

I proposed that Piero and Mario from the Lugano Funds paid one third of their share to Gianni while Roman and I paid a one third share to Roberto who I believed was the major asset in the whole scheme, so he proved to be. We did a calculation on all the readily available funds and came up with this settlement.

All four Regions in the fund would receive £6.5M or the equivalent in Dollars or whichever currency they desired to be paid into a nominated Account, within one month. The remaining £24M in Bullion and Diamonds would be split between a new main Offshore bank and the larger of the two banks in Switzerland in four separate Offshore Investor Trading accounts.

The new Company's name was agreed as Camillo Global Equity and Investment Corporation, Mario dealt with most of the top Law firms in Rome and Milan both Commercial and Corporate and assured us the new Company would be registered in Lugano, Rome and Milan by the following week, with serviced offices only at this stage.

The meeting with Raoul Esteban the Chairman of the Global International Panamanian Bank went very smoothly, we explained we were large investors in companies who had good track records but were undervalued in these difficult trading times, where we could see good positions, we could move quickly to make things happen and gain some very good assets and profits on the way. We were looking to expand our businesses in the States and South America also Europe, we were looking for a Bank with a forward looking approach to business.

Raoul explained his Bank was one of the oldest in Panama City and since the United States Government had given them special Offshore status it was a great time for investors to move in and get established in the area, as he believed Panama would become a number one choice for financial leaders in Commerce and Worldwide Dealings with the backing of the United States.

His bank was able to offer an International Trading Licence to operate worldwide from the Tax advantageous haven of Panama. He also thought we might be interested in opening an office in a new up and coming Offshore Licensed area called The Cayman Islands, a British run Overseas Territory.

I spoke with Roberto at length after lunch, and asked him if he would be making a deposit at Raoul's Bank, he affirmed he would and had already opened a Shadow Private Investment Account with them. I asked him to arrange a meet for me in Panama to open a Corporate Account, also to tie in a quick meeting in the Cayman Islands at a large Bank he could recommend for Private and Corporate Account Holders. Raoul set up a meeting with his Deputy to open my Account which had to be done with a personal visit, Roberto said he could come with me to Cayman as well.

I needed to get back to England to sort my base out and hire some experienced staff from the Corporate and Financial World. Mamma and I flew back to Heathrow and got a train back to Bournemouth.

I know today you can say everybody uses drugs, as though that's a good enough reason to join in. Kids, their parents, it's a social thing, thank god I never had the time for it or the inclination to even try it. My head was always buzzing with ideas that needed to happen right away, that was my drug.

Just taking taxis in New York seeing the Burger joints and Diners with their free and easy style made me realise there was a need for this style of eating back home in England. The Yanks with their music which had grown on us since the war in Europe, was now taking off in England as the young people wanted more freedom to think for themselves and to be heard by the grownups, it was a great time for change.

Camillo wanted to know all the ins and outs of course of the trip, I explained most of it to him and told him about my thoughts on modernising his Cafe and Fish Bar in Bournemouth and Poole which interested him and I hoped it would keep him busy and free me up for my own agenda.

I told him I'd get an Architect to do some plans to alter his two main buildings and see how quickly it could be accomplished. He had been interned on the Isle of Wight for a year as an Alien because of his Italian Nationality and there he had got friendly with a man by the name of Carmine Forte from the old country, he was a Caterer in London with big plans to develop a business all over England, he opened his first Milk Bars as they were called, in Regent Street and Leicester Square in the West End.

He went on to buy the Cafe Royal in the same street a few years later. He opened the first Motorway Services in England and he opened the first Restaurant at Heathrow Airport. He went on to found the Forte Hotel Group and at one time employed thousands of people in his businesses.

He was forced to sell his business eventually in a hostile takeover bid by Granada Group and was left with £350M. He retired and his son Rocco took up the challenge for his family name, now he has built and owns the Luxury Rocco Forte Hotels in various Cities round the World. Rocco`s daughter is Olga Polizzi a Hotelier in her own right, you know, Alex her daughter is on TV as the Hotel Inspector, che Famiglia meravigliosa Tonia certo?

Camillo had a contact number for Carmine but had never called him, I said I would give him a call and it would be good to go to see his operation in the West End, to see how he makes it work. I could also get going setting up interviews with Recruitment Agencies to start building my Financial Team, I set up three meetings at the Regent Palace Hotel, behind the Cafe Royal in Regent Street, in the West End."

"What car were you driving then Dad?"

"I waited till 1948 when Jaguar bought out their XK120 very innovative and aerodynamic, at that time the fastest car in the world, its top speed was why it was called the 120. I had a couple of American cars as well, then a car you will never have heard of the Borgward Isabella with a column gear change, German, also a French Facel Vega and BMW 1800 Ti all aluminium, with a Frazer Nash performance engine, it was so light, but the gearing was superb amazing on corners you need to ask your Uncle how it was.

I took Mike with me to London to look at an E-Type, I thought about buying, he drove the BMW behind a friend of mine in his E-Type. Mike had only passed his test 3 months earlier, he nearly lost it on a long sweeping right hand bend, as we climbed up a big hill with a 300 foot drop on the left hand side, with no guard rails. He was keeping up with us, my friend opened the E-Type up dropping a couple of gears Mike followed suit. I saw him in the rear view mirror change gear a fraction too late, he started drifting to the edge and the drop then I saw the suspension change, as he floored it out of trouble but he could have gone over, if he had braked.

Of course, he denied losing it but his face was still red when we got out of the cars. He did admit it days later and said as it happened, he remembered what I had told him once, sometimes when you are not sure if you will get out of a situation, drop a gear and flooring it will save you losing it, in the right car, but you need to know your car, so he admitted he lost it for a second or two, frightening the life out of himself.

There were restrictions on steel products for the home market, as we had to export or die, that was the Government drive at the time. Britain had borrowed millions from the U.S. and they wanted paying back, in fact it took us 50 years to make the final payment on the War Loans. As a favour to Roberto I gave him the nod about the new Jaguar and how they were earmarking 2000 of the first production run for the States, the price was going to be $4000 per car which was unheard of then, most of the top sports cars were around £1500 here. Anyway Roberto made sure a friend got the Import Licence, I went to Jaguar and explained to Sir William Lyons, Jaguars Chairman, I could guarantee the Licence and would be interested in a Concession for Europe and South America also Asia, that was one of my first export deals.

Do not forget what it was like after the War, Britain needed money to come into not leave the country, to be able to rebuild. One of the new Labour Governments top Economists went to the States on behalf of the Government to plead for a £8 Billion loan, which the Americans listened to, then refused.

They were very fearful of the Labour Socialists, which they believed were too closely aligned or sympathetic to the Marxists of Russia. It was only this fear of the spread of Communism that made them realize it was sensible to help to keep them out of Western Europe and Britain, by lending money to rebuild the economies that were shattered.

Churchills "Iron Curtain" was well and truly drawn across all the Russian occupied countries at the Wars end.

Incidentally Tonia, if you wanted to travel abroad you could only take £25 with you, that wouldn't get you far for lunch in Paris or Milan during Fashion Week today, for me luckily it wasn't a problem."

"Dad, I never understood why the people voted against

Churchill after what he achieved in the War, holding Britain together and bringing America in as well, It didn`t make sense to me."

"Tonia the people were sick of War, they wanted a change, the Labour Party under Attlee took power and started building the Welfare State, concentrating on getting the country back to work, they stayed in power till 1951 when Churchill led the Conservatives back for the next ten years.

In America they created The International Monetary Fund and The World Bank to help ensure the growth and ideal of Capitalism, with a stable set up of World Financial Institutions, as they realized they were the lead drivers of growth and prosperity in the world.

It was the Marshall Plan that helped the whole of Europe rebuild. America of course lent Europe and Britain some £14 Billion over the period with the supplies and Contracts going from Companies in the States, which enriched Companies and enabled them to grow and created some of the biggest US and worldwide names we know today, as many of them merged. The escalation in Technology and Defence with the Russian threat in the Cold War period was fast and prolific with Roberto`s contacts we were involved from the beginning, setting ourselves up as players to be reckoned with.

I had several meetings with Roberto in the States and with Business people in Panama and the Cayman Islands and decided not to enter the British Investment market during the Labour Government period, in any event there were more than enough opportunities Stateside and in Europe itself, so I deferred opening a British base till the next change of Government.

Michael how are the girls getting on? what are they up to now? it`s a while since I`ve seen them."

"Karena has just finished a three month Course in Data Analytics in the States, as you know she heads up our team in the Hedge Fund, on Sovereign and General Debt Purchase, Nikki has just completed a Secondment at an up and coming Hi-Tech firm in Japan and Australia on Data Analytic Algorythms and Business Intelligence,

This Technology is the way forward for the future of our business, we can learn things about an individual, or a Companies position in minutes, or analyse cause and effect on the play in specific markets.

Instead of teams of staff pouring over Data taking days or weeks, which gives us an incredible advantage over our Competitors, helping us make important decisions that need to be taken quickly, she has sent in a lot of exciting reports on results achieved in the last quarter."

"Fortunately that Technology is all beyond me Mike, but it`s good to know we are on top of it.

To bring tonight to a close as we`ve got an early start tomorrow, we bought this house here on Sandbanks on the front line, with this amazing view for £4800 in 1947 we waited for the one next door to come on the market, bought that, then the two behind in the `50`s which gave us the size we have today.

Once I`ve sorted Romans problem out, hopefully over the next few days, we can then decide the way forward with Max, I`ll see my Medics in Geneva, then go down to Forte for some R&R, we can all go over, Lara as well and Max as soon as he can be moved, we will know more tomorrow, I will call you from Petersburg around lunch time at the hospital."

4

Tommy, Able and Yuri, a former Spetsnaz Russian Special Forces Colonel cleared scrutiny at Polukinov1 Airport at St. Petersburg and headed to Romans Dacha ten kms. from the City centre.

Dachas were normally converted farms or small properties left unused after the end of Communism but were bought up and developed during Perestroika when Capitalism was encouraged by Brezhnev. They were generally second or holiday homes for Muscovites with money.

Roman had bought his ten years ago, a former Winter Palace for one of the last Russian Princesses, before the Revolution, small by former Russian Palace dimensions only having some fifty odd bedrooms, bathrooms, lounges and ante rooms all set in thirty acres with its own lake and moat in the French style, with a wide tree lined approach. One side of the property abuts the Fontanka River with its own Pier and massive embankments of Granite.

You can walk from here to the centre of St Petersburg, along one complete seven kilometre walkway, its particularly spectacular by boat and is known as the Venice of the north.

Able noted the walled turrets at every contour in the road behind the ten foot walls, with latest Hi Tech Surveillance Cameras, covering every point of possible entry. Two armed guards were at the impressive entrance columns with the Russian Eagle atop each one, highly ornate and gilded. He showed his passport and the gates purred open, to the two hundred yard gravelled drive, which stopped short in front of the ten yard moat, with the magnificent Palace in all its splendour filling the skyline on the other side.

Tommy asked Yuri what the notice said either side of the main entrance, over the access to the moat, he laughed "Do not enter the water unless you like Piranha" at this point, a ten yard tarmac covered metal bridge came out of a concealed inlet on the palace side, locking automatically onto the footings, where the party needed to cross. Able gingerly drove the Mercedes gently across the bridge up to the main entrance saying "James Bond really is alive and in Russia sir"

"Apparently so Able, it`s the first time I have visited Roman here."

"My name is Alexander please come in Mr. Beales, Mr. Orlov is eager to see you, if you will all follow me, staff will take your belongings to your rooms, he has asked me to take you to him directly, alone, your friends will be shown to their rooms, to freshen up after your long trip, he asks that you all convene in the Library in one hour, for lunch, informal dress if you please."

"Please lead on Alexander."

Alexander led Tommy through the magnificent marbled hallway with a massive double sided staircase, leading to the accommodation upstairs, every corner filled with beautiful sculptures, the walls adorned with landscapes and military paintings.

Going into the main salon or lounge, this again was a completely synchronized marble floor with marble columns the furniture all very Versailles, too ornate for Tommy`s liking, but all with no expense spared. Alexander led him down a corridor off the Lounge, stopping at a pair of fourteen by eight feet heavy lacquered 17th century doors, he held the door open for Tommy announcing "Mr.Beales sir"

Roman leapt out of his chair at the end of the library, the two full grown Borzois gracefully flowed in front of him, stopping and blocking Tommy`s advance

"Down Romy and Remy, Tommy my friend at last you are here, I am so glad to see you." after his monster bear hug he put Tommy back down on his feet.

"Roman, God it's good to see you, it's been too long, I see you still wear your Cavalry boots indoors."

"Always Tommy its part of my English Squire look, no? A drink before lunch Tom, some of my old favourite Marmont remember? we had a few bottles in Geneva the week we started on our adventure, or is it still Cristal."

"Marmont will be fine, plenty of ice please Roman, hard to believe but its fourteen years since that week at the end of the War, what we set out to do has served us all well."

"No question Tom, we will talk after lunch in depth, the two of us. Your friends can have a tour of the estate, I see you still have Able with you and one of our ex Special Forces Ops men, I know him by reputation Yuri, he was called the Mad Wolf, his Code Name was always Alpha 1, Leader of the Pack. We have much to arrange with little time, I'd appreciate their take on my security here."

"Are we secure here Roman, apart from the moat that is?"

"Everybody loves it except uninvited guests."

"We are totally secure here, I had the Palace completely rebuilt when I bought it, I have the latest Surveillance Technology and Counter Surveillance installed, every room is swept by my team on a daily basis, my staff are all either people I served with at some point, or sons of men I served with. Guests are unable to use mobile phones of any description on the premises or in the grounds, any signals are scrambled to be unintelligible except in my safe room, in the vault beneath the main lounge.

The vehicles are all armoured to withstand anti-tank grenades at fifty yards, with wheels that will drive for 100 miles on rims, if tyres get blown out, also individual oxygen inside for passengers and driver, in the event of a gas attack.

Two of the latest Alligator Kamov Helicopters with extras, in an underground garage locked and loaded, the only thing I don't have as yet is my own space vehicle. You had no problems at the Airport?"

"Nothing Roman, straight through. Are you in trouble? I thought you were uneasy in our last conversation I hope it`s something you can resolve, if there`s anything I can do you only need ask you know that."

"Thank you Tommy you`re right of course, as you suspected, I have a major problem, I can see only one way out but I will need your help."

"Anything old friend and brother what do you need?"

"I will tell you my problem, what I propose to do to resolve it with your help, the biggest ask is I need you to possibly put yourself in the target frame with me, at least until I am gone."

"Gone, gone, where are you going Roman? you will never leave your homeland."

"Exactly so Tom, the powers that be, here, now want me in Siberia for a long time or better still in the final furnace."

"I`ve heard what`s happened to some of the other big hitters in Russia recently, but you`ve always been careful what has gone wrong?"

"Quite simply President Chomski needs everybody`s money, he personally is one of the richest men in the world, worth in excess of sixty Billion Sterling, but he intends to stay in power and maintain his total rule, while embarking on making Russia one of the top two World Powers. The expenditure on modernising the Russian Army, the Fleets and Air Force alone will cost many Billions more than our present GDP, so he cannot squeeze the people like the old days and lose his populist support, he has to get it from the wealthy he helped create, he knows how much each one has. They were "invited" to join in his various investment projects, whereby he took a guaranteed Finders Fee from every investment, paid into his Personal Offshore Accounts, no doubt, in a couple of the Banks we own."

Alexander entered the Library.

"Alex get our guests into the Family dining room it`s less

formal, please seat them with drinks, Tommy and I will join them in two minutes."

"Tom, if you like to use my en-suite to freshen up, it`s the door next to the Presidents portrait down the end, by my desk, Alex will take the dogs out for their lunch."

"Roman may I use your Safe Room? as I need to call England to see how my boy is doing."

"Tonia hi, it`s Dad how`s Max doing?"

"Amazing Dad, he`s sitting up, the tubes are all out, not eaten anything yet, but he recognises us all, he`s exhausted of course."

"Let me have a word with Michael please darling. Hi Mike, better news on Max I am hoping to get back tomorrow night latest. There are some moves coming up here which I expect to quantify tonight, more about it when I see you. Have you spoken to Max`s girls yet?"

"Yes Dad, you need to hear what they`re convinced is coming up, they went to see Roberto and his son Enrico in New York, Roberto wants to meet with you as soon as possible."

"When I`m back Mike, we need to move the family`s security up to Amber alert, no one travels unescorted with no exception this includes Alexis, leave me to talk to her. I want us all to aim to be in Forte at the Villa within the next two weeks latest, where we can consider our next options, with no knee jerk reactions and we will make time for us all to come to whatever decisions we need to make."

"Dad, I`m due at the next Hedge Fund meet in New York in a week."

"Keep the meeting Mike, we will know what`s going on by then, we can change arrangements if we need to, at the last minute."

"Sure Dad, get back safely, see you tomorrow."

"Say bye to Tonia, love to Max, Alexis and the girls, a domani çiao."

"Sorry to divert Roman but my boy is out of danger and on the mend, I need to be back by tomorrow night if that fits in with your agenda."

"That would be good for all of us Tommy let us eat."

"What poor Russian food have we for our guests today Alexander?"

"Sir, we start with Marmont Vodka and with the finest Malossol Beluga Caviar on traditional Buckwheat Blini Pancakes and Creme Fraiche, followed by Finest Kamchatka Red King Crab from Alaska with the purest sweet white moist flesh, eaten on its own with nothing to distract the excitement to your taste buds. Finally, again a traditional Russian dish Pelmeni our answer to Ravioli, the lightest Pasta parcels filled with Pork, Veal and baby Wild Boar with a light jus inside each dumpling, topped off with a light bitter sweet sauce and a spoon of soured cream on top.

For dessert we have traditional Fifteen Layer Honey Cake with Hennessey Cognac 1920 and Louis Roederer Cristal 2006.

I hope you are all in need of refreshment Gentlemen please enjoy our humble offering."

"Excellent Alexander, please serve the Blinis with the Marmont now, then later we will have dessert and brandy in the Library."

Four bottles of Marmont later and half a dozen battles re-enacted, everybody was ready for Brandy and Dessert "The lunch was excellent Roman, you have done us proud, who`s for a Hennessey or Cristal? Able,Yuri?"

"Thank you sir, the excellent Vodka was enough for me today, I don`t want to miss the tour of the property and I am looking forward to seeing Mr. Romans private fleet of cars and shooting range."

"That goes for me too sir, if Mr. Roman is agreeable."

"Of course Yuri, I knew your father a little in Moscow, when Brezhnev was President, a good man your father, I was saddened to hear of his death. Alexander get the head of security to give the boys the Presidential tour wherever they want to go, Tommy and I will have coffee and brandy in the Library."

"Thank you Alexander, no sugar. So Roman, to continue from where we broke for lunch."

"Tom, several of the Oligarchs are in prison on trumped up charges of tax evasion or fraud they are tried in secret courts, no witnesses, then simply not seen again, their families are told which prison they have been sent to, but are not allowed to visit.

Their Assets in Russia are seized by the State, there is no appeal, you know a few fled to England, were left alone for a short time, then had what seemed like tragic accidents, Case Closed, by the British Police, Able and Yuri will tell you how easily it is done. Our State Secret Service wait for as long as it takes, no one ever gets away, the President has recently had "The pursuit and elimination by any means, of enemies of the State in any country", written into our Constitution."

"But you have enough money to live anywhere in the World, with friends in many countries, England or the US would welcome you with full Residency tomorrow."

"There are two reasons I cannot leave, as you said the Motherland is in my blood, bones and soul, I could not live away from Russia. The second and equally important reason is my Daughter Larissa."

"I never knew you had a daughter Roman, this is the first time you have ever mentioned her existence, how can that be?"

"After Stalin came Kruschev, I was still in the Red Army in Moscow, I was appointed Military Attache to Brezhnev who was second in command to Kruschev I was now a Lieutenant General, in '64 Kruschev was removed and Brezhnev became virtual President. He built up the Red Army to be the largest in the world and built up our Nuclear Armaments to the same level as the US, actually outstripping them in Space technology for a period.

Other parts of the economy were left out of the funding budgets, Agriculture and Health suffered badly. I had a Secretary Commissar appointed to my staff to report on my adherence to the Party Dogma, we became close, we kept it secret for both our sakes, Ludmilla was 28, a beautiful former Science Graduate from Leningrad, her parents died in 1940 during the German invasion in the War she had an Aunt in St. Petersburg. She had joined the NKVD Commissariat Internal Police, we became very close and she became pregnant, left the NKVD and had our Daughter, she went to live with her Aunt who was not married.

I had requested retirement but had been given a final Military Assignment, as an Aide to General Gorelov during the invasion of Czechoslovakia, which he felt was an unnecessary intervention, they wanted independence from Russia.

We went in on 20th August `68 with 2000 Tanks and 200,000 soldiers, fortunately the Czech Army offered no resistance, the people could not understand why we were there, but Moscow could not allow them to break away from Communism, as they saw the situation developing. Several hundred civilians were killed, maybe a dozen soldiers in the end. Our occupation lasted a year, the Dubcek Government replaced with a pro-Moscow team and we gradually withdrew our armoured forces. This was when Brezhnev created his edict that the Soviet Union had the supreme right to invade any Communist country, where Communism itself was under attack.

I returned to Moscow, retired from the Army and went to St. Petersburg to find Ludmilla, she had named my daughter Larissa, we had agreed to leave my name off her Birth Certificate.

Her aunt had died of Cancer and Ludmilla was in hospital with pneumonia, Larissa was being cared for in a home for ex Forces Personnel who would put any children out for adoption. I saw Ludmilla just before she died and swore to look after our daughter in her memory. In her few belongings was a necklace I gave her before I went to Czechoslovakia which she promised never to take off till I returned. I was so wrapped up in my military life, I could have got her to a clinic anywhere in the world if I had known she was ill, I had all that money sitting in Switzerland, but until I was out of the Army it was not in my thoughts, beyond changing the codes on the Assets I had left in the Big Banks."

"Don't beat yourself up Roman, we all regret things we did and didn't do, you can never go back."

"It's true Tommy, but it doesn't make it easier to live with. Anyway Larissa was adopted by a choreographer at the Mariinsky Ballet Company in St. Petersburg, so I knew she would have a good life in Russia, it is still one of the foremost Ballet Companies, their performers are treated like Royalty.

As a cover for myself after my involvement with the Military I set up a Trust Fund for Orphans of ex-military personnel who had served under me during my service years.

I was able to visit the parents or relatives who had adopted the orphans, so I eventually met Larissa and her adoptive parents at her new home in St. Petersburg and began to get involved in the Ballet world, wherever the Mariinsky was involved. I kept an eye on her as she grew up from a distance. When she was a teenager she was sent to Moscow to the KGB Training Academy for a year, before returning to the Mariinsky, she passed out with flying colours.

It was something the State required for any performers likely to travel to the corrupt Western Countries, to ensure they were fully indoctrinated in the Soviet States current outlook on the West, with basic training in assimilating any information that needed to be passed back to a Controller, it was all standard stuff at the time.

I bought a modest Villa here for visits and got involved in the Hermitage Restoration works as an investor."

"That's when you wanted us to join in the renovation of that other theatre years ago."

"Just so Tommy, I saw where the money for Brezhnevs military build up came from and knew as long as we were a State driven Economy there was no prospect for individual financial growth, things had to change. After Brezhnev, we had three different Presidents in as many years, the old guard were dying off.

That was when I visited you in London Tommy and agreed to

come in with you on several ventures in the United States, until we had found a love of Free Enterprise and a new style of Capitalism in Russia, in the `90`s, whereby we could buy into State owned Monopolies which eventually were sold off at knockdown prices to budding Entrepreneurs who knew how to grease the wheels of their good fortune, as you know we both made a lot of money in Gas and Oil.

When Chomski came to power in 2000 and up to now in 2008 he opened the floodgates for Entrepreneurship and made sure suitable contributions were made to his Offshore Accounts, from any and all sectors of the Russian Economy, the working one and the Illegal one, even the Criminal hierarchy realized they needed him onside and paid their dues, for which they were more or less left alone, unless they breached his red lines. Which brings me back to my current problem.

At a meeting with the Finance Minister last month he produced a spreadsheet of their estimate of my Worldwide Holdings fortunately they were wide of the mark, but accurate on all of my Soviet Investments.

He put it to me that my expected contributions to the Motherland were falling below acceptable levels, for our continued good working relationship, all my associates in Moscow were being squeezed to up their contributions. I was left with no illusion as to what would occur if I did not comply with the request, they have raided several of my Company HQ`s, removed documents, files and computers and slapped a temporary Court Closure Notice on the offices, alleging Tax and Accounting Fraud."

"Will you get a fair hearing in the Courts? will the closures carry on?"

"This is Russia not London Tommy, it`s Chomski`s Rules, in the end. I have decided to sell all my holdings in Russia, pay whatever contribution they come up with, I`m too old to serve in Siberia. I will transfer my Foreign Investments to you Tommy, my Assets in the Offshore Banks will be transferred to my

Daughters Trust Fund."

"Roman move to London, plenty of the Russian rich are already there, or move to somewhere warm, or the States."

"I will die in my Homeland Tommy, it`s where my heart and soul are, you`re an International Citizen with Italian and English blood, Panamanian, US, English and Italian Passports with family all over, I only have my love child who I can never publicly acknowledge, I know what would happen to her if they thought they could use her against me, in the blinking of an eye and as a warning to anyone else who thinks they are beyond their reach.

I have to tell you something now, I need your oath you will not divulge this to anybody else, until I am dead."

"Of course Roman, it goes without saying."

"Your daughter Tonia`s best friend and partner Lara is my daughter Larissa, but they must never know until I have gone. That is why I have no problem with transferring my Assets outside Russia to you, especially now you know what it means to me now, I trust you with my daughters life as we did with each others."

"Consider it done Roman, on all levels, you know if you change your mind you can come to England anytime, just give me a call with whatever you need."

"Thank you Tommy, at present my Passports are restricted by the Tax Authorities, I need the Account details to transfer my Assets to you by the week end, I will call you next week to let you know how things are going."

"Of course Roman, I need to get back to the UK tonight and get things in place for what you want arranged, also to get my son on his road to recovery."

Tommy came off the phone as he re-entered UK air space, heading for Bournemouth International Airport and home.

Able joined him "As of tomorrow I want all personal security beefed up to Red Alert no arguments from anyone in the Family, any problems come straight to me. We are moving Max to the Villa in Forte day after tomorrow, air ambulance to Pisa then converted Mercedes ambulance to the Villa, should take about an hour from Pisa. I need you to travel with him, I have to fly to the States for a few days then I`ll be back to the Villa. While you`re there I want a full complement of top guys at the Villa, nobody goes out unescorted not even for a coffee.

They will all be armed, I have spoken with our Police contact there Commander Luigi Berti a distant cousin, I have brought him up to speed and he is literally at our disposal, anything we need. We are licensed in Italy to carry firearms, for self-defence as there is a credible threat against us at the moment. Our Legal Team have faxed through to Luigi all he needs to cover the paperwork his end, but it`s important that you keep in touch with him on a daily basis, to update him on any situations. Also as soon as you`re insitu call him up tell him what time you expect me back and register all your guys with him, with their Passports obviously, they must be 100% clean, good with firearms and very experienced."

"Yes to all of that sir, I have at least four top guys known to me personally. I can get them to the Villa by the week end they are all ex military. What vehicles will be available there sir?"

"There are a couple of Hummers there, Max`s Lamborghini, my DB9 Aston, it`s a barely used 2003, that`s how I want it kept Able, a couple of BM`s and a Bentley Sport, all in ready to go condition, we pay a local Dealer to keep them charged up and Claude who lives in, keeps them turned over. Your first job after you`ve unpacked, is to check out total security on the site, contact me direct with any upgrades you think we may need, sufficient to defray a direct assault from up to a dozen assailants, fully armed. You can use your contacts to get quotes but they need to be fully installed by next week end."

"What kind of time frame are you expecting any situations to commence sir?"

"Not for at least a couple of weeks and maybe it could be a month or more after that, but you need to be aware and ready."

"Where is the threat coming from sir? so I may have an idea

of what specifics we may have to cope with."

Uunfortunately the Russians Able, from the highest level so all options are available to them."

"What support can we get from the local force sir?"

"100% within what`s legal Able any covert actions stay with us. The Russians came here in the `90`s and started buying up all the most expensive Villas, opened up night Clubs and took the drug business to a new level. It became known as Moscow by the sea. They are not loved by the locals as they think money is everything and they can do what they like. A friend of mine the biggest Estate Agent in Forte told me a true story, when the first Russians arrived with their suitcases full of Swiss 9000 Franc notes.

A husband and wife from Moscow went into his office saying we want the largest villa in town. Do you have any special requirements? Yes we need a helipad it must have at least 12 bedrooms, same number of en-suites, marble floors throughout, pool, tennis courts, gym and as close as possible to Gianni Agnelli. That`s not possible my friend replied. We will pay whatever your fee is but it must be near Signore Agnelli`s villa. Impossible says my friend. Why? asks the husband. Because he died over thirty years ago. They wanted to be close to the biggest playboy of his era, he owned Fiat, a Multi Millionaire Playboy, the first of his kind, but they had not read of his death.

In exclusive restaurants they would turn up in jeans and T-shirts order up most expensive wines and brandy and get drunk before eating, which never happens in Italy, throwing money on the table, when they thankfully left. They ride around town in Ferraris, Rolls Royces, with bodyguards in a limo behind the bosses. They park anywhere, upsetting the locals, walking along the streets they barge locals out of the way, even the elderly. They have no respect.

Eventually the Police sent in a Task Force squad with machine guns and full combat gear and closed the Clubs in the town overnight, the managers are still in jail, the clubs still empty.

Recently since 2004 the latest Russians have gone for property in land, they are buying in Umbria where they get more for their bucks. Those that remain are keeping a low profile in the town. Luigi has a good handle on them and their groups and what they're up to.

He has a link at Pisa Airport, the Harbour Police at Viareggio, Genoa and Milan Terminals as well, if any Russian or Eastern European Passports are put into the system he gets a message, also he is connected directly with all the car hire companies."

"That's good sir, we should get intel early, which will put us ahead of the game, how long do you anticipate being in Forte?"

"Until Max is back up to strength, then we will probably stay in Cayman for a few months, right now I need to be in Europe in case Roman needs me, plus I need to see my Specialists in Geneva."

The Hostess asked them to buckle up as they were approaching Bournemouth Airport landing in 15 minutes. They cleared arrivals in five minutes and were en-route to Sandbanks, it was 8pm. Tommy rang home Nikki answered " Grandad where are you?"

"Half an hour away is Karena with you? good, ask Albie to get a cold buffet ready for four people in the kitchen, it will be fine, some light wine, it's been a long day, love to everyone be with you in a bit."

"Able you and Yuri stay the night, it's late get an early start tomorrow, Yuri can go with you get an executive flight in the morning as you need to get to Forte, to make sure the Villa is ready for all comers, Yuri may have some extra pointers on what the approach is likely to be if Spetsnaz is involved. Call me direct, as soon as you've assessed the Estate and touch base with Luigi the Carabinieri Commander."

As the electric gates swung open two of Ables men came either side of the car both holding two serious black and tan Dobermans with fierce clipped ears waiting for a command. They acknowledged Able and waved them on. Inside the family waited.

"Alexis sweetheart, it`s been horrendous for you, with us all over the place, how is my boy? he`s coming back tomorrow and we all go to Forte for a few months, or as long as it takes to get Max back on his feet, it`s all going to be fine in the end.

Alexis, Nikki, Karena, Michael, God it`s good to see you all in one house together, I`ll say we should do it more often, but under different circumstances, have you all eaten?"

"Sure Dad, we were with Max for most of the day, he`s weak but Professor Lindsay says it`s ok to move him tomorrow. He can go to the toilet on his own, his wounds are healing well his visions fine, his memory is lucid in places, but he does not recall anything about the accident. Professor Lindsay says that`s normal. Max says he cannot wait to get back in his red bird and fly, got a real urge to get on the test track at Maranello again."

"Michael, you know Able this is Yuri one of Ables men, he`s going over to Forte with Able for the next few days to get the Villa ready for us, I`m going to get a bite in the kitchen with the boys then we can have a proper sit down while I bring you all up to speed with what is going to happen." Tommy set out final details with Able and Yuri.

"Gather round family, get comfortable there is much to discuss, the best way to get through it all I`m afraid is a mini business meeting, me first. I`ll run through what needs to happen starting tomorrow, with the reasons for it. I know it may not be what you all want to hear but you need to see the bigger picture, which will affect us all.

As I thought Roman has major problems with the Russian hierarchy, they have put a ban on him leaving the country and are after his Assets in Russia. He is transferring all his liquid Assets to me and doing a Fire Sale on all his Investments in Russia. Before you ask Michael his Assets in Camillo cannot be touched by the Russians. President Chomski has around twenty billion of his wealth invested through our Banks in Panama and the Cayman Islands. At some point I will have to meet him.

Now do not all start screaming at once, Karena and Nikki

especially. We need to move Max to the Villa in Forte, where we can provide armed protection with total back up from Luigi and the local Carabinieri, there is a Military Air Base at Pisa Airport and I have spoken with the Defence Minister for Homeland Security in Rome, he has assured me of whatever assistance the local police need. I want us all there for at least a couple of months, maybe longer we need to get Max back up to speed as soon as possible.

If anyone leaves the Estate they must be accompanied by an armed guard for safety`s sake. Alexis, Max will have all the care he needs, there is a brand new Private Neurology Clinic in the hills behind Lucca, state of the art helipad and top Consultants attending weekly. Max can attend as needed, they will send Physiotherapists daily to the Villa, it`s all organized, we have organized 24 hour nursing for the duration. Tonia you mentioned your friend Lara was coming to stay, I am sure she will be happier staying at the Villa with us as Milan shopping for both of you is only an hour awa, or Florence.

Michael you will have to stay in New York for a week, to reassure the American Cousins that it`s all business as usual, you can fly back as soon as you feel they`re ok.

Karena and Nikki I want you both with me in Forte, I know you have your own lives to lead but we have never been in this area of fragility with our security before, we`ve had death threats and kidnap nonsense that came to nothing, but this is more serious, very real, you need to understand. I hope to resolve the position over the next few weeks, so look on it as an extended holiday with some security training thrown in, you have no choice on this, I`m sure your Mum will agree with me.

Tomorrow Michael and I will sit down with you both and you can present the Financials on this upcoming situation you told Michael about, as you see it. We`ll organize a conference call with Roberto and his son after

Now one at a time your thoughts and any news, its ages since I`ve seen you girls, neither of you have got married yet without inviting me to the wedding? Alexis how are you right now?"

"Tom it was hard when I first heard about Max, but Tonia was great phoning me keeping me up to date, as soon as I saw him my worst fears faded as Professor Lindsay told me how things should develop, it`s a long road ahead, but he`s doing well so far. I am looking forward to having him close again, with all the help he will get in Forte. How about you Tom? all this travelling with Max on your mind and all this with Roman now. Will you be going to see your Specialists while you`re in Forte?"

"Yes sweet, they have sent me a long communication, there is a new Robotic Cerebral operation they have trialled in Lausanne, that they have had excellent results with, they want me to come in for tests with the Surgeon running the trials. I cannot go in while this is all in the air, we need a lid on it asap. Tonia baby how about you how are you coping?"

"I`m good Dad now the girls are back, with us all being together, life is a bitch when its going well watch out, that`s when it bites you on the back of the neck and throws everything into disorder, it`s like we are all pieces in one of those video games, but it`s a hard game to beat. I think what you`ve always said is right, never give in no matter how hopeless things seem, fight to the end, tough it out. That`s the best chance for you to turn things round, however big the problem and always trust your gut. You`re the best example of your own words Dad, we all love you for it.

When you go to see the Lausanne Clinic I am coming, I spoke with Lara yesterday told her what is going on, I am sure she will be up for Forte."

"Thank you sweetheart, now you two chicklets what`s going on with you?"

"Nothing serious with any men right now Gramps, we are both too busy, we will go into that with you in the morning. We had both agreed if you think its ok, to rent something for a while in New York then after speaking with Roberto he said we could stay with his son Enrico, he works in the Fed Reserve as Roberto does. Not a problem for us to stay a couple of months if Mums ok with it of course, see what you both think after we speak tomorrow."

"Michael, we have spoken a few times over the last few days, you are fairly up to speed with what is on my mind, more in the morning and tomorrow, unless you have got something I need to know now."

"Tomorrow will do Dad, get an early night tonight, I think we could all do with one, breakfast about 8am yes?"

"Michael and you girls, go on now off to bed all of you, I need a word with Tonia, sit down Tonia darllng, there is no way to ease you into this, I need to tell you something in confidence that Roman revealed to me, Lara your best friend was recruited into service with the KGB as a teenager and trained as a sleeper agent.

She was told lies about her Mothers death. She was told her Mother fell in love with a British double agent, who was her real Father, he had killed her mother as she had discovered he was betraying the Motherland, after Lara was born. She never knew Roman was her father because he knew it was safer for her not to be known as his daughter, as she would have been a target to be used against him.

As she became a formal Dancer at the Mariinsky Ballet travelling worldwide was her cover, for the targets she would be told to cultivate, while making links with important and wealthy families in countries she performed in. Sorry to be the bearer of such shocking news, we will talk with Roman later, how he kept it to himself all these years God alone knows. Try to get some sleep baby, see you in the morning."

"Morning Michael, Alexis, Nikki let's have a good breakfast then get down to it. Fresh orange juice and a full English for me please Albie, yes to lambs kidneys, some ciabatta toast thanks, how about you guys. Omelettes, Cotto Ham with Fontina cheese please Albie. Girls? Yoghurt and Muesli twice, with four Cappucinos."

"Is this scenario related to what we discussed last year

Michael, with some murmurs that got quickly buried about the Sub-Prime Market getting overheated?"

"That`s the one Dad, there are a couple of Fund Managers I am talking to, who are really getting worried, but if they speak to their Shareholders they cannot see it and threaten to withdraw their Investments, if we say anything public. Let`s be honest the Federal Reserve is not giving any guidance, they are helping the feeding frenzy along."

"Roberto and I have spoken about it and he is coming to Forte next week to give me his take on it all, till then I think we should keep our powder dry and not over react just now. I still want to go through the girls analysis of the situation. Let`s get our breakfast down then crunch some figures."

"That was a great breakfast Albie, when you have cleared away we will have another four Cappucinos then we are good till lunch. Take the rest of the day off Albie, we are fine we can knock up some toasted sandwiches or go to Steins for lunch."

"Thank you sir, as long as you are sure."

"See you in the morning Albie 8.00am, can you make sure the kitchen look after the security outside and their dogs, if they are allowed near them. Tonia and Alexis will come down when they are ready, we will get their order in to the kitchen then."

"Right girls what have you got?"

"What`s really interesting Gramps to us is that we both came up with the same seismic picture from opposite sides of the world, using different formats to get the results. So if you like it`s a disconnected cross check on the same answers, but it`s not good reading. However we believe we can make it work incredibly well for us, if we move at the right time, we think that time is not far off. If we miscalculate the timing we could lose, like everyone else, or lose less than the others, our best option if it works means we can make unquantifiable profits, really eye watering."

"Nikki do you agree with Karena?"

"As I was born immediately after Karena she thinks as the

71

older sister she should always speak first, but in this instance we are agreed on every detail Gramps."

In 2006 we had picked up on a big decline in house prices in the US, the ratio of Household Debt to Disposable Personal Income had risen from 77% in 1990 to 127% in 2007, this is beyond alarming, yet no one was saying anything.

We believe we need to short any Sub Prime Mortgages, Bonds or anything associated with that market in totality. If we don`t we are not going to catch a cold it`s going to be terminal pneumonia and I do not exaggerate.

We both agree from all the evidence we have, it may only be a matter of weeks to offload these toxic deals, before it explodes downwards. As at this week the major Investment Banks are still trading the Stocks and Bonds so we could get out while there is still time."

"Michael do you concur with the girls?"

"Having spoken with Enrico, Roberto`s son I am sure the girls are right."

"Get Roberto on the phone for me now."

"Roberto its Michael, Dads here he wants to speak with you."

"Roberto, I have got the girls with me they landed yesterday, they have brought me up to speed with the Sub Prime Loan & Bonds situation about to explode, what`s the Feds position on it as far as you know?"

"Tommy, that is what I wanted to see you about, you need to dump everything you have got in that market its totally Toxic, it will be completely worthless in a few weeks. Move quickly now, Short all your sub Prime Stock now, while everybody is buying everything they can get hold of. When the market collapses, buy, as the Fed will back Bond Holders Portfolios who bought at a certain point, with the two biggest Bond Dealers, so you will get a double Mac for the price of a bag of fries.

From all the inside chatter I can get at the Fed, the Government is not going to bail anyone out, they can all go to the wall, is going to be the position. They will allow the two biggest

Sub Prime Lenders Fannie May, with Freddie Mac, where did they get those names from? to take on another $200 Billion of debt. Only from Banks that package them into Mortgage Backed Securities, then you will be able sell them on Wall Street.

With what we know it's insane, they do not want it to get out of the bag, but you cannot keep a tiger in a bag for long. This could be a quick result for you with your connections. It's being announced in the morning, take todays price and run Tommy I am sorry about Max, if I can I will get over to Forte and see you there. Take care and do not hang around on this."

"Thanks Roberto, see you in the old country."

"Michael, Nikki, Karena get on to all our Fund Managers, Banks, Brokers in every Country, get them to liquidate all our positions in all Sub Prime Bonds, Mortgages, or Loans of any description. I want all positions closed by tomorrow night, at a Fire Sale price if necessary. They work round the clock, twenty four hours, till their Portfolios are empty of this junk. Sell only to other Banks or Brokers, we do not sell to any of our existing clients. The first couple of hours will get the best prices, till the word spreads, then it will start to get harder, call in any favours, do whatever they have to do but shift those Bonds.

The Annual Bonuses were paid out last month in May, we will pay the same again in two weeks for everyone clearing their Toxic Bond Accounts, it is a once in a lifetime earning shot for them all, so get them on it. Use whatever phones you need, there are two Satellite secure phones in my office and two separate lines in the lounge, speak with your own teams first, just tell them to get on it, their jobs depend on how well they perform in the next thirty six hours.

Any problems with any one give them to Michael or me girls. Get the hourly running positions put through to my office on the Internet, with our current updates showing on the six monitors.

Michael you and I need to be hammering down Fannie and Freddies doors on the phones now, with us first on their call list after mid-night tonight. I need to speak with some of our biggest

Investors, before they hear what is happening from someone else, leave the Banks in Panama, Switzerland and Cayman to me. Kitts and Nevis, Jersey and Isle of Man, yours Michael.

You need to speak to the Team at the Hedge Fund in New York tell them we`ve got a unique opportunity for big hitters only, coming up in the next seven days. Girls I need you to call the team at Camillo in Canary Wharf tell them I am flying in later today, but you are giving them my explicit orders, no deviations allowed without my personal contact, tell them to make us some money and about the opportunity coming in next week, which I will give the Department Heads the full monty on over the week end."

"We`re all on it Dad."

In January President Bush had announced a $150 Billion Tax Rebate to try to instil some Consumer confidence and get the people spending again. It was not working, the girls timely warning and Tommy`s quick reaction saved the Organizations position and increased their wealth base exponentially. Romans Assets were also put into the Short selling positions, adopted in the nick of time, as he had also got heavily involved in the highly Leveraged risky world of Toxic Securities.

From his connections with the Panama Bank, Tommy was made aware that Venezuela one of the largest oil producers in the world, was in two weeks time announcing Oil contracts for forward purchase to be quoted in Euros as a possible Hedge against the Dollar, which The Organization invested in heavily.

In March 2008 Blackstone Group, Manager of the Worlds biggest Buyout Fund suffered a 90% drop in profit in the last quarter, among it`s poor decisions was a $31 Billion takeover of a Casino Chain in the States, it simply overreached itself.

The same week the Government injected another $236 Billion into the US Banking System. Citigroup the Worlds largest Bank was forced to put $1 Billion from its Reserves in, to bail out six of its Hedge Funds.

The next week, The Carlyle Group, the largest Private Equity Firm in the States stated one of it`s funds could not repay its debts, the $22 Billion Carlyle Capital fund had a leveraged debt of $32 worth of loan, for every $1 of real equity. It collapsed under the weight of this unsustainable debt.

Bear Stearns had $10 TRILLION in Securities on its books, if it had gone under the Financial Markets would have collapsed, they and JPMorgan received bail outs from the Federal Reserve. Later in the year Lehmans Bank was allowed to go under with 5000 job losses in the UK alone. A rescue deal was put together in the UK for HBOS its biggest Mortgage Lender and Northern Rock Building Society was kept afloat with Government loans.

In the States AIG the Worlds biggest Insurance Firm was granted a $46 Billion loan to stay afloat.

The US Government announced a $700 billion loan Fund to bail out major institutions at risk of collapse from Toxic Assets.

In Europe a 200 Billion Euro Fund was made available for the same purpose. Slowly the fall bottomed out and confidence started to return, with stronger regulations, for the time being.

HSBC one of the largest Banks in the World wrote down its holdings in Sub Prime Mortgage Bonds by 10.5 Billion dollars. Millions of Homeowners in the US as employment fell due to lack of investment and lower spending, could not re-mortgage and were defaulting on their Sub Prime Loans. The bubble then burst all around the world.

"Well team Tommy how did we do? Michael first."

"Amazingly well Dad, as you said most of the buyers are in disbelief that there is a problem. We have across the board, sold off all our Sub Prime Linked products, I am still waiting for final numbers now and it`s just turned mid night. Traders are all reporting a feeding frenzy and saying it`s good to see you are not infallible, making a wrong call for once."

"We had better be right, my gut tells me it`s so, Karena and

Nikki have you both earned the latest Gucci or Prada bag for today?"

"More than that Gramps, we expect we should have enough to buy them both out if it all falls into place. Everything went better than anticipated, no problems with any clients or from our side, just a few more hours should clean it all up, we will have the figures by 2.00am."

"I spoke with Roman on the Satellite phone in St. Petes, putting him in the picture he has a meeting scheduled next week with the Interior Minister where he gives him his proposals to relinquish his Russian Investment Holdings. Our Banks and Hedge Funds are all clean as of close of business tonight. Panama has come up with some very interesting proposals and possible opportunities in Oil with Venezuela, where we could make a quick turn around, on large investments, if everything drops into place. I will go through it with you all tomorrow let's get our figures in tonight."

"Sure Dad, double espresso with brandy or Grappa 60% to keep you awake? only kidding and Mike double espresso?"

"Perfect Nikki thanks just coffee for me."

"Grappa for me sweet thanks, there will be Cristal in the wine chiller if you girls want a drink or do you want to wait for the final figures Mum and Tonia might like a glass."

"Have we got a total figure of what we needed to short Michael?"

"It's coming through in your office now Dad."

"We were in for just over $1.5 Billion at our maximum leveraged position of 30-1 across all of our Holdings, we are forecast by 2.00am this morning to clear in the region of $200 Billion profit which in a few weeks time is going to look as though God is definitely on our side, its unbelievable Dad, thank the Lord for creating greed in the Market."

"The Market is what it is Mike, the greed is in man, big congratulations to all Fund Managers Staff and our Banks send tonight to all.

Get the Accountants to work out the bonuses, get them paid in the next week, then get all Divisional Managers across our businesses and Banks included, to do a live Head Count on who maximised their Portfolios and who has become surplus to requirement, who are we carrying, who we do not need. We must be able to trim, now we have relinquished all those Portfolios. Any Divisional Leader who states he needs all his Traders needs replacing, as the first order of the day. You got your Gucci and Prada bags girls and more, well done it looks as though the business is in good hands."

When the final figures came in at 2am Camillo Holdings had cleared a total of $202.5 Billion in profit. The markets were shaken, Banks and Lenders collapsed all around the world, not seen since The Great Depression. In the end the true cost of the Toxic Debt was estimated at over a Trillion Dollars, the Governments had to buy back from the remaining Banks all their Toxic debt at a low interest rate to enable them to continue to lend to businesses. It has not been paid back in full to this day.

"Able meet us at Pisa, in two hours, we can talk on the way back to the Villa. Yuri and the rest of the team can stay at the Villa. Luigi is giving us a personal light armoured escort from the Airport. I`m coming in with Michael, Tonia and the girls now.

Bring one of the Hummers, they are ex special forces U.S. Max bought them last year as boy`s toys, he had them redesigned inside for comfort, but still keeping all the Armour etc. he never got round to getting one over to the UK.

Alexis is coming with Max and the Medics tomorrow late morning. The Italian Medics will take over late morning. The Defence Minister has agreed a no Helicopter fly zone, over Forte, for the next three months except for Carabinieri or Air & Sea Rescue and Ambulance."

"Is everything good there?"

"Yes sir, I have my assessment for security upgrade ready for you, I will see you in two hours at Pisa."

Tommy, Michael, Tonia and the girls cleared landing, went to the VIP Lounge where they had the usual family ritual in the Old Country, a real Cappuccino "Perfection, that`s when you know you have arrived in Italy, everybody makes perfect coffee, flavour, temperature and crema, every little café and top restaurant the same, how do they do that Gramps?"

"Tonia for them it is easy, they love what they do, they do not need a thermometer to tell them when the milk is ready, they listen to the sound of the machine, just like their engine when they are driving, or so it seems, I am only kidding.

It is funny but for me I always get the same feeling whenever I arrive here, my first coffee and walking from the Airport Lounge, I start to feel Italian again. I realize how hard it must have been for Camillo and his Brothers to leave this land, to go into the unknown, rest his soul."

"Able hi, Ciao Luigi, Commendatore e Cugino its too long since we have seen each other, how are Carla and the children?"

"Tom, good to see you all, is good with me and my family, I am sorry for Max, Alexis and all of you, of course. I have spoken with Able since he arrived, I am your disposal while you are here, I have some of my men to escort you to the Villa we go now yes?

Able spoke with me for the alterations you may make at the Villa I will visit in a few days we discuss how you need, yes?"

"Perfetto Luigi, bring Carla for a meal, lunch, or dinner we can talk then, Michael, Max and Tonia would love to see you both again, call me for the best day for you, thank you again for your help at this time."

"Qualsiasi cosa per la Famiglia, Tom come faresti per me eh?"

"Missed that Gramps."

"He said "Anything for the family, as you would do for me, Nikki. "

Two armoured patrol jeeps with two Machine Pistol carrying Police in each jeep, one in front, one behind covered the normal fifty minute journey in thirty five minutes, with lights and sirens blaring, ignoring the numerous red lights along the route.

"The only way to drive here." said Karen.

"Just like your Father darling, how many points on your licence now?"

"Nine Gramps nearly lost it last time I was pulled."

"What are you driving now?"

"R8 Audi, Gramps V10 engine 0-60 in 3.5 seconds, after yesterday I will probably treat myself to the latest Mercedes AMG GTR it's so beautiful, if I get one I'll have to buy a house so that I can drive it into the lounge and keep it in there. I couldn't bear to leave it in a garage overnight."

"And you Nikki? points first."

"I'm more sensible Gramps, I have all the latest Radar Trap avoidance kit installed, I'm more cautious, I'm currently running on three points, mine is a TVR Sagaris, it's one of the last made in '06, top speed 185 mph 0-60 about the same as Karena's, it used to be British Sports Car now owned by a Russian Oligarch's son, I've had it two years and need a change. Before yesterday I would have kept it for another year or so, but I could now get my dream car a Ford GTD 40 a real one, not a Replica, though you can pay up to £30k for a good Replica, the real thing is about £300,000, we'll see."

"Why are you girls in such a hurry to get anywhere?"

"It's not that Gramps, it's about with a bit of open road not having to follow a convoy going to the Supermarket."

"Do not start me on it Gramps, we are short of Police for crime, it's because they are all behind trees with speed guns."

"Karena you will soon get your next points then what?"

"I can afford a driver now Gramps, till I get my licence back."

"Able, give me a short version of upgrades at the Villa as you see it, with an overall cost and time to install. I will go through it in detail later tonight, you can walk me round the site in the morning, before Max arrives."

"Sir, it depends what level of threat you want to protect against. The whole perimeter wall at five metres high is adequate, some of the wooded areas between the wall and the Villa itself need cutting back, to give a better field of vision for cameras and field of fire against assault. Any vehicular assault from the sea front, assuming it`s not going to be heavy armour, would not get through the perimeter walls.

Video surveillance can be increased, with electrified razor wire on top of the perimeter wall just inside, one foot lower than the wall. Movement sensors in the wooded areas.

Armoured glass at all windows and all doors strengthened with blast proof heavy doors behind the front facings. Again you have to consider what level of penetration you want to stop. The harder the attack the costlier the kit to repel it in simple terms.

For instance, you can get armoured glass to withstand .50 calibre assault rifles only one quarter of an inch thick but what about the frames this applies to doors as well of course. You need to consider what level of protection you need in conjunction with your assessment of what the threat is. Everything is available at a price sir."

"Thanks Able, I will look at the detail tonight and decide what we need tomorrow."

Max and Alexis arrived next day with the Medics in attendance, Luigi provided an escort again with Police outriders, this time Able and Yuri took the two Hummers with two armed agents as well. The Villa was all set up by the Hospital staff from Lausanne who transferred Max with minimum disruption.

For mid May the weather was sunny at 60 degrees, with at least six weeks before the holidaymakers were due to arrive in numbers. The Villa was built in 1910 over three floors with twenty bedrooms, twelve baths. The entire compound is just over 3000sq mtrs. with two guest houses, one by the main gate, the other by the main pool and tennis court at the rear and with a helipad, three large garages, one covered outdoor pool with wave machine and jacuzzi.

The perimeters are mainly wooded set back from the

perimeter walls, with some areas coming within 25 mtrs of the main house. The only vehicular access being on a side road from the main sea front road, which runs from Marina di Massa in the West all the way to Viareggio in the East some twenty one kilometers of flat main road, known as the Lungomare di Levante, right on the entire sea front with end to end beach bars and clubs with their famous sea front cabanas to rent, on a daily basis.

Tommy and Able did a detailed inspection of the Villa`s interior and its grounds, then went to Tommy`s office.

"As I explained in the beginning sir, when the property was bought Security was not a top priority, you loved the Villa and bought it as a family home, but to get it ready as a secure accommodation from outside intrusion or attack it requires a fair amount of work and time to complete it, not to mention approval from the local Commune for any alterations, as it`s a listed building of historical interest."

"There is a possible threat against me and my family from the Russians, it`s concerning our business and our connection with Roman who you met last week in St. Petersburg. The Russian President Chomski is trying to exert any and all kinds of pressures on the Native Russian millionaires and billionaires who have access to large Assets in Russia, or Overseas, it`s become Romans turn.

His Passport has been withdrawn and he is facing charges of Tax evasion, in a few weeks, if he does not comply to all demands. He could end up in a Gulag or worse, he would not survive. He has transferred his overseas Assets to our main Hedge Fund in London and that could put us in the crosshairs of the Presidents best shooters. On present form it would be more subtle than that, you could tell me more no doubt Able.

I am calling for a meeting next week in Geneva with the Presidents top advisor and confidant, to find a solution, if I fail all bets are off."

"Sir, if I may say for immediate action, I recommend strengthening the team here with more weapons specialists, half a dozen tops will suffice, I have contacts who can supply good verified people. Electrifying the perimeter wall with razor wire. More lighting and surveillance, also dog handlers.

In relation to a vehicular attack on the entrance gates, as it is a side road which is on surveillance there is not much frontal space for anyone to get major speed up to penetrate all the way in. For now we can cover this with a couple of heavy armoured vehicles of our own, parked across the inside of the gates loaded with concrete drums with a small amount of explosive ready to detonate on a mobile signal from the surveillance office.

There is no danger they will go off accidentally and they would only be used if we were under a large assault from outside. We have to assume we are sound from the Air with the three month no fly exclusion zone. The only other unknown quantity is the sea, but again they have to get on the land to get to us, we will be as ready as we can sir.

In relation to guests being outside I had a call from a friend in the States last week in manufacturing, he has developed a new armoured boarding which can be decorated with any surface to look like screens, movable, to a height of three metres and two metres wide, they will withstand sniper or assault rifle rounds from up to thirty metres. They could provide a sun bathing area for family outside sir, we can put them behind the windows day and night, set back so as to allow sunlight in but still giving good cover, I can get what we need flown in by the week end."

"I think we need to go with this option Able, organize what you need in the morning. I will speak with Luigi tomorrow morning and brief him on what you are organizing I`m sure he will sort any problems with the Commune, in the National Interest with the Defence Minister involved, it`s a shame Berlusconi is not still the top man, you could always strike a deal with him, if there was something he wanted from you.

Most importantly none of the family goes anywhere without an armed escort. How many men have we got here now?"

"Myself, Yuri and six others sir, with the other four coming as well, we will be sufficiently prepped up to cope with what we may face, with Luigi's back up as well"

"Good, I will see you tomorrow evening."

Tommy went into the kitchen, saw Maria, who looked after the catering when any of the family were in residence "Buon giorno Maria come va oggi? Bene."

"Si signore Tolmino, anche lei va bene? poveraggio signore Massimo."

"Sicuro Maria e grazie, what are we eating tonight?"

"Always your favorite, my home made Sausage Ragu with Pappardelle, the sausages I get my butcher to get from Emilia Romagna a farm near your home town in Piandelagotti and then followed by another favourite, Osso Bucco e Saffron Risotto con Gremolata, is no too heavy for you together signore?"

"It will be perfect as always grazie mille Maria, ci vediamo un po piu tardi," he went into the main lounge, Michael was on the phone, Tonia and the girls were having a drink "How's Max doing guys?"

"He is resting Gramps, sedated after the trip Alexis is with him, he has been asleep a couple of hours."

"It's good he is resting, Maria's preparing tonights welcome meal, the usual, well it's my favourite, do not forget to tell her how you loved it and eat as much as you can or you will get told off for not eating enough in England. No problems to report Mike?"

"No Dad, just touching base with the office in New York and London, they are a bit edgy about the Venezuelan Oil Futures we are committing to."

"It is where we need to be Mike, we wait till it drops to $30 a barrel, that is our buy line, after that it will rise, we sell at anything over $50 a barrel, it is all good, we can increase our profit on the toxic junk we got rid of and our biggest investors will be happy."

"I hope your info is right Dad, even though they've never been wrong yet."

"Without a shadow of a doubt Mike, as Nikki always says."

"Alexis how is he? I will pop in after we have eaten if he is awake."

"He is still asleep, he needs to rest for the trip to Lausanne on Monday for his check up. The Medical Team from the Hospital seem very good, it is as though they looked after him from day one very impressive."

"That is great, it will all help to get him back to us again. Now listen up guys, you know we have a situation whereby we may be at risk from some people who may wish to do us harm.

That is why Able and Yuri and the others are here, we are getting more help in before the week end. We are tightening up the security around the whole Villa for the duration of our stay. I have had credible intelligence that it is possible somebody may try something against us in the next couple of months.

I am going to Geneva tomorrow to see my Specialists and hope to set up a meeting next week, to see if I can get to who may be behind this problem and sort it out. I cannot be more specific at this stage, but you must follow Ables orders for your safety, if I am not here understood? That is everybody, no exceptions, agreed all of you?"

"Ok Gramps, are we allowed out or what."

"Yes darlings, preferably together and never without an armed guard, no hide and seek, it's not a game they are armed for a reason and I want you all back here every evening. If we eat out, we all go together, with guards, no going out for a paper or cigarettes and definitely no riding alone in any of the cars. There will be extra security work going on here next week, so no going outside in the gardens after 9pm, there will be guard dogs trained to bring anyone down and go for the kill, with handlers outside all night."

"How long have you known about this Tom is this why we are all here?"

"Yes to most of that Alexis, for Max its where he will get the best attention and help to recuperate, for me with you all here I can provide close quarter protection for everybody with our ability to arm our guards in Italy, also with Luigi a relative and local Police Commander on side we will be fine. We need to do all we can to keep ourselves as safe as possible until I can resolve the problem, one way or another.

I had no chance if you were all living all over the place, in different jurisdictions this is our safest option, are you all in agreement? I need to know you are all with me on this."

"Yes from me Dad."

"Thanks Mike how about you girls?"

"Sounds like there is no other option for us all."

"Thanks Karena, you Nikki?"

"Sure Gramps, can we get the Special Forces guys to patrol without shirts? only kidding."

"Able will work out an area at the rear by the pool where you can stay outside, with a safe area, protected from any attempts by outsiders to enter the area, our guys will patrol the whole time, glad to see you have not lost your sense of humour Nikki."

"Tonia?"

"I am ok with it Dad, it is a shock though and Lara is arriving for a week, tomorrow, before she goes back to say goodbye to the Mariinsky, for the final time."

"That`s fine, the same rules apply to her of course, for her safety, while she is here ok. Aah, Maria shall we sit up, va bene Leo can we have a nice Tignanello for Michael and myself, some of the local white from the Cinque Terre for Nikki and Karena and a bottle of Cristal to start. Buon appetito a tutti e mille grazie a Maria, dig in everyone."

The following morning Max and Tonia in the Mercedes Ambulance, Tommy and two of Ables men in the lead Hummer with two more in the Hummer behind set out for the Hospital in Lausanne, on the Northern side of Lake Geneva. Tommy was staying with Max and Tonia for the day at the Hospital then staying over night at Hotel D`Angleterre in Geneva as he had an appointment with his Specialists first thing next morning, with a pre-arranged meeting at 4pm at the D`Angleterre with an Attache from the Russian Embassy.

On arrival at the Hospital in Lausanne Professor Richter a Worldwide authority on Neurological Problems induced through Trauma Accidents, met Tommy and Alexis in Max`s suite at the Hospital, while he was being made ready for assessment tests on behalf of the Professor.

"Professor my Daughter in Law Alexis. I understand you have all of Professor Lindsay`s reports and Scans etc. from the UK, how soon before you will have evaluated Max`s status for us?"

"Mr. Beales, Alexis, I have all the reports from England, I will have completed my assessment by tomorrow afternoon latest, at this stage shall we say I am optimistic we will achieve a good result with Max. His physical trauma will repair in good time as he is still young and fit. The psychological problems which may manifest could be a more long term care situation, we will have a clearer picture after a few days. I must go to Radiography now to ensure I get what I need from my Scans here. Max will come back to the suite and I will go over the results with my team. We may need more tests next day we will see. Max will stay with us for at least two or three days will you stay in Lausanne or travel back to Forte Dei Marmi and return on Thursday?"

"Alexis will stay at a Hotel in Lausanne I have an appointment in Geneva tomorrow I must keep, I will be back on Wednesday morning God willing. I assume there will be no problem with my Security people staying outside Max`s room, a twenty four hour watch, it is non negotiable Professor."

"That will be fine Mr. Beales, the Police Commander has brought us up to speed with your situation, I will see you both later with Max."

"Alexis let`s get you set up at a Hotel, one of Ables men will stay with you, with one of the Hummers and bring you back to the Hospital in the morning. Max is covered here, I am heading back to Geneva with the other Hummer and one of Ables men as I have an early one with the Specialists tomorrow. Also a meeting at the D`Angleterre at 4pm. I will drive back tomorrow evening. Any issues or problems of any kind call me on my mobile yes?"

"Fine Dad, I will see you tomorrow evening good luck for both visits."

The next morning Tommy was at the Geneva Hospital prompt at 9.00am he was seen by his personal Consultant Mr. Lindstrom who explained they had recently had great success with a new Trial of Stem Cell Transplants in reducing benign Brain Tumors, they were only recommending them for people who had exhausted all other types of treatments and he could benefit.

"What are the figures Doc how good are the results?"

"Mr. Beales I can tell you we have had a sixty per cent increase in longevity with patients who by all previous interventions would not be still with us today. Before you ask, the longest improvement is coming up to two years."

"Why was this treatment not made available to me at the time of your prognosis?"

"Mr. Beales a trial must have an exact number of patients starting on it at the commencement date, which preceded your prognosis date. Once its quota is filled the trial cannot accept new patients, till the results are validated either way. We are now going to commence a second Trial."

"When would I need to be available? and how long would I be likely to be out of action to my business?"

"We would need you here at the end of the month in ten days, of course it is not possible to say how long you would need to recuperate, though some patients from the first trial are back at work now after six or seven months rest."

"It is something that interests me, I need a week to sort some pressing issues then I will decide if that fits with your scheduling."

"That will be excellent, I will get my Secretary to confirm joining details with your office, we will look forward to receiving your confirmation in a weeks time, it would not be wise to delay or defer this opportunity sir."

Tommy checked in with Michael, explained the latest news and asked him to check all Investment Managers and their Teams were ready for the Venezuelan Oil Price spike to happen, ready to take the action he wanted. He told Mike he would talk again after his meeting at the D`Angleterre.

Tommy then spoke with Alexis "Hi, how`s my boy?"

"Champing at the bit, wants to drive back to Forte now, desperate to see the girls and wants to take me out for a meal tonight."

Tommy relayed the Specialists news and said he would see both of them at Lausanne that night.

Tommy had booked a suite at the D`Angleterre and was ensconced at 3.30 pm strictly on double espressos. At precisely 3.55 pm a Russian in Military Dress Uniform and two minders arrived and were shown to Tommy`s suite.

"Leonid Brezhinski, First Military Attache at the Swiss Embassy and these gentlemen are here to advise me if necessary, while correlating what passes between us Mr. Beales, shall we begin?"

"Please Mr. Brezhinski and gentlemen some coffee or tea or something stronger?"

"We are fine, if you care to start the meeting which you asked for, we are here to expedite answers to any questions you may have, so let`s get straight to it."

"Your Government has rescinded the Passport of a business colleague of mine in Moscow, a Mr. Roman Orlov."

"Personally I have no information on this matter, if what you say is correct he should seek clarification from his local Visa Office."

"I can see it could be difficult for you to have knowledge of each case of this sort as there are now so many of your top businessmen on a proscribed list, unable to leave the country."

"You seem to know more than I at this point, so I am at a disadvantage."

"Can we talk hypothetically about a possible situation?"

"Of course, if it will help to provide more clarity."

"This business friend of mine has been a good friend to President Chomski over the years, he has supported many charitable works in the country he loves, he had a distinguished Military Service Record and now through some possible mis-information is without freedom to travel on business and I understand may be about to face Tax evasion charges in the Courts."

"As I say Mr. Beales I have no knowledge of any such situations in Moscow at present, with anyone of that name."

The taller of the two other men spoke "If what you say is correct and this businessman faces charges in our Courts we could not interfere with our Judicial System."

"I understand, what I am asking is if it would be possible to settle this matter before any Court papers are issued?"

"That would be for a higher authority to consider Mr. Beales."

"Would it be feasible for you to put the possibility to that higher authority?"

"I will look into the situation you describe and contact the relevant authorities, to see if it is a situation we could deal with in this manner, I will come back to you before the week end."

"Thank you Mr. Brezhinski for your time and you gentlemen, much appreciated. I await your response."

Alexis came out of A L` Emeraude, one of the oldest and most luxurious Watch Emporiums in Switzerland since 1909. As a special treat to Max she had gone in to replace his beloved Ulysse Nardin which was damaged in his crash. She had sent it to be repaired which would take a month, he might not want to wear it again anyway. She decided on the Executive Skeleton Tourbillon 45mm, a stunning masterpiece in Watch design at a cool £32500.

The armed guard on the door opened it as it electronically clicked, Ables man went out in front of Alexis to the cars passenger door, holding it open for her, as two muffled shots spat out. Ables man died with a head shot to the forehead, Alexis was on the floor screaming in agony. The armed doorman covered her with his own body as the motorcyclist and pillion passenger screeched off.

Police arrived in a minute or so, swiftly followed by an Ambulance, the area was quickly cordoned off with armed police everywhere. Alexis was hit in the arm conscious and on the way to Max`s Hospital with a Police escort. Tommy was on the drive back from Geneva when he got the call from Able.

"Sir bad news, Alexis was shot at in Lausanne leaving a jewellers, my man with her is dead. I`m on the way to you in the Lamborghini, intel is sketchy at the moment, I will have much more when I get there, or sooner."

"We can guess who`s responsible."

"Initial thoughts from the Police, an attempted robbery gone wrong."

"When did they last have such an incident?"

"Exactly sir, the style of the shooting is signature Ndrangheta, Calabrian Mafia, two on a motorcycle, the pilot, with the shooter behind. It`s possible it was a Contract hit we will be able to find out. More likely, some Agency putting up a smokescreen. If there is any comfort for you sir, it is most likely a warning, the shooter could have killed Alexis with only two shots fired, he told us, by getting my man with a head shot that he is very accurate, he was ordered to only wing your Daughter in Law, it looks as though it is about to begin as you predicted."

"I will see you at the Hospital Able, have we got those extra guys yet? and how about the additional security items we agreed?"

"Yes to the men sir, all works are commencing later tonight, the defence screens will be installed tomorrow. I will be happier when everybody is back at the Estate sir."

"Good man, I need to see how soon we can get Max and now Alexis back to Forte safely."

Max`s Specialist was pleased with his progress since the surgery, given the circumstances, he had no problem with him going back to Forte, with his Medical Team in attendance there. He was to keep in daily contact by video link and the Hospital would expect him back in a months time, provided there were no new complications.

Tommy, Alexis, Max and Able arrived back at the Villa the next afternoon, the place was a hive of activity, workmen, electricians, technicians and the four new Security men, under Yuri's supervision overseeing the installation of the new improvements to the estate.

Tommy, Able and Yuri met in Tommy's office over black coffee "Do we have anything new Able from your contacts?"

"As I said at the outset sir, 90% sure it was a choreographed warning, well executed. My contacts tell me there are no Contracts out on any of your family members, on the open market anyway. This verifies the likelihood it is a Government Agency covert op, Yuri and I are agreed the likeliest perpetrators are Russian. The question if you agree with our analysis sir, is what response do you wish to provide how overt do you want it to be?"

"So as you say Able, they have proved they have accurate firearms professionals at their disposal, we either go to ground and dig in behind our fencing, or send them a message back, we are not playing a game. It needs to be an unambiguous message, one they will understand as meaning we are ready to do whatever it takes to gain the upper hand. It needs to be sent quickly, while they think we are all in disarray. How soon can you come up with some options?"

"We have a specific plan we can work on immediately. Part of our training in Mossad was when we worked for a Target Resolution, we firstly identified the main protagonists, know the lead targets exact daily movements, from the day he/she is identified. Get a complete working daily diary however complex. There are always repetitive scenarios that will crop up, even if it's only what time of day the target attends to his bowel needs. These can provide opportunities for action. It is impossible for a person to live every day differently."

"Have you such a portfolio for the Russian President Able?"

"We have sir, Yuri has provided us with some updates we did not have. His final six month assignment was spent on internal Security at the Kremlin."

"If we decide to make a play against him directly, how can we get access? he must have one of the most secure environments around him, all day every day."

"Just so sir, but our scheme would play out, God willing, from a distance, with nobody having any connection to yourself, or any of us involved."

"Give me the specifics, it sounds too good to be true."

"Like all plans sir there will always be an "if" or "but", here is what I propose. At the beginning of every month the President goes to the Kremlin Medical Unit used only by Politburo Members. He has a pre-Glaucoma weakness in both eyes controlled by eye drops. It means the pressure behind each eye must be monitored and controlled, otherwise the risk of blindness is acute. He has his check ups religiously, same day same time each month. This gives us our best shot at present."

"How do we proceed Able?"

"The President insists the Pressure Monitoring Equipment is checked every day, before his use of it, a Technician from the firm that installed it arrives at the Kremlin the evening before the Presidents test and checks it out, putting a sticker on it to verify it's been done. We intercept him on his way in, taking his ID, replacing his photo, we keep him out of the way till next day, having replaced him with our man who adjusts the equipment with one added extra."

"What is it Able?"

"Just before the President leans into the equipment, placing his chin on a moulded rest, the Medic puts coloured dye in both eyes to dilate both pupils, enabling the telescopes to read behind the eyes to get the pressure, it stings a bit, but what follows next will sting a lot more. Built into the two telescopes are retractable tungsten spikes eight inches long.

When the operator tries to focus the telescopes the spikes are ejected and propelled at 80mph, penetrating to the back of the targets head, instantly blinding him or resulting in immediate death more likely. As a secondary back up, the eye drops in the locked cabinets will have delayed acid release compound added to them. Even if by some extraordinary chain of events the scenario I have just proposed does not happen, the message will be sent and they will know we have serious intent, determined to keep acting, until we achieve the result we want. Over to you sir."

"I like the sound of it Able, go with it as soon as you are ready."

"All in place sir, just awaiting your approval, Yuri will handle the team from the Security Room in Forte, all signals are encrypted, we are capable of making it look as if they are directed from a Chinese Satellite, no trace back to us, not even from GCHQ in Cheltenham or the Pentagon, totally clean, with all traces destroyed after use."

5

Three days later on the evening before the Presidents eye test Olga Semyanova and Alexei her cleaning Supervisor were in the Medical Clinic in the Kremlin, doing their usual checks and routine, with extra care as the President was using it next day they knew he was the most meticulous client they looked after and they would be out of a job if anything was missed. Olga was dusting the equipment when she noticed the Opthalmic equipment had been moved off line from its normal position.

She moved it back to centralise it, switched the plug on at the socket to make sure all was well, touched the on off button on the Telescopic equipment and promptly shot Alexei in the back with both Tungsten Spikes. She ran to the guard outside and hit the alarm button, on the way out at the exit door.

Yuri`s contacts in the Military appraised him of the latest failed attempt on the Presidents life, with no Press Release being made, as the President was on the Campaign trail, with elections in a months time. Not that any upset was expected as his last result to remain in office was 99.7% of the vote in his favour.

Next day Tommy had a call from the Embassy contact in Geneva, the Russian Attache was asking for a meeting, at the earliest opportunity.

The additional Security adjustments were all completed to Ables satisfaction and the security detail had been increased to twelve, not counting Yuri and himself. Their firepower had been increased to max level to include everything except a Tank, a

Jump Jet, or an Anti Aircraft Missile System. The armoured vehicles were in place at the entrance gates, the electrified razor wire was all in place, with extra lighting and sensors. Luigi had placed a light armoured Personnel Carrier outside the back of the property on twenty four seven standby, Able and Yuri were ready for all comers. The Family were all behaving well, especially after Alexis`s episode in Lausanne.

President Chomski had called a meeting of his Personal Security Attachment he was not in a good frame of mind "how could anyone get that close to me? I should send all of you to a Gulag to sharpen you up, whoever it was came within a pubic hair of altering the course the Motherland is on, what do you have to say idiots?"

"Mr. President our Intelligence suggests the likeliest perpetrators are the Hedge Fund friends of Orlov the billionaire Investor, currently under investigation for Tax evasion to the State. His friends are assisted by Yuri the ex-Spetsnaz Colonel known as Mad Wolf, you will recall him. He now only works in the private sector not for any Government Agencies, it is his kind of operation."

"I want an open option Contract on his head from today a million dollars. His friends are a different proposition. How do we neutralise them now?"

"We have two options, the first is to rid ourselves completely of Mr. Orlov`s interference in our business by eliminating him and his Friends family, the second is to seemingly acquiesce to his terms of settlement and destroy him financially. We will try the first one as soon as you are ready to go, our plan is on your desk now."

The plan was straightforward by Spetsnaz previous strategies. The Russian Fleet had two Naval Amphibious vessels and a Cruiser Vlad the Impaler, on a visit to La Spezia, Italy`s largest Naval Port, on the Tuscan Coast, fourty minutes by road from Forte Dei Marmi.

The Cruiser carries a permanent Spetsnaz team of sixteen men who would deploy off the coast of Forte at night, as it left on its return journey home. They would carry all their assault weapons, no uniforms and they would find their own way to Genoa after they had completed their mission, where the Cruiser had a two day visit booked in. They were to leave enough traceable items to pinpoint the attack perpetrators as if it originated from the Calabrian Mafia. The President gave his approval and it was rapidly put into place.

Tommy wanted to get everybody out of the anxious state which had developed with the attack on Alexis, he booked for them all to go to Bistrot on the beach in Forte. As it happens it is only six doors from the Russian night club which remained chained up.

Bistrot is a Michelin Starred Restaurant, one of the Regions finest dining experiences with a top drawer brigade of chefs, most of them having worked there for many years. The menu is extensive and the wine cellar beyond stellar. Service is totally high end and of course utterly discreet. In the old days before the smoking ban, as you reached for a cigarette a gloved hand was at the end of your cigarette as you put it into your mouth, with a perfectly sized flame.

It is still strange today, compared to England, to see in Italy, wealthy people immaculately dressed exotic women and smooth men getting the waiter to lay a place at the table for their small dog. Some even have the dog on a cushion, on the table to feed it tit bits, they see nothing unusual in this.

Tommy took one quarter of the Restaurant area, having spoken to Matteo the owner when he booked. They had been friends for over thirty years, in fact Matteo owned five of the top restaurants in Forte, all catering to different clienteles with different styles of food and service. Tommy had invested in his businesses over twenty years ago, they were almost related. Tommy`s section of the restaurant was screened off, floor to ceiling with movable interlocking opaque heavy panelling. An armed guard was at all four corners outside. Matteo welcomed the party and gave his recommendation for the evening, Tommy said "Everything you do is absolutely perfect Matteo we leave it to you to feed us, five or six courses with your recommended wines and Aperitivos will be what we all need now, it has been a tiring week for us all."

"Tom my pleasure as always, so good to see you all back in Forte, so sorry to hear about your son Max, I trust we will see him soon. The girls they are amazing, Tom looking so spectacular as ever. Alexis, cos a fai? what have you been up to?"

"A long story Matteo, maybe next time it is so good to be back."

"Where is Tony the old Captain, as I always call him, he looks after everyones car outside?"

"Is a great shame Tom, he was diagnosed with Prostate Cancer, at the moment he is in Hospital with treatment, he will not be able to return, he is now eighty years old he has been with me fourty five years, poveraggio, is life, no Tom? alora."

"Yes Matteo, none of us know what is in store, make the most of each day, for today could be our last."

The waiter brought out some of their superb flatbread to share with the aperitifs they were puffed up about three inches high, nothing in the middle, but with Tuscan Extra Virgin Olive Oil on the top side only with Rosemary, still warm from the wood oven. This was followed by local mixed meat platters, served by the waiter with white gloves.

After the meats which were all served paper thin, with silken folds, they sampled some wines before the next course. This consisted of Gilt Head Sea Bream and local Sea Bass fillets served with a spoonful of quenelles on the side of creamed Asparagus, with three or four baby local potatoes. Next the piece de resistance was served at the table, under two large domed silver servery units, three Suckling Pigs on one and a massive Tagliata di Manzo from cows that receive a daily massage to ensure tender meat, with not a spot of fat on it, served to the plate, with a drizzle of extra virgin oil, softer than butter.

After more wine, a Cheese trolley, with an array of at least twenty different local cheeses including Burrata from Southern Italy, Alexis`s favourite, a cheese produced in the making of Mozzarella, the outside of the ball is Mozzarella the inner part is a stringy melt in the mouth texture made with fresh cream in the process, which oozes out when you cut into the ball. Finally, desserts, Millefoglie which translates to one thousand leaves. Most restaurants make it like a cream slice but Bistrot make it with a minimum of twenty sheets of paper thin crusty pastry that explodes as you cut into it, the Chantilly Cream with strawberries and raspberries embedded have the most exotic flavours, they are no bigger than marbles.

Matteo popped round to make sure Tommy had enjoyed his evening.

"Always Matteo old friend, everything is good with you?"

"Tom, I have to go round my other restaurants now to see if I can eat tomorrow."

"Grazie mille Matteo, we are here for a month at least, I will call to book again."

"He`s one of the richest men in Forte, rides everywhere on his bike for his health, he says, his staff say he doesn`t like paying for petrol. He opened a Sushi Japanese restaurant last year five doors away, you need to book three weeks ahead to get in. Everyone done? who fancies a stroll around the centre of town see what your favourites have in the windows, Tonia?"

"Good call Dad, girls?"

"Definitely Cavalli, Gucci, then Prada for me."

"Ok Nikki, we can get a coffee at one of the bars, we have missed the shops tonight maybe you girls could have a day out shopping tomorrow, forecast is a bit cloudy."

Next morning the girls were up with an early breakfast, Alexis stayed in with Max as he had physio booked and was sitting in the lounge, glad to be out of bed at last. Tonia and the girls headed off for a days shopping and lunch out, with a two man escort team.

They stopped in the main square of Pietrasanta in the hills behind Forte, for a coffee, in a bar where there is a plaque outside the building saying " Michelangelo stayed at this Inn, when he picked the marble for his work on the Sistine Chapel" Tonia said it made her feel as though it gave them a connection with the history this little village had with the past, every time she read the plaque.

Today it is a centre of excellence for Artists and Sculptors who travel from all over the world, to work and learn here. You can wander into the Sculpting Studios and watch the Artists at work. The three or four roads are all lined with Boutiques and Art Galleries as well as local restaurants and bars.

Not far from this place of beauty and peace is S`ant Anna di Stazzema, where on August 12th 1944 the Waffen SS massacred 560 local Villagers and Refugees in reprisal for Partisan attacks on German troops, they were all locked in the Church, men, women and children, machine gunned through the windows with all the bodies burned alive.

"Michael how is the Venezuelan Oil deal panning out?"

"As you thought Dad, the price per barrel bottomed out at $30 dollars its now steadying at around $60 dollars a barrel I told all our brokers to sell, that`s happening as we speak."

"Well done Mike, what figure did we pay out on the Bonuses on the Toxic Sales."

"It`s coming in at about 50 Million Sterling Dad."

"Let me know what we clear on the Oil, I am going to have a walk round with Able and Yuri see you in a bit."

Able and Yuri took Tommy on a guided tour of their preparations at the Villa starting with the two sniper posts on the roof, which had total vision over the whole estate. Weapons and ammunition were ready for use, with hand held Rocket Launcher anti Armoured Vehicle weapons locked and loaded, Night Vision Binoculars were on tripods ready for use. Tree lined avenues to the Villa had been tidied up, clean cut, with all avenues covered by arc lights on sensors.

One tree on the edge of each avenue was colour marked at the edge to give the exact distance in metres from the villa, for precision targeting which the Sniper Scopes could easily use for total accuracy. Inside the wooded areas there were countless trip wires rigged to Shrapnel Grenades at head height. Sewage manholes were booby trapped to detonate if lifted from underneath.

Emergency generators would cut in immediately should the power supply fail.

Able and Yuri were confident that any attack could be stopped, before it reached the Villa itself. The girls and Tonia came back laden with their designer packages, all the usual suspects Cavalli and Gucci the most dominant.

"Right girls, get ready we're out for the next two nights in a row. I've booked us at Gilda's on the beach tonight as its only ten minutes away, it won't be a late one, Max is up for it in his wheel chair, just a nice chilled evening."

"Great Gramps, all this shopping is exhausting."

They arrived at Gilda's at 9.30pm, their Reserved Area was outside under the arbour on the sand, between the Restaurant and the Cabanas all in precise military lines.

The restaurant was heaving as usual. Gilda greeted Tommy with a kiss on either cheek then the rest of the family "It's been too long Tom, how long you stay now?"

"Maybe a month Gilda, how is Mamma? is she running the kitchen tonight."

"Of course Tom, without her we would have to close."

"Ricardo, he is well?"

"Yes, he doesn't work tonight he is at football."

"Our menu has some changes so have an Aperitivo on the house while you decide."

"Grazie Gilda."

Tommy and the family sat in the warm evening air, gazing out to sea, Karena said

"That`s a big ship to the left out there Dad."

"Yes, probably Italian Navy patrolling for illegals or a cruise ship on its way to Genoa, travelling up from Sicily."

Yuri recognised it as a Cruiser Russian Navy, from the silhouette. He messaged Able "Could be on tonight there`s a Russian Cruiser off Forte, looks as though it`s anchored up. I will be back in ten, the family are sound, they will be safer here if it`s going to happen now."

"Yes Yuri, speak to Tommy, so the others don't hear. Get your men to take them to that big Coffee bar with music on the beach front in Camaiore, always packed, get them to stay there till mid night, then you get back here fast."

Yuri got to the Villa at 10pm, they were all set. The Snipers were all set in place, on the Villa roof, the Armoured Vehicles placed in chevron shape at the main gates, with headlights on. Ables best men were all in their positions, the dogs locked up for the night, Yuri was glad he couldn`t spot all the shooters. The staff had been sent home. He joined Able in the control room.

"Looks tight out there, hope they`re not long coming I`m getting changed."

Yuri came back in an all black one suit, Martial Arts style, on the belt at his waist he had a short two foot Samurai blade in its scabbard, he had gone to Japan to the most famous Swordsmith in Longquan and got a customised short sword in folded steel.

It involves a long manufacturing process, but gives a virtually indestructible blade that cuts lesser steels with one blow. Low slung at his hip was his Glock G48 Rail the belt had two Glock field close combat knives in the webbing at the back, finally a Beretta Nano strapped to his other leg.

"That`s what I call ready for work," laughed Able.

"I had to let Luigi know we may get some action tonight, he said he will deploy a Squadra Speciale team behind the Villa, he has given us a call Code to get them in, and he say`s he will get a police helicopter overhead at mid night."

"Not before we have some fun I hope Able. We can assume

they will come from the sea with the Cruiser offshore, how about a Fisherman on the Pier with a set of night vision eyes for an early warning."

"Send one of the boys, tell him to give us the shout and get back here before they arrive."

Able kept monitoring the compound, ensuring all the Hi Tech kit was in order, checking in with all the team at each set up. Twenty minutes later Able's earpiece announced "Spotter one to base, Trojan Horse 200 yards out, fast approach sixteen peas in a pod out."

"They're here Yuri fifteen and a pilot, I'm staying inside on the comms, you do your thing outside, keep your earpiece on."

Able made a quick call to Tommy "Sir we will be under attack in the next ten minutes or so sixteen targets coming in fast from the sea, we are ready. Luigi is sending a Squadra Speciale for back up if we need to call them in, I notified him with a courtesy call saying we expected a visit tonight. Do not return till you get my or Yuri's, All Clear call."

"Thank you Able, God be with you all, give them hell."

The spotter arrived back, went straight to Able "Sir they're pro's armed to the gills, automatic Assault rifles, Side Arms, Grenade belts, the lot."

"Good job, get in position, make every shot count, fire on my order only."

Able went back to scanning the perimeter, two blacked out SUV's slowed on the seafront opposite the Villa the first one went left down the side road and parked close to the wall on the pavement, the second one went round the back and up the other side road back to the seafront parking twenty yards from the entrance gates, again up close on the pavement.

Able gave Luigi the call sign for the Squadra Speciale, asking him if they could take out the SUV near the main entrance.

"Certo, Able it is done."

Able saw the Squadra Team ram the back of the SUV,

immediately surrounding the vehicle before the occupants had even got out.

The other Suv's occupants were on it's roof, having put ladders to the top of the perimeter wall and rapidly scaled and somersaulted down into the compound retrieving their assault weapons which they had lowered before they jumped.

Able told the drivers in each of the armoured vehicles to move them from the entrance gates so the Squadra Team would be able to enter when ready, they had all the SUV occupants on the ground cuffed and neutralized, without a shot fired.

The eight intruders split into two teams, four men stealthily approaching the Villa down one of the tree lined approaches, the other three leaving a driver in the van went swiftly to the rear.

Able told all his team over the comms "If you have a clear shot take it, take them out now."

Two shots rang out two attackers dropped, taken out by one rapid fire Sniper, one of the men slipped into the wooded area he triggered a trip wire and the Shrapnel Grenade cut him to pieces. The other Sniper took out the last frontal assailant.

"Snipers targets now at rear of villa, three men Yuri come in, where are you at?"

"I am at the rear behind the Pool equipment hut."

"Two of them are closing on you ten yards out, the other one is coming round the side of the Villa approaching the steps to the rear doors."

"If he goes inside he is yours Able, the others are mine."

The one at the back doors to the Villa opened and entered, the other two kept coming to the Villa keeping close to the Pool hut. Yuri went round the back, they were no more than a yard in front of him in a crouching position Assault rifles at the ready, to follow into the Villa. In one synchronised movement Yuri sprung at both men, the one on his right he put two bullets in his forehead as they both spun round on his command "Spetsnaz Soldaty" the one on his left had the top of his head completely cut off, with one deadly stroke of Yuri's short Samurai Sword. They didn't get a chance to fire a round. Yuri leapt up the steps and through the doors into the lounge which was empty.

"Yuri one of them is still on the ground floor."

He instinctively spun round saw a slight movement behind the heavy full length curtains, drew one of his two Glock Field Knives and threw it with one mighty overarm throw deftly into the body behind the curtain. As the man fell forward, Yuri severed his jugular with one swiping movement of the sword, it was all over.

"Stand down all teams, intruders dispatched."

The Squadra Speciale drove into the compound and parked up at the main entrance, the second team of Assailants were all cuffed, hands and feet in the SUV with two of the SWAT team monitoring them.

"Captain Moro, Signore Able at your service, our timing was good? we looked after half of them anyway, we will remove the bodies back to HQ, the Commander visits in the morning."

"Thank you Capitano, well done to all your men, we took no casualties you were a big help."

Yuri had dragged the two bodies outside to the lawn edge and put his two targets in black body bags, they were all removed by the Police.

Able called Tommy "All clear sir, seven targets neutralized no casualties on our side, there were two teams, one team apprehended by the Squadra Speciale without a shot fired."

"A bloody good nights work, well done Able and to all your boys, we will be back within the hour."

Next morning around 10.00am Luigi arrived at the Villa and was shown into the lounge "Tom good to see you, are all well, after last night."

"Luigi your Squadra were outstanding, if I can make a contribution to the Widows Fund or Holiday Fund for children?"

"Very kind Tom, but is no necessary "For them it was a good exercise, I am glad nobody was hurt here, how long do you expect to stay in Forte? can we expect any more visits?"

"I hope it will not occur again, I am staying till the end of the month only, I hope to talk with the people behind this situation, to get a resolution."

"Keep me posted Tom, the Press will carry a story tomorrow saying eight illegal immigrants all male were found dead on the beach at Palmaria, from an open boat. Cause of death dehydration and starvation, we have not yet decided where they embarked from. The second team we snatched with the driver, from the second SUV, they will all be serving very long prison sentences in high security detention. Oh, there was one other thing, the Coroner wondered how two of the bodies both had an eye missing. Just a small detail, I will see you shortly Tom, I hope the remainder of your stay is more enjoyable."

"Thank you again Luigi."

"Able, I`ll leave you to sort the mystery of the missing eyes."

"So, what was it about Yuri?"

"Old habits Able, in the Chechen War some of the soldiers especially Spetznaz used to cut the ears off dead Chechen troops, to make necklaces. I don`t make necklaces but when somebody puts a price on my head open to all comers, I like to send them a personal message from me. It means keep YOUR eyes open, because I will be visiting any day soon. I am going to the Post Office this afternoon and posting them to President Chomski care of the Russian Embassy in Rome."

Max`s physiotherapy was doing wonders for his rehabilitation, but he was getting more and more frustrated at being house bound.

"Dad, great food again tonight, I think I might visit an old friend tomorrow for an hour or so if that`s ok, one of the team could drive me as Alexis is out of action. There is far too much excitement going on here."

"Ok Max, as long as you`re sure you are up to it."

"Yes Dad, it will be good for me, we can take a Hummer,

easier for me to get in and out of."

"Ok Max let's get to bed it's been a long day."

"Night Dad."

Max got into his room, Alexis was sitting on the edge of their bed in a nightie that would have graced any catwalk in London or Milan "I don't know how this will work, back in our room, but if you are not comfortable I'll have your bed moved back tomorrow."

"I don't want to interrupt your sleep that's all darling, I don't get much rest, mainly nightmares which I hope will change, after I have been to the Specialist in Rome next week. Max sat on the edge of the Emperor size bed beside Alexis, who put her arm round his shoulder, stood in front of him and unbuttoned his shirt. She gently laid him back on the bed removing his socks, trousers and underwear, lingering near his pubic area, she cupped his testes in her hand, gently fluttering over and up and down his member which started to harden.

"It's too soon for me Alexis, my head is all over the place, it is not that I don't want you, but I am afraid I am not my old self at present , I could hurt you without realising till after. I have horrific flashbacks and vivid nightmares, it is most likely from the medication drugs I am on for my head.

Whenever I close my eyes even in daytime for even a minute, my eyes have either a vivid red or black background then in the distance like on a TV screen I see a small figure or object coming towards me, a mouth or an eye, or an animal getting larger all the time, the eye is particularly unnerving it comes right up to mine, a beautiful oval Asian shape and colour, the lids open very wide and it starts dripping blood, so real I wake up choking on the blood.

The second I open my eyes it vanishes, when I close them the sequence continues till I fall asleep and wake, usually in an hour. Sometimes there is a wall of kaleidoscope colour, like a monster wallpaper of weird designs, which change all the time, then I have really weird scenarios, like every woman I have ever seen I thought as good looking, could be from a supermarket, or some of the local Policewomen in their jackboots with side arms, full make up, thick lipstick and highly coiffed hair or even Actresses in some film with hundreds of guys I recognise, all in a huge Roman Style Orgy.

I am not in it, just watching them all, it seems to go on for hours but is in reality only a few minutes or so. It drives me nuts, sometimes I have lashed out knocking things off my side table I don't want it happening to you, so let's wait till I have seen the Specialist."

"Of course Maxi, a black eye is about the only thing you haven't given me."

Next morning Max was having his physio session while everybody was at breakfast, the girls wanted a day round the pool with Tonia and Alexis, Michael was on the phone to the offices, Tommy was outside with Able checking out the set up for security again. Max was wheeled out by the physio to the main entrance, one of Able's men pulled up in the Hummer and loaded him in. Tommy came over "Send two with Max Able, get him back by mid-day latest no arguments son."

Max told the driver to go along the coast road to Camaiore just past the Dune Hotel, he took a left turn to a small selection of retail shops in a layby "Park up in front of the sign saying Modelli con Portfolio e Esperienza* then one of you can offload me inside, I'm seeing an old friend, you can wait in the car till I'm ready to leave."

"Maxi how good to see you, why you no call me, what has happen to you? you have an accident? come through to the back room, is wide enough for the chair no?"

"Gianpiero, it's good to see you, it's a long and boring story, I had a car crash I am here at Forte to recover."

"Are you wanting some of your old friends? many of them are on "tour" but will be back by the end of the month."

"No, my tastes have changed now, I am more adventurous

since I am lucky to be here. I have some special needs now."

"I need you to get me a drug, it's a special one, the price is not important, the girl I choose will take the drug with me and obey my every word, as though her life depended on it."

"Max the name of the drug is? I have a beautiful tall Russian blonde model arriving for one month, next week, she has worked with all the Catwalks in London, Paris and Milan she may be interested, if you like her Portfolio. I have plenty Eastern European, who will do whatever you want, at a price, but you will have no conversation, no simpatica you understand?"

"Of course Gianpiero, the drug is DMT in liquid form, a dripper bottle will be good, DMT is derived from Ayahuasca a Psychedelic drug the most powerful one on earth, which is made deep in our brains in minute amounts, it gives us our dreams. My source was damaged in my accident, one side effect is an extreme desire to have near death experiences. The Drug elongates seconds to minutes, when used sexually and seems to make it last hours, with highly intense reactions and orgasms. If used without control it can bring on heart attacks, strokes or death."

"I can supply Max is no problem, I know the Drug, I have something which may amuse you, the latest Hi Tech Reality Sex Doll from Silicon Valley, you can have a free test run as you are a special client, her skin, hair, make up, voice is perfect, she is 100% compliant. She will follow your voice round in the room, you can have a proper conversation with her if you wish, they retail at US100K."

"If the Russian is up for it book me with her, the week she arrives, a normal double suite at the Principe in Viareggio will do for the afternoon. Call me when you have the Drug I could have a test run on one of your Romanian girls or Thai."

"Always a pleasure to deal with you Max, I get your driver."

Tommy asked Alexis to have a walk with him round the Villa before it got too hot.

"Well sweetheart, how is my boy progressing? I mean in his inner self, we can see his physical results get better each day, the physios tell me he is doing really well."

"To be honest Dad, I`m worried about him, it`s probably too early to pass judgment, but I have noticed some changes in him."

"How so? I guess knowing him he`s very frustrated right now, but that should pass."

"It`s deeper than that, he seems to have a burning resentment for what happened to him, not all the time but it comes out at odd times, in completely innocuous moments, for no reason. He gets erratic sometimes, then defensive, then very aggressive, not physically but he seems to feel he was always the lucky one and now he is not so sure. I think he feels he needs to keep pushing it to prove who he is."

"When we get him back home and he is fit again to do a days work, I want him to get involved in the business which he has never done. I want him to team up with Michael, it will mean more flying but we can build him up slowly. It will give him something to concentrate on rather than dwelling on the past.

Also it would be good for Mike to get closer to Max for back up. You know I am not going to be around for ever, I have booked in for my operation in Geneva next week. What do you think about him going to work? I have a proposal to put to the family which I hope will excite them as much as it does me.

We`ll have a slap up meal the evening before I go for my surgery, I will set everything out and you all have a key part to play."

"It could be just what he needs a purpose outside of pure self amusement. With a Playboy Dad it`s a miracle the girls turned out as they did, both grafters like Grandad and Nonna."

"The Genes will out in the end, I am in Geneva tomorrow with the Russians again then back there Tuesday next week for my op. I`m glad we had this chat, anytime you know you can talk with me Alexis, I will always make time for you, as to me you are another daughter."

Tommy's meeting was at 4pm at the D'Angleterre with the Russians, this time he took Able with him. Yuri was keen to go but Tommy decided not to provoke them to that degree. Brezhinski arrived with the two minders who attended the previous meeting, with a short well dressed man who was introduced as a special adviser to the President, who had his ear. It crossed Ables mind that the President had some spare eyes in the post to him from Yuri, but he managed not to grin at the thought.

"Some refreshments gentlemen?" asked Tommy, they declined.

"Mr. Beales I contacted the relevant authority in Moscow with your proposal, the details that you offered at our last meeting. It is possible that this could be a way forward to alleviate Mr. Orlov's, situation that is the reason for Mr. Richter being in attendance today. It is for you to set out your proposal to Mr. Richter, he will advise the President and we will respond in due course."

"Thank you Mr. Brezhinski, Mr. Richter I will commence by saying I have known Mr. Orlov for many years and have always found him to be one of the most upright principled businessmen I have ever dealt with. He has an overwhelming love of his country, he would in my opinion put that above all else. All of that aside, I would make a simple offer, if his Passport is re-instated, I am prepared to deposit into any nominated Bank Account of the Presidents choosing, a Billion US Dollars on the appointed day that Mr. Orlov lands in Geneva Airport, unescorted."

"On the face of it Mr. Beales that might sound like a generous offer, but to me it is not what I would call a high price to pay, for someone who made in excess of £200 Billion profit just under a month ago, thereby becoming the 6th largest Hedge Fund Manager in the US."

"I accept what you say sir, but the two are disconnected. On the one hand how I drive my business is one thing, my sentiment for my friends is another. Next week I may lose £20 Billion."

"That is not your reputation Mr. Beales, you do not play the market, you are always ahead of what the market knows will happen, you have sufficient funds to move market prices on any given day, £5 million on a position in the Forex Exchange moves it your way, you don't get moved by Spikes, you create them, with good friends in all the right places."

"That is what I want to be to your President, as a testimony to this, I will double my offer to $2 Billion, on the same terms, with a sweetener of allowing him to enter my special Fund of Funds Account in the Cayman Islands that has been closed to outside investors for five years. It currently returns over 60% profit year on year."

"That does indeed sound interesting, I will report back to the President on my return and I will contact you directly by Satellite Phone, my number is on my card. I bid you good day and by the way, I hope your operation in Geneva goes well next week."

"They know everything as soon as I do Able, I only confirmed the Op yesterday, it was obviously a warning from the President that he knows where we all are, whenever he wants to reach us."

"Agreed sir, it was a shame the optical attempt failed, but we can work on a second attempt, as I don't think he will let it's failure lie for long."

"Same thoughts exactly Able, I need you and Yuri to come up with something special asap."

On the Monday morning Max got a call from Gianpiero saying he had his drugs in and he had booked a session for him at 2pm with a Thai and Romanian girl in a purpose built BDSM house, one mile inland from his Agency in Camaiore. His driver dropped him at the house after picking up the drugs at Gianpiero's. He managed to walk in on crutches with a support boot for his ankle.

The Villeta was on one floor with a surrounding garden and parking out front where the driver and security waited for a call from Max.

The windows had reflective glass all triple glazed so no one could see in. The interior had a couple of shower rooms a couple of bathrooms one with disabled facilities a decent sized kitchen and four bedrooms. The main interior room was all in white with all the walls and doors soundproofed. There were numerous contraptions around all the side walls with various attachments to the ceiling with chains and leather belts and restraints attached also on the floors. there were two massage tables in the middle of the room. The two girls had two flimsy beach dresses on with nothing underneath.

"I am Miko, my friend is Antanasia, which means one who will be reborn."

"Could be wishful thinking" Max replied and they all laughed "It`s my first time girls, so I need you to show me the ropes, so to speak, if I get comfortable on the massage table you show me your routine nothing too tame though."

"Of course, we are here to please, there is only one rule here, we use a code word which we agree at the beginning, if or when we use it the session is over immediately. Our fee is being settled by Gianpiero, so you only need to relax and enjoy, you may join in at any point if you wish, in which case the code word will be Domani."

Miko explained that she is normally subservient, as Antanasia is dominant, but they can switch if requested.

Both girls undressed and Max could see they were totally oiled with a delicate smelling sunscreen. Soft background music was playing on a system and the lights were dimmed on a remote built into the massage table. Miko laid on her front on the table with her face down into the hole, that ensured her spine was correctly aligned, her legs were spread to the edge of the table her arms loosely down the side.

Antanasia went to the side away from Max to give him clear vision, as she drizzled warm Massage oil with Aromatherapy oils added, from Miko`s neck to the base of her spine then onto her arms and legs. She massaged Miko for ten minutes then gently dabbed any excess oil off with baby wipes.

She pulled a small table on wheels over to the end of the massage table and joined them together with two metal grips attached, locking the wheels tight. Out of a side drawer she lifted a mechanical device which she placed on top of the table plugging it in to an in-built socket. Max recognised it as a massager he had seen used in porn movies. Antanasia half lifted Miko's body, then placed a large cube of dense memory foam underneath her pelvis making her buttocks arch upwards, so she was in a low kneeling position, she strapped Miko's ankles to the massage table and her wrists.

She lubricated Miko's orifices with lube then Antanasia adjusted the machine with an adjustable extending arm with a large double Vibrator attached, so that it touched Miko's lower areas with just the right amount of pressure before switching it on. Miko groaned " perfect" Antanasia passed the remote control to Max, to adjust the speed and depth of penetration. She went to the top of the table reached up and brought a hoist down which had a seat attached, with a hollowed out bottom to it. There was a belt attached to the pulley for safetys sake, before climbing in she dropped the hinged top, facial part of the table, so Miko had to keep her head up or drop it right down, she then climbed into the seat, strapped herself in and hoisted herself electrically up to table top height. She positioned herself with her pelvic areas directly over Miko's mouth and could make adjustments to tilt or move backwards and forwards all from the same control.

"How is it sweetie?"

"I am loving it mistress."

"Don't get too comfortable it's my ride don't forget."

"Of course mistress."

Antanasia told Max to increase pressure and penetration when she lifted her right arm to him, which she did, Miko groaned.

"I can't feel you Miko, harder" raising her arm again.

Antanasia raised the tilt on the seat, so her buttocks were

enveloping Miko`s nose completely, raising her arm again."

"You haven`t hit my spot yet bitch, you`re not working hard enough."

"It`s nearly on maximum " said Max as she raised her arm again.

"Are we getting hot darling?"

"Yes mistress."

Antanasia lowered the hoist to Miko`s head height and proceeded to grind over her head for at least two minutes, then gently lowered herself to the floor.

Antanasia went to the side wall, pulled out a hose extension, switched it on shower mode and played it on Miko`s head.

She switched the vibrators off, she adjusted the table at the top to realign Miko`s body then pushed the table and machine to a side wall leaving Miko in the original angular position.

"Would you like to join in sir? it`s time for some manual corrective treatment."

"I am happy to watch today, you seem to know what you are doing, very entertaining girls."

Antanasia then proceeded to paddle Miko`s backside with a large leather fly swat on a long handle, going harder and harder, till weals started to appear on the skins surface.

Miko finally said "Domani" and Antanasia immediately stopped and released her, embracing her as she climbed down from the table. Antanasia sat on the table, legs apart and said "You haven`t thanked me properly for the pleasure I just gave you"

Miko went down on her knees in front of Antanasia and buried her head in Antanasias groin, when she got up and helped her off the table she said "Me on top tomorrow mistress" and they both laughed.

Max went out into the sunshine and told the driver to head to his favourite bar in Forte he wanted a cold beer.

He called Gianpiero "You did well today Gian I want Antanasia alone next week, as a warm up, same place, before my

Russian model arrives. Text me what I owe to date, I will bring cash with me on my next visit, Ciao"

Tommy had arranged for the two top Chefs from Bistrot to prepare his favourite dinner for the family at the Villa. He was not eating as his Surgery was scheduled for 9 am. next day. Everybody was excited to hear what new scheme Tommy was about to come up with, Karena and Nikki were running a prize draw, with everyone putting their ideas into a champagne bucket, only one each with a prize of £500 for the closest to the actual idea Tommy was about to reveal.

The staff were clearing away and everyone moved into the main lounge "Come on Gramps lets have it, how can you bear to keep us all waiting?"

"This one you will not believe Alexis, I can hardly believe it myself, I have been thinking of a project for the family for some time.

The first hurdle with any project is funding, we are rich beyond most peoples imagination, but this needed to be disconnected from any of our business resources or normal access to funding, then I remembered reading about a Chinese Billionaire who took a punt on the English Lottery. There are a finite number of one line entries to every Lottery, if you back the total number you are guaranteed a win.

Fantastic you may say, do it every week, not so, because the problem is someone else, or more than one other could also have the winning line, so that's the real gamble, sharing the jackpot. Anyway, the Chinese flew into Heathrow in his private jet placed, I think from memory £40 million to cover every possible line, then promptly flew home. He won £100 million jackpot, on his own. There was uproar in the Commons saying it should not be allowed, the Government response was he is a British Passport holder and he placed his wager on British soil as required, there is no problem with his win.

The Euro Lottery with more numbers required £70 million to

guarantee the jackpot so I waited till it went to £160 million with a lot of rollovers, then laid the bet from my private account, which I won with one line and no other winners! So my project will be funded with lottery winnings, which is the second luckiest event to happen to me in my life."

"Dad that's the most ridiculous chance to take, that I have ever heard of, I could never even dream of it," everyone else was speechless for at least a minute.

"Agreed but to realize my dream that's what was needed. If there had been one other winner, I would have only broken even.

So to get to the project, the funds are in place, but what is the project? It is about our family and its origins and to create a legacy, so that people will use it and remember our family name, way after I am gone. What I want is all of you involved, if anyone doesn't want to join in, it is a non-starter.

It is to be based in Piandelagotti I want Max and Michael to come up with a Project Karena and Nikki to come up with a separate one. The first person to get on side, is the local Priest, they always need funds for a new roof or something, so that should be a boot in.

I suggest setting up some advertised meetings in the village hall, to get the locals in and get them to say what the village needs. Obviously there are the remaining relatives who still live there. You will need to tread carefully, they will not look kindly on outsiders coming in with fat wallets, trying to change their lives as they will see it.

Why did Camillo never return to the village? He bought property in La Spezia but never went back to Piandelagotti. I think a proper sculpture as a First World War memorial, in Marble, would be a good addition, with all the names on the base, there are four Bulgarelli`s named on the Church wall, again the local Priest will have all the family records. So first reactions one at a time please."

"You have really surpassed yourself Dad this time, we were running a book on what your idea was. £2000 in the pot, but for sure no one got close to this one."

"I like the idea Gramps, can Max work with me? To my knowledge, Dad won`t argue diffrently, he hasn't done a full day in his life so far. He has people skills for sure, but applying himself to get something done, not so sure."

"Nikki and I are definitely up for it Gramps only worry is time management to spend on the project we settle on. How is the winning project selected Gramps?

" One vote darling, mine "

Tommy travelled to the Hospital in Geneva where he was admitted for his operation Tonia and Lara came with him, Able, with three of Ables men in the second Hummer. Tonia and Lara were booked into the D`Angleterre for two nights, with two of Ables men on their door in turns.

A day later the Specialists were ecstatic with the results, Tommy had come through with best possible prognosis after the op. It was now a waiting game to see how well he would recover and how soon. The family were all elated, Tonia and Lara went on a shopping spree in Geneva as next day Lara had to return to St.Petersburg to sign off formally from the Mariinsky, as she had decided she was moving in with Tonia at last.

6

Next day Tommy was still under heavy sedation in his suite with all the attendant drip feeds and breathing apparatus in sight as Tonia and Lara spent the morning with him. Nurses and Specialists came in and out every ten minutes checking on this and that with Able or one of his men outside the door all the time. Tonia and Lara went to leave as Lara had a 2pm flight to St. Petersburg Lara said "you go ahead to the car I need the loo again, I will get you at the car park entrance."

"Sure thing sweet, we have plenty of time."

Lara went back into Tommys suite saying to Able`s man she had left her lighter inside and was going to use his loo.

She immediately opened her bag took out a syringe and put it gently into the drip feed to Tommys arm she squeezed the small amount of mercury into the drip feed and hastily left getting to the front entrance as Tonia pulled up.

"Thought I`d save you the walk."

"Thanks darling lets go."

"Oh I nearly forgot, Dad asked me to give you this envelope, if he didn`t come out of the op alright, I don`t know what`s in it, I don`t suppose he will mind now it`s all good, read it in private on the plane."

Back at the Hospital all hell had broken loose, a quick thinking nurse had gone in to check Tommy when an alarm went off she immediately spotted a kink in his drip feed on the bed where he had moved and disconnected it at his wrist, switching over to a secondary supply, unbeknown to her in the nick of time, the mercury had not entered Tommy`s system.

Lara boarded her flight on time and waved to Tonia in the departure lounge reaching for her bag and Tommy`s letter.

She opened it quizzically, as Tommy had never communicated with her in this way before. Inside, Tommy explained in detail that Roman was her real Father giving her as much detail as he could and reassuring her he had always loved her, but kept her protected in the best way he knew, from any retributions that could fall on her, if the powers that existed in Russia knew he was her father. He enclosed the only photo he had of Lara, her mother and Roman, as well as the necklace he gave her mother when they married.

Lara was distraught, she realised she had been used and lied to by the system in her Homeland, when she had been told her mother had died at the hands of a British Double Agent, she worked with during the war, Tommy was the Agents Controller she had been given Tommy as her target only a month ago.

She composed herself emailing her Controller, saying she had completed her mission and Tommy was dead she asked to meet with the President, as she had information for him only, regarding his Offshore Accounts in Tommy`s Banks, she had promised to deliver the message to the President alone, and asked to be able to return permanently to her Homeland.

She then emailed Able explaining what she had done, telling him it was essential that they put out a Press Bulletin saying Tommy had not survived a Critical Operation at the Geneva Hospital. She emailed Michael telling him he could expect the Russian Rouble to nosedive by the morning, she was on her way to guarantee it.

She told him to freeze all of the Russian Presidents assets in all their Banks blaming it on a Chinese Cyber Hacking attack, as a temporary explanation, as President Chomski would be dead in 24 hours.

Finally she emailed Tonia explaining everything, telling her how she was made to integrate with Tommy`s family, so she was close to her target, though she never knew the actual identity of who the target was until she arrived at the Villa. Agents always carried at least two methods of killing their targets. She then told Tonia she really loved her, begging her forgiveness, but she would never see her again.

Lara received a response from her Controller, the President agreed to meet her but only at the Mariinsky in St. Petersburg that night at 9pm, as he was kicking off his re-election campaign tour from his home town. The result was a foregone conclusion as in the previous election he had won with a 97% turnout and a majority win of 94% with 3% of the vote being scrapped as illegible.

Lara arrived at the Mariinsky at 8.45pm and went straight to the Directors Office where he greeted her effusiveyl "My favourite Butterfly, I understand you are to meet the President tonight, before our performance honouring his Presidency. Such a shame he has not seen you in his home town, his party is due now, they will be using my Office, come next door, till he calls for you. I am so happy to see you positively glowing, your rest in Italy was overdue."

"Thank you Comrade Director, it is good to be back to my spiritual home, I will quickly use the toilet and wait next door till I am called."

Lara calmly went to the toilets and found what she wanted in her handbag, checked her phone, which she had bought at the Airport and that the message on it was correct then went back to the Office, next to the Directors Office and sat inside.

The door opened quickly, two bodyguard type men pushed in ordering Lara to stand, as they strip searched her, after frisking her with a hand scanner.

They frog marched her back into the Directors Office, where the President sat at the Directors desk, he asked her to convey Tommy`s message, she told him she now knows she was set up to kill Tommy, he was not involved in her Mothers death.

President Chomski denied any personal involvement, saying it was part of a systematic culling of people Worldwide who the State deemed to be enemies of the People, they had to be removed, the Homeland demanded it. She slowly produced her mobile, which she said had Biometric Iris Identification on it, which needs to be activated after her fingerprint sign on, within 10 seconds, or it will combust. There is a one time code she has to enter which will give the user access to Tommy's codes for his Offshore Accounts.

The President invited her round to his side of the desk followed by his minders, she opened the phone with her fingerprint ID, put it to her IRIS and it displayed ENTER CODE, on the screen, she tapped in digits and letters then put it gently on the desk in front of the President, he leaned forward to read PRESS ONCE, to receive data. He eagerly, but gingerly pressed the active button, the message came up FUCK YOU ITS OVER, as he turned to her she grabbed him with one hand behind his head, forcing her tongue down his throat clamping his jaw shut, biting through her tongue, as she had her throat cut from ear to ear by one of the Presidents bodyguards. Too little, too late, the President died in seconds, as did Lara from the two small 5mg capsules stuck to the underneath of her tongue. It contained Tetrodotoxin the most readily available Toxin to man, from the Puffer Fish, among others a great delicacy in South East Asia. One milligram gives a normally healthy person the shakes as it mildly upsets the nervous system, 5mg will kill any adult in seconds.

Lara's phone display read MISSION ACCOMPLISHED sent automatically to Tonia, Able and Michael on the desk.

The next day the Russian State News agencies announced the death of the beloved President Chomski from a fatal heart attack, as he worked on papers of National Importance, he was being treated for an Aneurysm, which had burst unexpectedly. The top Specialists at the St. Petersburg Hospital had fought all night to save him, but in the end he had gone to meet his ancestors in the City he was born in and loved all his life. Two weeks National Mourning were declared and his deputy was sworn in as President. The Elections to be held in six months were declared open to all Opposition Parties and any Leaders held were to be released from Detention, marches and demonstrations were to be permitted, but limited to no more than ten thousand people, the first march of over 600,000 ended peacefully with no arrests.

Michael had acted on Lara`s message and gone Short on all their Russian Rouble positions. Keeping it strictly in the family.

Tommy told Michael to transfer all the dead Presidents Funds to other Banks, ones they were Major Shareholders in, without any Russian connections to the Main Boards. He called a meeting of all the families in Forte for the next week end as Tommy could not yet be moved never mind fly anywhere. Roman confirmed he would arrive mid-week, his travel restrictions had been lifted. The Americans would arrive on Sunday.

Max had his usual Physio-Session before breakfast then took one of the Hummers with a driver, making his way to Gianpiero`s in Lido di Camaiore, he picked up his bottle of goodies and paid his tab up to date. Gianpiero told him the Russian Model was arriving on Monday coming, she was looking forward to seeing him, for a two hour session at the House of Fun, rather than the Hotel.

Antanasia was all set up for him at the House, the lights were dimmed, the air-con hummed away in the background and chilled Crystal on ice with two glasses were on the table by the massage couch. Max was able to walk in slowly, with a stick and he still had his support boot on.

"I am pleased you wanted to see me again sir, welcome."

"I liked your attitude you could be my kind of girl."

"Do you have anything special in mind for today?"

"I have a new drug I want to try, I need you to take it with me, it`s not a big deal, like a soft style LSD, prolongs the pleasure so they say, Gianpiero got it for me so I know it will be legit. If we have a drink first, then you give me a gentle massage, we take our shots, then see where we go, is that ok with you?"

"Sounds good."

Antanasia undressed Max, she could see his new scars and handled him gently, helping him onto the double massage table, he propped himself up on one elbow while they drank their Crystal, he laid down as Anastasia started with his shoulders, moving down his spine to his buttocks, then down his legs. She moved his legs gently apart and caressed his buttocks lightly running her nails under his body, down his member and slowly up his back crack while pouring warm oil down the run.

She inserted her middle finger gently Max whispered "yes more" she obliged, Max said "Harder", she complied.

Max turned over, asked for another glass of Crystal and for the dropper bottle of liquid he had brought with him. Antanasia took three and gave Max three.

Around the edge of the massage table were leather covered metal clamps for wrists and ankles. Max got off the table, instructing Antanasia to lay face down with her head where his had been. He clamped her wrists and ankles to the outer edges crucifix style. He slowly finished the bottle of Crystal, by the neck, climbing back on the table.

"Is it kicking in yet?"

"Just starting to feel good."

"I am getting rock hard, lets do it, I have been out of action for months I really need this."

He turned the music up really loud, a heavy metal beat as he covered Antanasia`s head with his, they French kissed and he bit her lips and tongue making it bleed a little, it tasted good, as the room started to move in kaleidoscope shapes in tune with the music. He did not hear her cries of discomfort, as he moved roughly over her body. Antanasia was shrieking stop, stop! but Max heard nothing, he was way way out of it.

He got off the table going behind Antanasia`s head, dropping the hinged piece down he forced her mouth onto his member and with both hands on the back of her head kept it there, rammed tight for what seemed like ten minutes. Max tightened his grip on Antanasia`s neck pushing her head down over the back of the table as she tried with all her strength to resist his force. He held the grip until she no longer struggled. After a few minutes Max steadied himself, managed to get to the intercom, ordering more Crystal before slumping into a tub chair. Gianpiero brought another bottle with ice, opened the bottle poured two glasses, it was then he realised Antanasia was not moving. Max was sat in the chair, his eyes glazed over, smoking a joint.

"That was outstanding Gianpiero, your girl has earned a bonus today."

"Are you crazy Max? what have you done? the girl is no longer breathing, you have throttled her."

"It was just a game it is not possible" he mumbled.

"We need to get you away Subito Max, I will call Signor Able, he will take care of the situation we must resolve it quickly, you are confused, the girl is Miko the Thai girl, Antanasia`s friend", he got Max out of the room to his car and told the driver to take off quickly. Able was there in twelve minutes.

"Mr. Able, Max is out of control, he is using Ayahuasca for amusement, he loses total control when he is high. He lost it completely with one of my girls, he maintains it was an accident, the Thai girl is dead, the Albanians will want compensating, they will be here in the morning for today`s take. This cannot get out, it will finish all of us they have her passport of course."

"Where is the girl?"

"I have called in a favour, two friends have her, the Albanians will want to see the body, they will dispose of her after. They will see Max`s car on the CCTV, which they check every morning, for the count on visitors, also before you say wipe the video, is not possible there is a lock on and they would wipe me if it does not work. Safer to pay them for the girl and it all goes away."

"Call me as soon as they have been in the morning."

"Of course Mr. Able."

Able reported in to Michael, about the possibility of an Albanian financial play on the family, he got the call from Gianpiero at 10.30 next morning, the local Capo insisted on meeting Able at 4pm. that day, at Gianpieros.

Able was at Gianpieros at 3.30pm precisely with Yuri and one other shooter in the back of the Hummer, with the necessary firepower.

"He has gone to see the body, before coming here Able, he is not too happy shall we say, but an accommodation could be possible. His name is Cekicin which translates as the Hammer, he is an ex Cage Fighter and Para Military from their Army. Here he is, early, he runs all their girls from Genoa to Livorno, a real tough nut, he knows Max was here.

"So, we need to talk Mr. Able, a client of yours has damaged some of my goods. You are a businessman like me, I treat you with respect. I am accountable for my employed goods and my Bosses demand a good annual return for their investment. We know your clients background and connections, nearly as diverse as our own."

"Mr. Cekicin I accept all you are saying, I am only the messenger here, I have to report to my Bosses as well. It is an unfortunate interruption to your cash flow, here in your operation, if we can resolve it to everyones satisfaction it would be ideal."

"Mr. Able I don't know if you understand our operations, we have partners with expectancies, who we work with in Italy, as well as many other Countries the UK, USA, all of Europe and South America. Our goods are shipped everywhere, there is a big market in Italy, our Partners are the Ndrangheta or Calabrian Mafia as you probably know them."

"I know them we have had dealings in the past, Mr. Cekicin, their net turnover last year from their Businesses was larger than Deutsche Bank, the largest Bank in Germany, in excess of 40 billion Dollars,"

"As you say in your country, they are big hitters, serious players."

"All of the preamble accepted, Mr. Cekicin, what figure are we looking at to make the problem go away? my clients are not in the market trading business, but they are practical men."

"Mr. Able, I prefer that my bosses do not know I have lost a piece of their merchandise, through neglect on my part, so it will be made to look like suicide, I will still be expected to make up the trading deficit, by recruiting a new piece of equipment, so the cost will be less. In such circumstances we require 250000 in Swiss Francs deposited to our account in Lugano in five working days."

"If my client is agreeable, we require the girls passport, we will dispose of the body. I will get back to Gianpiero by ten o`clock tomorrow with my clients answer."

Able reported back to Michael word for word, sayingd they were being reasonable, unless they thought they could revisit the deal again in the future.

"Mr. Michael it doesn't feel right to me, not the deal, nor the guy, somethings definitely not kosher."

"I will bow to your inside knowledge Able, but what do you suggest?"

"If you are up for it sir, go along with the deal, at this stage it`s not cash in hand, but going into an Account which is good, we have nothing to lose at this moment and we can pull the plug if it doesn't fit in the end."

"Agreed Able set it up, say nothing to Max right now."

"Gianpiero set the deal up with Cekicin, I want to see the body first."

"I`m sure all will be no problem, I take you this evening at seven."

"Fine."

Able spoke to Gianpiero who confirmed the deal was on and took Yuri in the Hummer to the meet, at a single storey apartment in Camaiore, he saw the dead Thai girl who they had crammed into a top loading freezer, with ice cream still in it.

"It was the best situation we could have no? Mr. Able."

They returned to the House of Fun.

As they went in Gianpiero switched the lights on and went through to the main room followed by Yuri and Able.

"A drink gentlemen to seal the deal?."

"I think so Gianpiero a good idea, Vodka and lots of ice" said Yuri, two bottles later Gianpiero was slurring his words and Able decided to move it on, turning the music up, he said to Gianpiero "How do they use some of this kit, how far do they take it with the client?"

"Depends how well the girl knows the man or woman" he slurred, taking another double, down in one. These leg and arm restraints keep the body locked in position, till they are released, I show."

Yuri helped him onto the massage table and arranged the leg bar, two feet apart and locked them on to Gianpieros ankles, the arm bar the same, vertically over his head.

At this point Able and Yuri took their jackets and shirts off, Able stood at the head of the table, Yuri half way down.

"Ok boys is a good fun but I no gay, no like where this is goin."

"I can promise, you will not like it at all, Gianpiero" Able forced his mouth wide open with the Speculum the girls used on willing clients and kept pouring the half of the remaining bottle down Gianpieros throat, while holding onto his nose he coughed, spluttered and swallowed more.

"Why you do this to me?"

"You are lying Gianpiero, Yuri hates liars, you and your friend today are not the real deal, tell us the truth. We have all night but you will not last long. Yuri is a Russian Special Forces operative from the Chechen War, he has castrated more prisoners and cage fighters than you have had Aperol Spritz. He can take every bit of skin off the pipework while leaving the orchestra in place, but useless, a bit messy but effective, I would talk before he starts if I were you. First a little gentle waterboarding or in your case vodka boarding I think."

Able went to the lounge bar and got three more bottles of vodka.

"Drink Yuri?"

"Thanks, no, never while I`m operating. From his jacket pocket he took out a leather sheaf containing six razor sharp Japanese Surgical Knives of varying size laying them near Gianpieros face, in his line of sight.

Able went to the sink got one of the hand towels and soaked it under the hot tap wringing it out placing it over Gianpieros face. He was strapped to the Massage tilting couch with arms and legs locked tight, as Able lowered his head to the floor his feet in the air, his body in a straight line. Able put a nose clip on him, while slowly pouring the vodka over the face towel. Gianpiero choked continuously, begging them to stop. Able put him back to the horizontal leaving the towel over his face.

"Last chance to come clean Gianpiero, or you will be no use to any of your boy or girl friends, I am going to have a drink and watch my friend at work, all yours Yuri to make it stop Gianpiero all you have to do is tell us the truth, about the girl and your Albanian."

Yuri took the towel off his prisoners face and smiled at him while showing him the tools of his trade up close "Now I perform my best artwork on you my friend, you have lasted longer than I thought, now you move into a different league, with the pain as well."

Able pulled a piece of sheer silk from his sheath and put one end inside the nose clip on Gianpieros face and let it drop onto his cheek it was black, he picked the other end up with a forefinger and thumb gently, in front of the prisoners eyes holding it taut, he then proceeded to gently cut GIANPIERO into the silk with simple clean movements. The knives were like a laser.

"Impressive no my friend? of course there will be pain, it`s been a long day I haven't eaten and I am getting a bit tired, so forgive me if my hand slips at any time."

Able went to the middle of the table gently picked the head of Gianpieros penis up with a rubber gloved hand, massaging him to an erection.

"It's easier this way quicker, ok, soon be done."

At this point Gianpiero passed out two minutes later Able slapped his face, jolting him awake pouring another vodka down his throat "Come on, you will miss the main event, wake up Gianpiero, are you not using any Anaesthetic Yuri?"

"Just some numbing cream, its afterwards he will want the Anaesthetic, we could drop him to the hospital outside Forte, they have A & E, drop him at the back door?"

"Sure, good call."

Yuri rubbed some numbing cream in and picked up the largest scalpel, pulling the scrotum sack taut, saying "Softest, saggiest bits first" slicing gently into the surface of the skin and a thousand nerve endings, Gianpiero nearly hit the ceiling but he was restrained, it was like a major electric shock, his piercing screams resonated round the room, above the deep throbbing music.

"The restraints work really well Gianpiero, I suppose it depends on how much blood he loses Yuri, no?"

"Exactly Able, it's partly down to my knife skills of course, remember Hannibal Lecter, he made lampshades from dead peoples bodies he had murdered, I think. I'm not that patient, so now we go down the main member, around the base and a circuit at the top gently easing away, all the way down, nearly half done then, Bravo Gianpiero."

"I wouldn't mind doing a bit Yuri, if you are ok with that", as Yuri picked the tip of his penis up again Gianpiero screamed "Ok you guys you win, STOP I will confess all to you, please stop now."

Yuri put on his most disappointed face, but cleaned off his scalpels and tidied up the prisoners nether regions, using some super glue on the loose flap on the scrotum. They sat him up at a

45 degree angle, releasing him from the leg and arm rigid S&M kit, but keeping him shackled to the massage couch.

"So what was the plan in the end Gianpiero, tell all and you will be a free man. Miss nothing out, it had better be good for you to walk away."

"You were right Signor Able it was how you say a ruse, an idea which presented to me from Mr.Max`s situation, for me to leave this business. When he asked me for Ayahuasca drug I knew he was far gone, it will kill him or someone with him, family maybe anyone. He knows how far it takes him to a different planet. I substituted the girl, when he was on the drug for my reality Thai doll, from America, she is so real he was convinced he had killed her, I got him away to his driver quickly. I then got one of my weight training friends to play the Albanian Capo, with the idea to make enough to leave Forte for good. What made you suspect?"

"You didn't ask for enough money, who the fuck was the body in the freezer?"

"A friend of a friend works in the local mortuary, he borrowed the girl for the night."

"So you got one thing right, you had better leave Forte, you have made an enemy of a powerful man in this region, with powerful friends, not to mention the now ruined reality sex doll, which your Albanians will want paying for."

"I will be gone by the week end, I have a cousin in Milan in the same business. Tell Max nothing personal and get him off that junk before it`s too late, can you free me now please?"

"I think we can leave you where you are, to think over what nearly happened to you, the girls will let you go in the morning, Ciao e Buona Notte Gianpiero, we must never see your face again Certo?"

Able narrated the whole events of the evening, except the graphic bits, to Michael on the phone, who was much relieved, now more determined than ever to get on Max`s case he said to Able "Lets keep the Thai Doll bit to ourselves, it will have more impact if Max thinks he had gone too far, it could speed his will to get clean."

"Not a problem sir, sounds like a good plan."

Able asked to have a word with Michael after he had completed his business session at 12 am. before lunch. Max kept a low profile under an umbrella round the pool, chatting with the girls and Karena, who were all consoling Tonia.

Alexis`s arm was healing well and she was now down to light bandaging, with anti-biotic creams. Tommy was due to return on Monday.

Able spoke with Tommy on the phone and asked if he could now get the booby trapped trees returned to normal, as all the guests were expected next week, stressing he would keep all the men on with all other security aspects maintained, till any change was authorized by Tommy.

Tommy agreed with Ables assessment and he arranged to have them removed over the week end, as well as the detonators from the two armoured vehicles.

Able went into the office after 12am and Michael was ready for him. He bade Able to sit down as he closed the door behind him.

"What`s on your mind Able? not thinking of retiring yet I hope? you`ve certainly seen us through a beauty this time."

"No sir, I wanted to give you an update because Mr .Beales is not back till Monday, I`ve spoken with him to put him in the picture, he has authorized a downgrading on all the equipment installed here by this week end.

"Thank you for the update. First off Max goes nowhere without you, I need to let him know that I know about it, then we decide what happens next when Dads back."

Michael took Max out for a coffee in the Bentley Continental GT Convertible, left hand drive, he had bought it for Tommy for when he was retired, at the Villa. It had been delivered a week ago, still under wraps in the garage for a week. Too much had been going on, Mike had forgotten it was there. It was a stunning Azzuro Blue, all White Doeskin Interior, a 6 Litre Petrol Engine, from 0-60 in 3.7 seconds top speed 207mph.

Able followed behind in a Hummer. Mike turned off the coast road at Ronchi to a wooded park area, pulling into a designated picnic area.

"What`s occuring Mike? is this where I get a bullet to the back of the head?"

"We need to discuss what to do with you, Able had to tell me what went down yesterday. Before you start, he works for us now, but if he goes to someone else he takes that knowledge with him, he could bring it back to haunt us in the future assuming you`re still alive. What the fuck is going on in that worthless head of yours now.

He got rid of the body last night it remains to be seen if we can kill the Albanian interest in the girl or whether they come after you, or us. Don`t you think we have enough going on right now? you worthless piece of shit. What Dads going to make of it is anyones guess, could even give him a stroke. As for Alexis, can we keep it from the kids for fuck sake?"

"I accept all you say Mike, especially about me being a worthless piece of shit. Over the years you`ve made it obvious that`s what you feel about me. I think it started when Alexis preferred me to you, as she started off dating you, then she saw the life she would have, with you flying all round the world super successful, but no time for her or any other woman."

"That`s right, I chose the business Dad created, you chose to spend as much money as you could and always be Mr. Affable without a care in the world, because someone else always picked up the bill, because of your name. Thank God Mum`s not alive to see you now."

"Ok, does that feel better now Mike?"

"It does actually, but it does not solve what to do about it."

"How much better that made you feel is exactly what my indiscretions do for me. You are right I am a disgrace to Mum and

Dad, but thank God they do not know and if you`re the loving son you make out you`ll protect Dad from it, as well as Alexis and especially the girls.

I can change with your help, I realize how bad it has become, the evil eats me up, I have thought of ending it all but, I love my kids to see them every day is everything. I need to see if I can get a different medication to kill these depressive urges that take me over. I know Dad wants me to come into the business with you, but I could not say it to him, I am not capable, you and my kids do an amazing job. Dad should have kicked my arse out a long time ago. The best I can hope for now is to get back to being a better person, but I need your help."

"If you mean it of course, for now we keep Dad, Alexis and the girls out of it, when we get home we see Geoffrey in London and see what we can sort out, you may have to come to the States to see someone, you can stay with me. Over here you go nowhere without Able or Yuri. You need to keep a low to invisible profile, as that other girl Antanasia will recognise you whatever Gianpiero says."

"All fine by me."

"Give me that shit in your pocket."

"Here you go bro, thanks for the chance, I will not let you down, I promise."

Mike turned around and headed back to the villa with Able following. Michael phoned Geoffrey in London explaining the situation with Max, Geoffrey agreed to do some research and get back to him with an appointment for Max to see someone in a weeks time.

The Villa gardens became a hive of activity as a team of Bomb Disposal men arrived from the Military at Pisa Airport and started to clear the grenades. The family had been told to stay indoors till the all clear later in the day.

Next day Tommy arrived at mid-day all the staff were at the main entrance to the Villa to welcome him, as his Ambulance drove in through the main gates, Able had all the security men in two lines either side of the entrance, presenting arms with their assault rifles and bayonets fixed. No shots were fired however.

Tommy was bedded down, Maria popped in to see him, asking if he was ready for some of her Chicken Soup in Brodo, a favourite old Nonna recipe, when any member of the family is under the weather. He could not say no, but a little later please. He wanted all the latest info on the Markets, how much did we make on the Oil Futures, what are the latest positions we are involved in today.

Michael gave him the latest and he said "I can see I have no need to rush back to work, but I will be glad when I can move around again", Michael told Tommy that he had fixed a visit for Max to see a top Brain Specialist in London, they were just waiting for Geoffrey to finalise a time slot with who the best person was. The medication he was originally on did not seem to be effective enough, he was getting panic attacks. Michael said he would fly back with him and Able possibly in the Company Jet.

Roman arrived next day and was glad to see Tommy to talk about Lara with Tonia as well.

"Here we are Tommy, two old soldiers at the end of the road, we have come a long way crossed a lot of bridges, lived and loved, fought and nearly died. Made fortunes lost loved ones, but in the end, what was it all for? if you outlive your children it all counts for nothing. There is nothing left of you when you die, no living part of you to carry on as you did, or to make better choices. With my Lara gone I wasted all those years thinking I was protecting her, watching her from a distance, when I could have had years with her, taking her to school, her first job, coming home, spending time with her all lost. It was all so pointless."

"Roman we have had our time as you say, we made our choices, often afterwards we can maybe wish we had done things differently, but we only get one moment in our lives to make a choice, whatever it may be, right or wrong and it will never be right all the time. We do things, cause and effect, we influence things around us and others lives, family and friends. They react, go off and do their own thing, we cannot blame ourselves or them if it does not work out, as we would all have wished, every time.

You did what you knew to be the right thing for Lara and you at that time. Life got in the way in the end. If you were back there now at the exact moment when you made the decision to protect her as you did, without knowing what has just come to pass, would you have made a different decision? Old friend I weep with you, for your loss, I ask you to befriend my daughter Tonia who Lara loved and was going to live with. She will let you read Lara`s last letter to her, I am sure, before she went to see the President. She knew in the end what you had done for her and loved you for it, she asked Tonia to give you back her locket and photo as she went to her certain death."

Next day the Americans arrived the Brothers, Wives and Children, it was like a London Hotel at Christmas week. Maria drafted her two sisters into the kitchen to help, as the staff were at full stretch, some of the security men were washing up after meals. Tommy was in good spirits and Roman and Tonia were spending time talking together in the grounds, going for early morning walks along the beach front with a guard and one of the Hummers following.

Michael got a call from Geoffrey who recommended an American he knew who was on a Lecture Tour of Europe for the next two weeks. He was based at his villa near Rome. Geoffrey had impressed on him it was an urgent matter and as an old colleague he agreed to see Max in Rome next day, the only time he could slot Max in.

After breakfast Max kissed Alexis and the girls goodbye said his farewells to Tommy, Roman and the American family and got into the Bentley. Tommy said he was waiting to try it out with

Michael beside him. Able was behind the driver with an armed guard.

They headed down the coast road to Viareggio turned inland past Lido di Camaiore following the Autostrada signs for Roma, the approach road was a winding circular road down to the toll booth ahead.

It was an automated payment booth on the drivers side. As the driver reached out extending his arm, he could not quite reach the machine, he had to open the door and manually feed his note into the machine, which rejected it. At that moment two men came round from the back of the booth one took deliberate aim at Max. Before he fired, the back of his head split wide open with two quick silenced shots from Ables Glock, as he had gone round behind the booth, where the men came from. saving Max`s life. The other shooter had dropped his gun, arms in the air, Able dispatched him anyway.

Able spoke to Michael, gave him the news and asked him not to say anything till he was back, just to say there had been a crash and they would be back later today as soon as the Police released them all. The only good news was that it had all happened in Luigi`s district of Command.

After statements and witnesses had been questioned they were allowed on their way. The two shooters were taken to the Mortuary in Viareggio, the Bentley to the Police pound for forensics and Ables Glock kept as evidence.

Michael had phoned their Doctor and asked him to attend the Villa with some sedatives for Tonia and the girls and whatever Tommy might need, he went straight into the lounge as the Doctor then arrived. Michael explained to him what had happened and asked him to remain there till he came down for him, he went upstairs to Tommy`s room. Alexis and the girls were just coming out of Tommy`s room.

"Able and Max were attacked on the road, they`re both unhurt, on their way back now, they are fine, Alexis my love, Nikki, Karena come down. Luigi thinks it was either mistaken identity or a mix up on some crossover of a contract between the Ndrangetha and the Albanians he is reaching out to his contacts to get a clear picture, he believed it was most likely a localised drug deal gone wrong, the killers had identified the wrong targets and were all dead.

Alexis wanted to get Max to bed and sedated. Michael asked Roman to explain to the guests Mike was sorry but he needed to make sure the girls and Alexis were stable, to this end, please accept his apologies, he and the Doctor would take the girls to their rooms and Michael would explain everything fully to the guests in the morning, Michael asked Able to put Security on high alert for the next few days. The Doctor eventually left, having given the women a strong sleeping draught to get them through the night.

In the morning at 8.00am. Maria went up quietly to Tommy's room with his morning coffee and tapped gently on his door before she went in, she placed the coffee on his bedside table and opened the heavy curtains to let a little light in. She went over to straighten his bedclothes and raise his pillows.

"Buon giorno signore Tom, una bella giornata oggi sta bene lei? " she got no reply looked closely at him to see if he was still asleep, she realised he had died in his sleep, as she turned to raise the alarm Tommy said "Due croissants grazie Maria e buon giorno a te."

Everybody was at breakfast at 10am as Tommy entered in his wheel chair, gently manoeuvred by one of the nurses. The Nurse set him up in his automatic recliner chair reminding him he had a one hour Physiotherapy session at mid-day.

"Just a double espresso please Maria. Hello everybody, it's good to see you all together in one room, it's been too long since we have been able to do this. There are a couple of reasons I wanted us to get together, on a face to face basis.

Firstly, with my health I was not sure if I would even be here when I asked you all to come, but my operation was successful and hopefully if recovery goes well, I may have some more years to play with.

Secondly, we have recently put to bed a situation that threatened our organizations position and possibly even its continuity. Following on from that it could be a good time for each of us to evaluate where we are today, with each other, also the organization and whether we wish to continue as we are, or enter into a different agreement for the future.

Let us take the time to re-affirm our commitment, or go our separate ways, if that is what we decide. Guys I suggest all of us at the sharp end of the business have our meetings between 2pm and 5pm here at the Villa, everybody else can hit the Designer shops in Forte, have a great lunch at Gilda's Beach Restaurant on my tab and we can either eat in with Maria and her team feeding us, or we can dine out at one of the many local eateries.

7

Girls, Florence is only about an hour and a half away, if you want to make a day of it, you decide, Yuri and one of his team will escort you. Max you stick with Mike today, see you boys at 2pm. here in the main lounge after my Physio."

Tommy arrived back at 2pm. sharp, to find Mike and Max deep in conversation in a corner of the lounge with laptops being passed one to the other, both with very animated conversations going on, between them. At the dining table Karena and Nikki were engrossed in laptops and lots of A4 sheets of paper with a steadily growing pile of rejected sheets of paper in a large waste bin.

"Good to see you committing to the task people, how is it going? your initial thoughts, girls first."

"We are trying to think of ways to make the village a place for people to want to live, with work available. We need to get up there for a look around at what may be feasible, there is a certain amount of information available on line, but as you said Dad the people on the ground need to approve whatever plan we come up with, for it to succeed.

From Satellite Surveying there are quite a few buildings available to utilize, bearing in mind whatever we want to do will have lots of red tape and protected environmental issues to get approval for. Piandelagotti itself has more of a middle aged plus population, but there are a dozen other villages and a couple of sizeable ones within a short distance. So our initial thoughts are firstly to create a manufacturing base in the village either for goods or foodstuffs for export and distribution in Italy.

With the internet, worldwide sales is a realistic possibility. Emilia Romagna is renowned for its Pork products we would need to look into costings, to set up a speciality range from scratch with an up to the minute facility to manufacture, package and export products at one site.

Our second possibility is to encompass the dozen or so other villages in Cross Country Skiing. This would involve creating B & B facilities in each nominated village participating. There is already a Cross Country Skiing Season at Frassinoro, a few kilometres from Piandelagotti. In summer the region is geared up for walking also cycling is very big, as in the rest of Italy, they have certain Championships throughout the year with entrants from all over the Country and Europe competing. The snow season runs from Christmas to end of March, with cycling taking over till the end of the summer.

Still in sporting mode, our final possibility is to create a Hill Climb car racing track as close to Piandelagotti as possible, we would want to get Sir Stirling Moss and Sir Jackie Stewart involved, as two of our most famous drivers known all over the world. Gramps, you used to tell us about when you went to the Prescot Hill Climb Championships before we were born.

Stirling is still a legend in Italy, as the driver who set the fastest time ever for the famous Mille Miglia, at an average speed of 104mph in a Mercedes. This race was a thousand miles from Brescia in the North to Rome and back, on roads that were open to the public, with sheep, cows and hand carts around any upcoming blind bend, unimaginable. It was considered too dangerous in the end and discontinued. Again, depending on costings, if feasible, it would be good to add an oval race track for pure speed trials.

That's where we are at the present Gramps, we think we need to have two ideas to present to the meetings. Ultimately we need to firm up basics on costings and likelihood of approval on planning. So, there is a mountain of work to be done to even get the idea in front of you, it's something we are keen to get going on."

"Wow, you girls are certainly the A Team. Very well done, a lot to take in and think about. I agree with you both two projects are plenty to keep you focused, with your day jobs as well. I propose a time limit of six months, to come up with a feasible plan for both projects, so the sense of urgency will get your final idea to me quicker. Again, well done girls have a half hour in the pool before the families get back, see you at supper.

Well boys, the girls have set the bar high in a very short time, how are you both doing, any thoughts from you?

"Dad, I have come up with something that will be a driver for me, Mike is worried about the nuts and bolts, but it is just an idea at present. There is a building for sale on the edge of Piandelagotti, an old Monastery, with several outbuildings closed down over twenty years ago. I am thinking of renovating it, seeing if we could with your contacts at the Vatican get a Religious Order of Monks to reopen it as a Sanitarium for Drug and Alcohol rehabilitation, they would be self sufficient producing their own food, Solar Heating etc. basic accommodation open to all Religions.

The Attendees would help in the running of the Sanatarium, we could get ideas and costings from the Specialist in Rome. This is something I could really get into, while easing in gently with Mikes schedules. The outbuildings could be converted to a Gym and Pool with Hydrotherapy as well. Accommodation in the main building would be for the Monks with a Chapel, kitchen etc. there could be Ski Type Lodges no more than four people to each lodge, only family or close friends of the Patient.

This would be a stand alone project, but depending on Funds we could construct a small to medium Ski Lodge Hotel with 4 star facilities and its own Helipad as Milan is only a half hour fly time away what do you think?"

"Well, again you have surprised me, it's definitely worth

pursuing to see if it's doable, I would love to see you bring it to fruition. Could be worth seeing if you can get Roman interested in the project, it would be therapeutic for him to have something concrete here to get involved in, talk to him privately.

This is completely unrelated, as an aside to something you said the other night, about confessing your misdemeanours to Alexis, just think about this Max, confession should only be given to a Priest as he cannot divulge it to anyone. Your mind may make you feel it's the way to free yourself of any guilt, but when you see the look on Alexis's face you may regret your decision, but you can't take it back.

Personally I think bearing the guilt is the cross you need to carry, the price you pay, it should go with you to the grave. She doesn't need your indiscretions pushed into her face, she is a good mother and wife think on. It's your choice of course, in the end. There is this idea nowadays that everybody tries to get a headline by "Coming out with personal indiscretions" it's poor judgment, are we all so stupid that we think because some film actor, tv celeb, or pop star shares a secret with some headlines, we are sharing in their lives. It's media feeding frenzy gone nuts, it's the only way the third raters get a headline, every day someone is coming out, is that what you buy your paper for? or to be able to comment on Twitter or Facebook what worthless lives they are leading. Public flagellation doesn't make you a better person it shows you, how weak you really are, that's how I see it anyway."

"Maybe you have a point Dad."

"How's it going with you and Mike?"

"We have cleared the air, I think we can work together, one step at a time, I've got a lot of catching up to do, hopefully genes will get the better of me in the end, with the right help."

"Exactly so Max, here are the girls loaded with parcels, looks like Alexis has hit your credit card for sure.

How was your day girls? just to let you know, I have booked an open air concert in Lucca for us all tomorrow night, Andrea

Bocelli with Zucchero on as well, with Georgia and a young singer Jessica Brando, I don't know her. Weather forecast is good so we can eat at a restaurant there, everybody up for it? You as well Roman, it will do us all good to get out for a few hours.

Guys, Nikki and Karena can we get an early breakfast and get into the conversation about our futures as an Organization, kicking off tomorrow at ten in the morning?.

Girls. if you are all done on shopping for a few days. it`s warm again tomorrow so the pool is all set to go, or you can drop round to Gilda`s with a Beach Cabana, great lunch Menu and service, it`s only a ten minute walk or take the Hummers, a couple of the security guys will accompany you discreetly."

Next morning Mike, Max, Roman, Roberto, Nikki and Karena the two other Brothers and any of their children who were involved in the business had breakfasted well by the time Tommy arrived, they were all on their follow up cappuccinos, in the main lounge.

"Good morning everyone, I hope you all slept well last night. In two days we say Arrivederci to our American Cousins and families, today I want to know from each one of you that you are still committed to our Organization. If you have any reservations or suggestions to help us move forward, today is the day to bring it up, while we are all together face to face.

I am not going into P & L or individual Balance Sheets today, we all know how well we have done recently, since the Banking collapse of 2008, we have prospered. Our current systems and intelligence gathering are second to none in our markets, with the latest Hi Tech systems and equipment we are able to get a maximum percentage on entry and exit levels with in excess of 92% of our trades. The way we share our inside information works well for us all, giving us a near fool proof method of maximising our leads at point of entry.

As a matter of interest lets go round the room individually and each of us give a brief overview of what we have going on at this moment in time. Roman can be excused at this juncture as he has had major trauma to deal with the last few months and is taking some time out, to stabilise his holdings. Mike if you and the girls kick it off."

"Hi guys, I will be brief, I speak with most of you on a weekly basis. A snapshot of where we are as an Organization, Cayman, Isle of Man, Panama are still our main entry and exit points in the Financial World. We have recently opened in Delaware in the States, Roberto will tell you the advantages of this as a base. Simply put they are one of the best regions outside Switzerland for non-disclosure of Clients Acccount Transactions and Holdings of Assets, under their umbrella.

We are currently doing deals on the African Continent as the Chinese and Russian Governments are getting very involved in anything to do with Raw Materials and Precious Metal Mining.

Cayman and Panama is where we tend to keep our Military and Aerospace Projects and Contracts, away from inquisitive eyes and ears. At any given time we have two dozen or more growth situations we are working on. A couple of examples of this, we are currently supplying a South American Country with two Naval Destroyers being taken out of service with our Royal Navy, we are doing the refurbishment in a German Dockyard delivering early next year.

We are also supplying a new Land to Air Missile Defence System to Jordan, delivery later this year. Our more normal business transactions number in the hundreds whereby we take a position in a Company we see as undervalued and underperforming, build up our position to enable us to remove unwanted Directors, sell off underperforming Divisions and reform the Company enabling us to get it to the Market at a much higher worth and valuation.

We also have a very active Debt Purchasing Division which seeks out opportunities Worldwide, whereby we purchase debt from major businesses at greatly discounted cost, work very hard to realize the debt at the original cost or minimal reduction thereon, giving us an expected return of in excess of 50% profit after all costs, this is all run from the London Office Canary Wharf. Max you took the last Board meeting as I was in New York how did it go?"

"Very well Mike, all Divisions reported up by over 40% year on year with totally diverse operations, from a new acquisition, a Worldwide Franchise Hairdressing & Beauty Company to Craft Brewing Operations and Textile Companies in Taiwan to name a few."

"Thanks Max, the girls are our Tech Masters they have just come back with the latest developments in Algorithms as applicable to our businesses, with really impressive systems to be put in place, in all our offices asap. Enough from me, now Roberto the floor is yours."

"Hello everyone, as you know I am due to retire from the Federal Reserve this year, but we are still well placed with Enrico my son taking my place on the Investment Committee for Federal Funding. He has built up a contact list with movers and shakers in both Democrat and Republican Parties which will serve us well for the foreseeable future.

Investment wise, the American Family is fully involved in our Offshore Banking Investments in Panama and Cayman Islands. We are particularly involved in Asia, India and Africa as we see major growth in these areas, where we want to counter some of the Russian involvement, in providing cheap loans to facilitate projects, to tie those countries into a new Russian mini Empire of influence.

The individual deals we are doing are all specified in detail on our Website available to all Organization members only, with our projections and up to date P & L positions. From the American position, we endorse the Status Quo for our continuance in our Organization for the foreseeable future, we look forward to many more years collaborating with Tommy and our Russian Cousin Roman, so I pass the platform to our Italian cousins Mario and Piero."

"Ciao a tutti my friends, Italy also is committed to the continuation of the Organization, as you know Piero joined Alfa Romeo as a Designer in their Racing Division after the War and left them with young Enzo Ferrari when he set up his racing team, he is now head of Research and Design for the whole Ferrari Group and a major shareholder. His son Mario has joined our Head Office team and is doing well in our Commercial Debt Division. Italy is a special case compared to the other Countries we all invest in, it`s all about our stability. We have had nearly fourty different Governments in as many years, so Government spending is difficult to bank on.

When Berlusconi was in power, situations were easier to plan for, also lending was easier. We have our Blue Chip Shareholdings in Italy and we did well from shorting Alitalia Shares months before it went into liquidation in 2008. We currently have large holdings in six of the most reputable companies in Engineering in Italy, particularly Road and Bridge Repair and Maintenance. who are currently working on all repair works on previous and new Government Contracts found to be in need of structural repairs, for Public Safety, with so far over 250 sites identified and in the quoting stage, with our Companies at the forefront of preferred suppliers.

Through Cayman Holdings we also are invested in India and Africa. We also are in Mining and Minerals in various countries in South America with good medium term returns. We are major Shareholders in the top ten Italian Fashion Houses with no let up in demand from around the world, also Fiat with their Military Contracts, Ferrari and Lamborghini. We are involved in half of the Companies supplying the Italian Army, Navy and Air Force with equipment. Also in sales to Peru, Argentina, Spain and Chile. So, in conclusion Tommy we are all looking to keep on going for years to come, we all hope you will be with us for the journey that you started, all those years ago."

Roman stood up "Friends I am going to change my status in the Organization, from active to passive. Tom knows all of my reasons for this, but it is now time for me to retire from active investing. I no longer have any family alive except Tom, who is like a brother to me, I will leave my investments in the Organization in place and Tommy will take all investment decisions for me. Now that the Government in my Homeland has changed I have more than enough Property and Investments there to see me out, for sure. My Shares and Investments in the Offshore Situations will be passed to Tommy to add to his personal Portfolio, my decision is final."

"Thank you for that Roman and our other Cousins, your vote of confidence in our business is heart warming and empowering, we will continue to face problems we will resolve, growing our Businesses to all our benefit. Michael, Max, Nikki and Karena are embarking on a new project here in Italy, in the Family village of Piandelagotti which is something I have wanted to launch for many years now.

Shortly they will present finished projections to completion, of the Individual Projects, if any of you would like to become involved sit down with them while you are here, to get a feel of what is being considered. We will keep you updated as we progress with planning and costings. On that positive note, if there is no further business for discussion, we can break for a buffet lunch which is about to be served.

"Dad just to say, I have had an email through this morning from Rome, the Specialist will see Max on Monday, so we should get some idea on time frames depending what he recommends, we could set up a first meet in Piandelagotti that week end Dad."

"Sounds good Mike, I think it would be worth getting a helicopter up to the village for the initial trip, it is a long winding climb by car, see what you think. I will sound out some of my contacts in the Vatican to see if there could be interest in one of the Orders of Monks opening a Sanitarium in the old Monastery, at our expense, it could be an offer they cannot refuse."

Over the next few days Tommy reached out to his contacts in the Vatican particularly Cardinal Benelli who he had known for over ten years. Tommy laid out the basic idea of what he wanted to achieve in Piandelagotti and the Cardinal was empathetic, but cautious. He explained there was a Drug Rehab Clinic, part of an existing Global Group in Piemonte, where treatment was available to all Religions and all Colours and Creeds, for habitual drug users or alcoholics. He suggested Tommy visit to see if that was the sort of involvement he wanted to progress.

In relation to the Monastery it had long been deconsecrated, the Chapel was in disrepair and essentially the entire building was available for sale. For a worthy change of use Benelli thought the Holy See could support such a sale, he would be interested to see the projected plans. He felt to open the Monastery as a Sanitarium run solely by an Order of Monks could be a step too far, but was interested in the possibility of having a small Seminary attached with possibly ten or twelve Monks in permanent residence, being self sufficient from the Estate, providing a Religious Slant on Rehabilitation while allowing all Religious beliefs to participate.

A percentage of Patients would need to be on a Pro Bono basis for all treatment. Michael made contact with Father Leo who had been in residence since 1975 and knew all the Parishioners individually by name and reputation, including all the direct descendants of the Bulgarelli family. He was keen to meet with Michael to discuss what he had in mind and said best keep their initial meeting private, until he had digested what the Family proposed.

Michael and Max were heading back to the villa in Forte on the Autrostrada Del Sole the A1 which runs from Milan to Rome, having had a meeting in Rome with the specialist recommended by Geoffrey in London.

"He was very positive about his diagnosis Max, I think it is all looking good for you, as long as you stay positive with the family`s help."

"He certainly knew what he was talking about, which was a comfort, to get me weaned off the Ayahuasca, where it's made from two separate hallucinogenic drugs combined, he has had good results in getting users clean. Hard to imagine people going to the jungles of Peru to visit the Shamans, staying for a "holiday" experience. It's incredible it is used to treat depression, when it can make people psychotic as well."

"That's why they usually have a medical practitioner on hand, when they try it for the first time, in case of emergencies Max.

"I think what will help me Mike is Dad's new scheme, if we can get him to agree to our idea for a Rehab site in Piandelagotti, I thought it was a good idea of the Specialist's for us to visit San Patrignano, the revolutionary Rehab Estate near Rimini on the Adriatic."

"Absolutely, they have over a thousand residents, all hard drug users in the past. But I think it may be a bit extreme as it is also a complete social reforming enterprise as well. Most of the patients stay in residence for two or more years where they learn many different life skills, if they wish. They have their own Factory set ups, Vineyards etc. which have been established for over thirty years. Maybe something between a normal Drug Rehab Centre and this gold standard would be better to aim for.

We need to be talking to the experts in the field, to get an idea where we want to be, we need to get costings on salaries for experienced staff and equipment."

"Mike, I will call Father Leo to set up a meeting about our idea, after a visit to Rimini it will need two nights away is that ok with you?"

"Sure thing Max, we need to get going, or the girls will leave us behind that will never do."

"Shall I see if the girls want to join us, to see Father Leo for the initial meeting?"

"I think they should make their own way, could be overkill all four of us putting different ideas to him at once. Better that our plan is first in his mind to work on."

It was just after 2am. in the morning when they arrived back at the Villa in Forte and everybody had bedded down for the night. Next day Max and Michael were down for a late breakfast at 11 am."

"Morning Dad, we had a good trip yesterday very productive, with the American Specialist in Rome, he is very optimistic with Max, he is going to liaise with the Clinic in Lucca and set up a treatment plan with them for Max. We had a chat with him about our proposed scheme in Piandelagotti and he had some ideas for us to look into. Max is setting up a meet with Father Leo later today, we will be gone for a couple of days."

"You need to change your day boys, the girls have gone by helicopter to Frassinoro early this morning, with a meeting set up with Father Leo this evening, wining and dining him at the best hotel in Frassinoro."

"It's ok Dad, Max I have arranged for us to see Father Leo tomorrow evening. I have fixed a visit to San Patrignano, it's a specialist Drug Rehab Agriturismo Dad near Rimini, we could pick up some ideas there. The Specialist in Rome said it would be worth our while to have a look."

"I'm pleased to see you are taking this seriously Max, good for you."

"We need to leave after lunch Mike, we can stay on site, basic but clean and tidy is what the Manager said. I'll pack a bag and one of the Hummers should be comfortable, it's a fair bit of driving, Rimini today, Piandelagotti then back here day after tomorrow."

Max went to his room, Alexis was just in the en-suite wet room, he undressed and quietly went in behind her, she had her back to him her naturally curly reddish brown hair covering her shoulders, smothered in shampoo, her eyes shut. He put one arm gently but firmly round her waist as he startled her, pulling her gently to him "God you smell fresh and edible", she felt his eagerness at the base of her spine, turned and said "It's good to have you back, it's been a long time, how was the trip?" she turned facing him, cupping his manhood in her hands. She gently soaped him from head to toe and led him back to the bed, laying on the massive Egyptian cotton bath sheet towels, she had spread out earlier.

"Mike and I are away for a couple of days, Rimini today after lunch, Piandelagotti tomorrow evening, back next day. The Specialist believes he can sort me out, he is working with the clinic in Lucca, so not too much travelling. I would say come with us, but it's a lot of driving, then only basic accommodation in Rimini we'll be back soon."

Max took the moisturiser from the side table and worked some in to Alexis's shoulders, moved down her back in soft effleurage strokes, as he had enjoyed himself so many times, gently pressing his thumbs into her buttock cheeks feeling for any stress lumps putting extra pressure with his thumbs on the knots till they eased, followed by soft swirling movements going down each leg, all the while using body oil, warmed in the palm of his hands first.

"That's soooo good, if I turn over can I get some extra's?"

"Surely that's my line he" laughed.

Alexis turned over pulling Max level with her face and kissed him full on the mouth her tongue forcing itself along his gum line, wet and warm as she tried to suck the air from his lungs, her hands caressing him as far as she could reach. Max's tongue probed hers darting in and out, her warmth exciting him more, he kissed her ear lobes gently licking inside each ear, the nape of her slender neck, the sweet smell of her shampooed soft wet silky long hair all over her face, as she moaned expectantly.

He felt his heart beat faster, as he reached down and into her body exploring, feeling it as he remembered he used to, enjoying it again. He kissed her breasts, circled her aureola and puckered her nipples which always annoyed her, she didn't complain this time as he softly tweaked the ends with his teeth. He licked down to her navel and around it going down to her groin slowly, she breathed more heavily now in anticipation, as he parted her legs carefully using his saliva on both side creases of her groin.

He was glad she always favoured a proper Brazilian and was as smooth as a baby`s butt cheek. She was ready for him, as he floated his wet tongue around her clit and lab areas, he flicked her gently clit from the base with his tongue to kissing the tip then entered as far as he could go with his tongue rolled like a cannoli, all the while making soft slurping noises, faster and slower alternately. Alexis moaned and ground her hips down onto his head with her legs wrapped tightly round it. She orgasmed twice, in quick succession, she was on fire now, as Max came up for air forcing his mouth onto hers, sucking the breath from her lungs and the wetness from her mouth, he orgasmed over her navel and lowered himself to her side embracing her and stroking her hair, he spoke first.

"I`ve missed you it`s good to be back with you again."

"I never went away, but I`m glad you`re back, at last."

"Mike and I will get a bite here before heading off, the girls have gone to Piandelagotti, we are there tomorrow night, then back next day. We must see Father Leo to get his take on our plan, we are seeing a rehab spa tomorrow, staying there tonight."

"How are you and your brother getting on? will you get your ideas off the ground? It would be good for you to get involved in a project no?"

"Absolutely, darling initially the start up will be pretty hectic as Mike is limited in how much time he can spend away from the business, so most of the leg work will be down to me, but we have agreed to work closely together in the future, which I am looking forward to."

"I`ll do your bag for you, if you want to stay down with Dad till you leave, do you want a suit or casual."

"Casual to travel, jeans and t- shirt, one of my Ferragamo suits, blue shirt, a couple of quiet ties thanks darling. See you down when you are ready, I will call you when we are an hour away, day after tomorrow, so I can catch you in the shower again, kisses."

"Twice in a week it`s been years."

Max went down, Mike and Tom were engrossed in conversation with Roman as he was saying he would be interested in becoming involved in the Piandelagotti Scheme if the boys would like him to be, he would be happy with any scenario, where they could make use of him.

"Hi Max, Maria just came in for any lunch orders, she has a local Beef Tagliata on the bone with garden tomatoes, cooked in the wood oven and French fries, the fish option is local Sea Bass, catch her in the kitchen, if Alexis is coming down get her order in so she can eat with us, before we go, Dad said we could take Able with us for the driving, Yuri stays here the girls, so they have got cover with them, what do you think?"

"For sure Mike."

"I was just discussing with Roman your plan and where he could help you with all his project management skills, but we can have a round table discussion when you have finalized your plans."

"Dad, what we are seeing at San Patrignano is not a Rehab Clinic as we know it in the UK or USA, for a start they have about 1200 residents mostly youngsters, the accommodation and everything provided is free to residents and their families.

Over the 40 or so years they have had over 26000 Attendees. They do weekly residential courses for social workers, teachers and anybody interested in helping young people with a Drug problem, they charge nothing, everything is all in, lectures twice daily, food and accommodation. The Government give a grant around 50%, they have to raise the rest, we will be eligible for some Government money, I have put our Property Acquisition Department onto it.

They use no drugs for treatment, but work on the psychological reasons people become addicted, the aim is to make the individual earn their own self respect."

Mike, Max and Able pulled into the driveway at San Patrignano at 5.30 pm."Good time with the traffic Able just under 3 hours."

One of the Assistant Managers met them at reception, took them to their room, four to a room, for all residents and showed them the Refectory where all students eat together and said he would meet them back at the dining hall in half an hour for their evening meal.

Luca showed them to their table and joined them for food, which was served military canteen style with a great offering from local produce and wine. "Guys because you are here for such a short time I am going to talk at you till you are exhausted, hopefully you will retain enough, to realize what our ethos is about.

Attendees come from all over the world, they normally stay up to 3 years but it can be shorter, a minimum of one year. We aim to not just take them off Drugs or a dependency, but to re-build the inner person to create his own self respect and respect for each other.

How do we do this? We make them all work, everybody gets up at 7am. for breakfast, then join one of our 50 Life and Training Sectors, of their choice, all the food and drink is produced here, we offer gardening, forestry, animal husbandry to name a few of our courses. We have direct links with the Universities of Milan and Modena and many Government Agencies.

When they leave they may have a new work qualification or profession. They can join a workshop at any level, if they have previous experience. During Rehab they work also to rebuild their relationship, with their families who are discouraged from visiting for the first year, after that, they may come up to 3 times a year.

The State saves 30 million Euros a year from the Attendees being here instead of being a problem in their communities. Independent polling and Academic Research proves over 72% do not return to Drugs.

A Mentor is appointed in each room with Attendees, eventually as the Attendee progresses he/she is promoted to Mentorship status to help the others. We are founder Members of Drug Policy Future, a Worldwide organisation working for a new

Drug Policy Debate based on health. So what we do is unique to us, tomorrow we will provide you with two Mentors for the day, to let you see exactly what we do at close quarters over the entire clinic.

We allow play time as well, we have our own theatre, television rooms, games rooms and so on. We have our own Sports training areas and we organize various teams that compete in several Leagues throughout Italy.

Do you have any questions for me now as I have to return to my Office for a few hours to catch up on Admin.

Feel free to wander around, talk to some people make yourselves at home, I am finishing off a folder for you, with lists of useful contacts who can help with costings and supply of whatever items you will need for your own project, it will be ready by tomorrow evening. Get a good nights sleep, as breakfast is sharp at 7am. in the morning, same table, your Mentors will be waiting for you. Buona Notte".

"Thank you Luca, most impressive and informative, we look forward to the morning, I think we are going to be sorry we are so short of time, thanks again for your time Buona Notte."

They had a continental breakfast, canteen style at 7am. then Mike and Max went off with a Mentor going round the various workshops talking to lots of the Attendees while they were working on their projects. They watched Sculpture Classes, Art and saw a team creating a Wallpaper from recycled material, on hand operated looms which had won a prize at an exhibition in Milan. There were Jewellery Workshops, Graphic Design & Engineering, Woodworking, Furniture Making and Metalwork.

The Attendees all seemed very involved in their courses and committed to achieving Certification and satisfaction. There were Language classes, Writing Tutorials and even Clothes Design, Amateur Dramatics, Photography, Film Production and Vehicle Maintenance.

Many other courses too many to list. They broke for lunch in the afternoon, they visited the Vineyards with over 150 hectares in production for over 36 years, which is sold all over the world, the Horticultural and Farming departments with 300 Cows, 200 sheep & 100 goats all for the cheese and dairy products. They had no idea the clinic had a recruiting base in London, who were the first stop for any UK applicants who wanted to attend, on a not too dissimilar basis to the Kibbutz system for young people in Israel which Abel was familiar with.

Mobile phones are banned. They make and sell Artisan foods and goods to include 32 different Cheeses, Biscuits, Cakes and Olive Oil which are exported around the world, including high end retailers in Londons West End, even Teddy Bears for Christian Dior. A Stud Farm with Livery Stables, Horse Riding Lessons and 3 Day Eventing. Kennels for Dog Training, Breeding & Pet Therapy.

There is the Conference Hall with seating for 1000 available for outside Hire, it also doubles as the Attendees Cinema. A Health Centre of Excellence is on site.

Half of the paid Staff on site are employed in Marketing the Clinic and its Products, which is the main source of its ever growing success. That evening when they had an hour with Luca they could hardly conceal their gratitude for having their eyes opened to what is achievable, to develop what is operating today, all started as a vision by one man.

"Luca we can honestly say we have never had such an empowering and enthralling single day, ever before. The visit has given us so many ideas and if we can take with us even a little of the enthusiasm and dedication to our new project, which we have seen here, we will be truly enriched and motivated."

"You are Molto Gentile, Mr. Michael and Max, reaching out to people is what our project here is about, we have been successful, so our founders dream lives on, but we cannot rest on our achievements, we have to grow and push forward every year with more endeavours all the time.

I have here for you the folder I promised, with many important contact details who will give you whatever assistance they are able. You may benefit by talking to a new colleague who has embarked on setting up a clinic in Australia, based on our model, he did reside here for three years. He took a 10 year Lease on 50 Acres of Rural Land, at a peppercorn Rent, with planning consent for the buildings he needs, funded and supported by local businesses, a great project. The same applies to yourselves, if you need any help, or advice please contact me Subito, I eagerly await the final details of your plans and God speed to you all, just keep in your mind exactly what you want to achieve and it will come to pass, Arrivederci, as you say until we meet again."

The drive back to Piandelagotti next morning after breakfast was a non stop brainstorming of ideas, from what they had seen at San Patrignano "It was incredible Mike, I had no idea of the size of the project there, the commitment to their Attendees and Staff, what they offer, how they have grown from nothing, they deserve all their success."

"Right on Max, reminds me of the old saying when someone says you are so lucky, the response is, yes the harder I work the luckier I seem to be. I don't think we can be even mentally committing to something of those dimensions. We can take the ethos accenting on rehabilitation, through useful productive employment. That side we need to set up, to what level we want to go to, at San Patrignano they start at NVQ level up to University Level, because they focus on the young. Nothing wrong with that, but we need to look at costs, to hire Staff to cover what we want to achieve with our target market."

"I think it was a good lesson, seeing how important it is to get Marketing right, at the start, also seeing if we can get Sponsors involved. We are lucky we have a connection now, to such a terrific role model, at such a successful stage, for us to be able to cherry pick the best bits to fit our model."

"Couldn't agree more brother, we need to get on with talking to the Vatican to see if they can help with pushing any levers, when we have agreed on the size and scope of what we want to do, hopefully Father Leo will know about San Partignano, certainly the Vatican will. What did you think Able? did you ever do a Kibbutz when you were young?"

"I certainly did Mr. Michael, it was a rite of passage for all young Jewish males and thank God young females, partly to help develop the captured territory, after the constant wars with neighbours, bed and board only, basic military training provided. The girls were the other main draw though. It's true the feeling of contributing to your homeland, especially with Israel surrounded with every other Nation bordering her wanting to annihilate the State, at any opportunity, was a good feeling.

What they have achieved in Italy is beyond belief, especially with no drugs on the premises or substitutes, to help with withdrawals. It is definitely a collective effort in every meaning of the word, seriously impressive."

"Mike we are seeing Father Leo at 5pm. at the Church, we are booked in at a Ski Hotel in Frassinore, I hadn't realised we would be away so early from Rimini, we should be there by mid-day, we could have a scout around the old Monastery site get a bite in Piandelagotti and drive back to Forte, if Able is up for it, or stay the night at the Hotel, what do you think Able? it's a long day driving for you and a real cliff hanger mountain road, back to Forte."

"I honestly don't mind Mr. Max, I am used to long hours at the wheel if necessary, I'm sure you would both rather be back in your own beds tonight, it's your call."

They arrived in Piandelagotti at 12.40 pm parked up near the Church, went into the cluster of shops and had a quick pizza and beer in the bar, 2 minutes from the Church.

The bar owner directed them to the Monastery site, 15 minutes from the village. The site itself covered approx. 40 acres, the Monastery built in the 14th Century was basically of sound construction built with local stone with the roof requiring repair in various places, in and out, from the report Max had received. It had its own water supply from a well close to the building itself.

Set back from the road with its own driveway edged with very old trees either side. The backdrop behind being the foothills to the approach to the more mountainous heights and Ski runs. One side was protected from winter squalls, by a 30-40 metre high hillock, running the full length of the Monastery with sturdy trees along the entire length on the top side. There was a gentle slope away from the site to the valley clearing in front. Several outbuilding remains were evident close to the site, but no other residential buildings in sight.

"We need to get a Surveyor and qualified Photographer up here as soon as we can Max, to see what we can do with the main building, get him to get any ideas on how we can sort the inside, to get the most from it, with regard to local planning. He will have all the planning contact details, but he will need to know what we want to achieve.

We can get the principle on a computer at the Villa, we have a CAD design team at Canary Wharf that can complete a totally finished project from scratch, which is what we need, they will get us a 3-D model of the entire Project and we can design it as we go along, they have Architects, Engineers and Surveyors to solve every problem but they need basics to get started, give them a call tomorrow morning, to set the ball rolling, they need to appoint a project Manager who reports only to us. I need to spend some time on the phones tomorrow, making sure the teams are not enjoying their holiday from my presence too much."

"Sure Mike, I will get back on to our contact in Rome, bring him up to speed with where we are, how impressed we were with San Partignano and especially with their ethical stance across their whole project, which we are keen to emulate, though with a different flavour on a much smaller project. I will say we will be seeking their help as needed, which should please him, as well as saying we need to get inside as soon as possible with our Surveyor etc. to get more of an idea on where we can go with the main buildings, telling him we will be in touch, as soon as we have a plan for him to look at."

"Have you got any Paracetamol Max?"

"There will be some at the Villa tonight, have you got a headache Mike?"

"No but you will have by tomorrow night, you aren't used to working to deadlines ha, ha."

They arrived back at the Church with ten minutes to spare, the main door was open with Father Leo smoking on the doorstep.

"Father Leo, I am Michael my brother Max and a close business associate Mr. Able it is a great pleasure to meet you, after the last few days, shall we go inside?"

"Michael, Max and Mr. Able come into my office, forgive me smoking on the doorstep, but the man upstairs would never forgive me if I did it in his house, follow me through to the office behind."

"I am really happy to meet you Michael and you of course Max, what a lovely pair of daughters you have, I spent a great evening with them yesterday in Frassinoro and I must tell you both before you ask, I am sworn to secrecy as to what was discussed.

It is always good to meet relatives of old Parishioners, though I never met any of your Grand Parents. Originally I served in a parish in La Spezia the big Naval Port along the Versilian coast, I was moved to Milan for several years and went to a Diocese in Rome when I had ignoble ambitions to gain a promotion by studying religious Theology in Rome itself, where I felt if I worked hard I would be rewarded with promotion. My ambitions were my undoing, for my penance I was removed from Rome, to several ever reducing Diocese until I landed here, to see the rest of my days in peaceful contemplative semi-retirement. Enough of me, I understand you have a family Villa in Forte."

"Yes Father, Michael lives mainly in the States whereas I live in Surrey, in the UK, we are a close family as we all work in the family business which in a roundabout way brings us back to our roots here, with a Project our father Tolmino, or Tommy in English, has challenged us to bring to fruition. We are a family who originated here as you know, the brothers Bulgarelli, some of whose names are on the Church inscriptions on the outside walls, having died fighting in the First World War.

The Sons of those brave boys emigrated at the end of that War to England and the US. We have achieved great wealth and it is our fathers wish before he dies to see the family re-establish its name here, where we originated. We are the Grand Children of Camillo, you have met my daughters Nikki and Karena our father is under medical supervision, so at present cannot travel to be here but he will come to see you as soon as he is able to travel.

He has put to us a challenge, to bring to him in rapid order, an idea to bring a benefit to the village here, it has to be totally self supporting and must provide a real benefit for the people who live here, our project must be totally transparent and we have a matter of months to present the plans to him when he will decide, which plan or plans will go forward.

There is one main proviso, it must have the backing of the people living in the village. Which is why we came to you Father, when we are finalising our plans we would like to hold an open meeting in the village for everyone to register a secret vote, we would come back to you with a set of the plans and a 3-D model of our project to be on display, where we will answer any questions prior to a ballot vote at the end, supervised by yourself, you are also eligible to vote, the result will be disclosed before we leave.

As a vote of confidence and a show of our good intentions, if you approve we would like to donate to the Parish the cost of any repairs required for the Church to date. If you are agreeable, we would like to have a permanent Marble Monument to all those who fell in the Great War and WW2 inside the Church grounds. This is a part of the project for the village. We are very excited about the main part, hoping to get your approval and with many other hurdles to jump through, to bring to fruition for the sake and also the future growth and prosperity of this our original family home."

"I hope you are both optimists, but with Gods will on your

side, you can achieve what you may seek. As you say I am all ears for your proposal."

"Father we want Piandelagotti to be as well known as Frassinoro but Worldwide not just in Italy. We propose to create a Sanatorium for those with Drug or Alcohol dependency beyond their control. We have approached contacts in the Vatican to enquire about the possibility of reinstating the old Monastery to make it the main building for our Clinic.

It would with the Vaticans approval have a small family of Monks from an Order of the Vaticans choice in permanent residence. They will provide all the requisite Religious Services for all their Attendees and be totally self sustaining there. We have visited San Partignano which I am sure you know of and they have pledged to assist us in achieving our aim.

Wherever we can we will emulate their model with Marketing, Tutoring, Re Education and various Mentoring Projects on site. They will be self sustaining for their food and aim to produce foodstuffs and goods which will be marketed to help their sustainability. Like San Partignano there will no Drugs used for rehabilitation but unlike that famous Clinic we will charge fees, for those that can afford to pay and we will offer a percentage of places, for those who are unable to pay. We will hire only from the best in their fields and strive for an excellence second to none.

It will create many jobs in the area, to service the facility and its growth. We will build accommodation for Staff on site and we envisage Lodge Type Chalets for Residents Guests and Visitors to the area to enjoy. We have a lot of work to complete to achieve the final plans, but with your approval in principle, we can commence tomorrow, we know it's a big decision for you to ponder but time is of the essence for us and we really need your blessing, we will call you in the morning at 11 am. unless you have a Service in Church?"

"11am. will be fine Michael and Max, I have much to consider tonight with some prayers to help me decide, for the benefit of the village. Either way I thank you for your courtesy to me and having met you both, from what I have learned of Camillo he would be proud of your business drive, he lives on in you both. Good night and God go with you and your family."

"Home it is then gents yes?"

"Yes please Able if you are good to drive."

On the drive home Mike and Max agreed it was 60/40 ultimately that Father Leo would vote against the plan, as he would feel his Parishioners would not want a Business Consortium taking the area over, the only caveat being the big carrot of spending on his Church. They agreed they should go full steam ahead, whatever his decision, as they felt if Tommy went for their project, he would ensure it prevailed with his contacts anyway.

Max phoned Alexis and asked for some cold meats and salads to be left out for them saying he hoped to be back by 10pm. which he was. Able went off for an early night, while Mike and Max gave Tommy and Roman a brief run through on what had occurred in the two days.

"Are we showering tonight Maxi or are you done for the night."

"I will shower off to clean up, after all the travelling darling, but I am too bushed to provide you with what you deserve tonight, I'm up early tomorrow, it will be a big day and I can`t think of a better start to the day before breakfast, than to carry on where we left off the other night."

"We will see, I will give you an aromatic oil back massage when you are out of the shower then just snuggles up yes?" Max fell fast asleep, before Alexis had got half way down his back. Next morning at 6am. Max gave Alexis a long slow oral wake up before bringing her coffee and croissants, to bed, while he then had a shave and was downstairs on his laptop, before anyone else was up.

By the time Michael had come down at 9am. Max had a brief outline of ideas for what might fit at the Monastery site for him to look at over his coffee. The main Monastery building would have a rebuilt Chapel, the original Monks Cells would be renovated, with en-suite showers. All floor and walls would be rebuilt with original local Stone, from the local quarry.

The dining room would be rebuilt to cater to the Monks requirements and Attendees alike, a separate Reading Room and Study would be reinstated. The three separate outbuildings would be joined in a horseshoe shape built in local Stone and Wood and would have another storey built on top. The whole would be designed for Tuition Areas and Mentoring Workshops a further block would be added to house up to 150 Attendees in 4 Star Type Hotel accommodation with its own Canteen and Kitchen with a Library, Games Room, and Cinema with a Bar, serving only non-alcoholic Cocktails, Wines and Lager.

There would be a Gymnasium and Wave Pool for exercising with a Sauna attached. In the grounds away from the main buildings and in separate areas would be the Chalet Style Lodges for guests up to 4 Guests in each Lodge, with all mod cons and mini bars, the contents only to be consumed inside the premises. Land would be cleared and laid out for Vegetables to be grown. Meat would be sourced from local suppliers of which there were many in the famed Emilia Romagna Region especially all the Pork specialities, a plan would be put in place to get local suppliers providing them to the Monastery, to market the produce from the Monastery ultimately for export.

"Morning Mike, I've done some work on the plan for the Clinic all laid out for you in Dads study, I am going to talk to our contact at the Vatican to see if I can firm up costs to take the Monastery and land on for the project, then talk to the Commune in Modena, which is the Region which governs all planning for the villages and surrounding areas in Emilia Romagna, after we have got our results back from the Regional Surveyor and Photographer.

We will use their feedback and any useful contacts they

provide. Obviously it's a moveable feast, but we have to start somewhere. Let me know what you think before you start on your day. We will have a sit down later this afternoon when I will let you know how far I have got."

"Sounds good Max have you seen the girls yet?"

"No, everyone is still in slumber mode, except Roman, he is doing thirty lengths in the pool before breakfast. We had a brief word earlier and he is happy to stay on the site, as soon as there is suitable accommodation for him, which would be a good move. He would be a good Liaison Manager between all the Italian professionals and ourselves don't you think? I have asked him to join me in the study when he is ready, he can make contact with the Cad Team at Canary Wharf, while I am chasing the Vatican contacts, hopefully we will start things moving by close of business today."

"Definitely Max, having dealt with the Military in Russia for years and since the war, he is a no nonsense guy, but used to handling every kind of crisis. I don't know if he has had many dealings with Italy, but I reckon it will be a learning curve for both parties we will talk later."

Karena and Nikki came in and reported on a successful meeting with Father Leo, who suggested they hire a venue in Frassinoro together, to present their schemes to the public of Piandelagotti and all interested parties, which they confirmed would suit the girls, while giving away none of their details. Able came into the lounge with a coffee in casual clothing, ready to take Nikki out for the morning, to give her some defensive driving training, as Tommy had arranged.

"Nikki, trainers will be best, comfortable driving clothes, with jeans, prescription sunglasses with shatterproof lenses, if you have them, I am ready when you are. We will be done for today by 2pm. Luigi has kindly arranged for us to use the Carabinieri Training Centre in Viareggio, used by their Drug chase patrols. We are not using the Lamborghinis, 180mph plus, the Alfa Sport saloons will be sufficient."

As they drove to Viareggio Able explained some principles to Nikki "Some of the things we go over today are good fun, but they have a real purpose and you need to understand the reason for them. It is harder to show a woman than man because women are not naturally predisposed to want to physically attack or kill an enemy, which is what an attacker is. One of the key things is awareness, all around you when you are driving, spot the problem before it becomes one.

You may not have many seconds to decide what to do, so you need to get some practice in as time goes on."

They met the Sergeant at the Centre entrance, going to a small classroom for students. On the wall was a site map showing the facility, Guido said "I have set up the situations as you requested Mr. Able, if there is anything you need contact me on the walkie talkie, I see you in a while."

"Thank you Guido for your help."

"Ok Miss Nikki, lets go through some basics, first forget all the films you have seen where the guy drives through a hail of bullets, grenades bounce off his car, doors get shot off and he gets out after he has rolled it and kills all the baddies. I am going to go through the likely scenarios you would face, if someone was trying to kill you in your car. I will use the blackboard, any questions as we go along, ok."

"Yes sir, whatever you say."

"Can we get one thing straight here, your Grandfather who employs me, asked me to show you some routines which could save your life, your mother nearly lost hers in Switzerland, shopping for jewellery, if you remember, so the least you can do is engage and take it seriously ok?"

"Not a problem you have my attention."

"What I want to explain to you, is to try to maximise the chances of your getting out of a serious situation. Here and now we are talking about vehicles. The car you normally drive will be different to the cars you will drive here, I expect you like an automatic, what do you drive at home?"

"I don't mind auto, or manual I am changing up to a Ford GT 40 when I get home."

"Well that will get you out of trouble on a quick exit, if you can handle it. As I said to you earlier, the single most important thing is acute awareness, of possible problems anywhere around your vehicle, when you are driving. Forget music, smoking, chatting to a passenger, any distractions. I am going to chalk up some scenarios on the board and I want you to tell me the right and wrong approach in each diagram."

Able drew a couple of roads with sharp bends a roundabout and a crossroad with traffic lights.

"What I want you to imagine is that you are on these roads and because you have been following the idea of 360 degree surveillance, you think someone is following you. Two men in a Sporty SUV, quite tight on your tail. You go along the two bendy roads straight over the roundabout and left at the traffic lights, talk me through your every move."

"I am using my rear view and side mirrors all the time, I maintain 60mph on the bendy roads, they are no closer, take a correct route to the left lane, round the roundabout and straight over, watching them all the while, then indicate to turn left at the lights, which are green."

"Ok, that's all very good for your driving test, but let`s suppose they mean you harm. If you can handle your GT40, you can lose them if you need to and you have a clear road. If you are convinced they are following you, its best to find out early to get your brain thinking of possible solutions to your problem.

The best option then, was to drive at much quicker speeds on the bendy roads at your safest speed. Use the clipping points on the corners, if you have good frontal vision use the whole road, ramp the speed up within your safe handling capacity. If they follow rapidly, they are either after you because you are a young woman driving faster than them, or they really may be after you to do you harm.

If you know the road you are on, think about points where you can utilise your speed to get away, or if approaching an urban area drive into the centre, if you can get the car number, model and type, memorise it. If they follow you over the roundabout, you should be out of sight by now and coming up to the crossroad with lights which are just changing to red there is no camera on top, so if safe go straight over, if they jump the lights you do have a problem.

But it really is about forward thinking and using your best weapon, your car, any questions?"

"What about jumping the red light?"

"Notice I said if it was safe to do so, if you believed you were in possible danger from a car chasing you, that would be a justifiable defence for jumping a light in court. If you were at the lights stopped and either of the men got out of the car, you would see. Again if it was safe, floor it through the lights and don't stop till you get to a busy area, if you spot a policeman or police car, pull up and tell them what occurred. Everything I show you today you need to practice and when you get home try out some country roads you know and get used to 360 degree surveillance, even when you go to the shops, it could save your life."

"This brings us to the next scenario, if there is more than one car which could be a problem or the worse case, a road block to stop you. You must try to escape and not stop under any circumstances, as you will be a sitting target for a shooter or a kidnapper. I will give you the textbook answers, then we will go out onto the training circuit and see what you can do ok?"

"Fine as long as no one is shooting."

"I promised your Grandfather I would bring you back alive."

Able rubbed the board clean, then drew a wide main road with two cars parked facing each other as a road block and with a lorry parked way beyond them across the road as well with no occupants visible.

"You are approaching at 60/70mph what are you thinking?"

"Where are the drivers? I must not stop, there is not enough room to go round I need to slow down, turn round and get out quickly."

"Not bad, the drivers could be killers or kidnappers, anyway you don't want to give them the opportunity to prove it. As you say, you can judge you cannot go round as you slow down. First option when you are 20 yards from the cars, drop your gears down to 1st or 2nd then aiming at either the front or back wheel of the smallest vehicle accelerate to the floor, the momentum as all the weight transfers to your front wheels will ram the hit car out of the way, you will be through. Because there is a lorry in the road 100 yards ahead, which you cannot get round or hope to push aside, you use option two, which you could have used on the two cars initially as well."

"Hand brake turn, I have done on a skid pan day, no reverse driving or getting out of Kill Zone techniques."

"When did you last do one? let's see how much you remember, you need to practice it, especially when you change your car, to be familiar with the change of response between you and your car. When you get your GT 40, I presume it will be a replica which should cost around £130K, the real thing would be over a couple of million at least, you don't want to be doing hand brake turns in one of those.

It's a 5litre vehicle, rear wheel drive with 5 speed manual box so it needs to be driven. If its standard you get top speed around 170 mph tuned about 200mph for track eventing. It's mid-engine so really well balanced and great to drive, totally responsive. If you haven't already sourced one I have a friend in Holland with a showroom who specialises in them and Ferraris I can take you up there, if I can get a couple of days off.

Anyway, let's get out on the track and see how you get on. They use Alfa Brera's here, front wheel drive 0-100mph in just over 6 seconds, 5 speed manual good little throw abouts, let's see you drive it to its max."

They both put helmets on and Nikki adjusted steering rake and seat position, checked rear and side mirrors and made her way to the centre of a waste area, concreted and with a couple of dozen oil drums, randomly scattered around and variously positioned hay bales, water sprays were covering the whole area as if it was a golf course at feeding time.

"Start at the beginning, follow the arrows and keep your speed to about 30 mph when you come to a red cross painted on a road sign, slam on the brakes and see where you end up, avoid the oil drums and straw bales, there are 10 drums and ten bales you get 10 points deducted for every one you hit, you start with 200 points and the drums are empty, it's all spread over the area you will drive on, get going, don't let your speed drop below 30mph between handbrake turns."

In the first 7 minutes Nikki had taken out 3 drums and two bales with no comment from Able "I see what you mean about keeping up the practice."

Able talked her through the rest of the course and she managed to avoid all but two of the others.

"Not bad, go round once more, then we go to the Kill Zone area that's real fun."

She went round quicker this time and only clipped one drum and no bales. Able pointed to the remains of some old buildings at what looked like an old industrial estate there were some Paramilitary Police in combat gear moving through the buildings.

"Don't worry about them, they know why you are here and they know to avoid any drivers in vehicles, that's part of their training, so I want you to follow the arrows on the roads through the estate, full on observation yes, when I shout a command just do it quick, keep your speed to about 50mph."

Nikki went off with a screech of rubber and through the deserted roads at an easy 50mph there was an arrow showing a left turn ahead, she cornered tight to the kerb then saw the two cars parked across the road 25 yards, ahead braking hard " take option 2 out of the kill zone NOW!!!!" in the moment Able said that, automatic fire shot over the roof of the car from the buildings to their sides. Nikki did a fast hand brake turn, straightened out without thinking and raced away the way she had come "Jeeeeez you could have warned me."

"Turn around and get through the roadblock, remember what I told you, slow to 20mph drop to 2nd gear don't hesitate, foot hard down through the floor, take the back or front wheel off, whichever looks the lightest car, GO!! and don't let go of the wheel."

She went for it and the smaller of the two Fiats nearly rolled over on impact she kept on going shaken, but not stirred. Able said "How was it? you did well, on both counts, the firing was blanks for effect, the adrenalin kicked in and you did what you knew, instinctively, a good job, time for lunch on the way back, you deserve a Prosecco, you can drive."

They parked up in Gilda`s car park at the Beach Club, it was rammed as usual outside, so they were happy to sit in the Restaurant in the cool. Ricardo was doing lunch looking after all the local businessmen, immaculate as only Italian men can in the heat "Ciao Nikki how are you? I have not seen you for a while, I hear you were in town, how long you stay? An Aperitivo before you order si?"

"Please Riccardo Aperol Spritz is fine, you Able?"

"A small bottled beer is fine thank you, what do you recommend from the menu Nikki?"

"For me always the same, either the Saffron Lobster Risotto with Champagne or Fresh Sea Bass dusted with flour and side salad."

"That will be for two please Riccardo."

"Ma Nikki, questo bell`uomo e tuo fidanzata? dimmi che non e vero, dammi qualche speranza."

"Not yet Riccardo, is Gilda here Riccardo, every time you see me you ask to marry me."

"One day you may say Si."

"Then you will run."

"Only towards you my Bella, I fetch your Aperitivo."

"When he asked you if this good looking man is your

boyfriend you said not yet?"

"I didn't know you were bi lingual Able."

"French, German, Italian and Hebrew of course."

"Tell me your life story, an abbreviated version. To me you are a man of mystery, obviously I know the capacity our family employ you in. Are you married? do you have any children? How did you get into the security business? where have you worked? who have you looked after?"

"Is this an interview? are you hiring? could you afford me? I am not married, my life style would not appeal to a woman, I had a close girl friend ten years ago we were serious, she died"

"I am so sorry I should not have asked, it`s too personal, I apologise"

"It was a long time ago I still blame myself. We lived in Jerusalem I was in the Mossad Secret Service we had an apartment, her car was at the garage for a service she left early for the school, where she taught young children, it was my day off, she took my car keys got into my car started it up and blew herself away.

A Palestinian bomber fitted an IED under the drivers footwell, it went off automatically, meant for me, but they were not concerned who they took out. After that I volunteered for every assignment going, the more dangerous the better, I only lived to kill terrorists.

My Code Name was Goel which is an old Hebrew name meaning the Blood Avenger, from the Bible. In old Jewish Law a close relative or clansmen to a murdered person has the right in Law to kill the perpetrators as an avenger of God. I became expert. One day I literally woke up and thought I am done with this, I cannot go on and resigned, to keep my sanity.

I was head hunted by an International VIP Security Firm worked for a few different firms in Europe and the US ending up in the UK where your Grandfather hired me and I now work solely for him, that's the short version. How about your life story?"

"Able I am so deeply sorry for your loss and pain, but I am glad you have found a new way. You have so much to give to life yours and others. Here are the drinks, thank you Riccardo is Nonna in the kitchen today? give her my love I will see her before we leave."

"When will you go back to the States Nikki? Is there someone waiting for you there?"

"No and don't know, there is no special person in my life now, I am too busy, the business is very time consuming, the good thing is I can do what I do from anywhere in the World, but with Grandads new wish list and Mum and Dads problems I am going to be based here, for at least a year I think, my sister as well. It's nice to be with the family all together for now."

Nikki reached across the table and held Ables hand, which he did not withdraw "Friends?"

"It works for me."

"I did worry about offering my hand, because I remember I read about a Jewish situation, probably with more Orthodox Jews, where they will not shake a womans hand because it should be reserved for your wife only, you should not touch her body, as any sexually overt situation starts with touching a part of the womans body, albeit even a handshake,"

"We are definitely not there yet, so no problem, I'm not Orthodox anyway, this food looks good, thank you Riccardo."

"Try my Risotto, I defy you to take only one fork full."

"Wow, you know your food, great flavour, the delicate pieces of lobster with the saffron rice, really make the dish."

"Yes its strange, all the Coastal Regions of Italy specialise in Seafood but their Lobsters are all quite small, when in the UK we can easily get 3 or 4 kilo Lobsters in Season, it must be our cold water or they just like them small here."

"Changing the subject, how is your project going for the old Homeland without giving any secrets away, I promise not to give any tips to Max or Michael."

"We are where we need to be, it's very early days yet, we

have had a first meet with the Parish Priest Father Leo, we have agreed for him to organize a joint date for a girls and boys presentation to any interested parties, local or otherwise. Roman is interested in joining the winning project and apart from increasing the financial pot he would bring added value, with his organizational and people skills, no doubt about it. We must share one of Nonnas Millefeuille strawberry and raspberry slices, it`s to die for, not that I should say that to a former Mossad operative."

"Many more lunches like this, I won`t get my seat belt done up for your ongoing training."

"You are not giving up on me yet then?"

"Your Grand Father wanted me to do some Krav Maga training with you and your sister, if you are up for it in the gym here, so as long as you want me around I will be."

"That's Israeli Special Forces training right?"

"It depends what level you want to take it to, no harm in learning a few moves."

"I`ll mention it to Karena and see if she is interested, yes I wouldn`t mind."

Able settled the bill and they drove back to the Villa. Michael, Max and Roman were deeply in conversation in the main lounge, Karena was sunbathing round the pool, with Tommy under the gazebo dozing, Tonia was doing lengths in the pool.

"Hi sis, how did you get on?"

"Could do better, needs to apply herself more, was the report I think, I did enjoy it however, worth honing up on, you should do it as well. Are we going to do a few hours on our presentation after supper what do you say?"

"Can do, can`t be left behind by the boys Nik, you are right, I was talking to Dad and Uncle Mike earlier and we talked about our projects, what do you think about us joining together now, as one big project and we all work as one with the four of us, Gramps won`t stand a chance, not forgetting Roman."

"No prob with that, I guess the boys needed our help in the end, downstairs in a couple of hours for drinks it is then."

Before the entire entourage came down for pre-dinner drinks, the two boys and girls sat down and agreed it was a sound idea to get their plans unified and to work together on the presentation to Tommy on the following Monday morning.

They all agreed the Clinic and Spa utilising the Monastery was a good way forward to put the Village on the map, they also agreed to incorporate a four or five star quality Hotel with Helipad and a Hill Climb Course based on the British style of Hill Course, where an entrant can even drive a standard road production car, in specific fun Classifications. There is a European Championship Hill Climb Course at Gubbio in North East Italy, in Umbria, but it is a totally asphalted course with high speed entrants whereas Nikki`s idea was for a more rustic finish, more akin to a Rally Track as in Wales or similar courses.

"Hi Dad, we have to report a development on the planning status, with all of the participants, we have decided to present a united front to you on Monday, we are combining our projected ideas into one big plan so we can concentrate together."

"Mike, I always wanted you to end up in that position, it makes sense for you to want to put all your efforts into your own ideas, as long as it works in the overall plan. It`s beginning to sound as though my £60 million is going to be short on funding without even seeing your plans?"

"Not necessarily Dad, I have been reaching out to some of our Investors with a Philanthropic interest who are always on the lookout for projects with Humanity and Tax Concessions to encourage them. I have over £21 million in "interested" pledges so far.

Bernard Ecclestone could come on board, if he likes the final plan, he will fund one part of the Project completely. I haven't spoken to him for a while, I reminded him he owed me Commission from when I worked at his showrooms in Bexleyheath, when I left University. I had to pick up a new driver for his Brabham F1 Team, Pedro Rodriguez, who was a schoolboy hero of mine, he had flown in from Mexico to sign up,

Bernie had a Roller he was going to sell him, which I picked him up in at Heathrow.

Driving back he said to me, can it go any faster? as we were coming back on the A2 over Blackheath, loads of roundabouts. I got on really well with Pedro told him I had all his newspaper and Motorsport cuttings in my scrapbook and what heroes he and his brother were to me, his brother died in a race crash.

I reprimanded him jokingly, saying this is a luxury car Pedro, not a race car, I gave him the specs on it and said it will go faster, but you don't throw it around, it is all about Grace, Pace and English Quality and Style, which he loved.

Anyway I got him back to the showroom, Bernie took him upstairs to his offices eventually coming down with Pedro, who shook my hand profusely thanking me for the drive, when he was gone Bernie turned to me asking what I had said to him, saying he was most impressed with me and what I had said to him. I didn't say much to Bernie but he had sold the Roller to Pedro and I reminded him he owed me Commission with interest on the sale, as I had set Pedro up for him."

"You would need to get up really early to catch Bernie out, he has never been any different. He has never paid the asking price of anything he wanted, he was never happy until you agreed his price. He has done well for himself and his Sport. He is meant to be an Atheist, he may have second thoughts now he is coming to the end of the road. If there is a God he will try to cut a deal for a second visit to sort out F1, or his daughters spending. His favourite meal is egg and chips and his daughter spends £1million on a bath cut from one rock of Crystal, having met Bernies Dad a few times, a lovely guy, whose every third word began with F, I can only imagine what he is screaming down now."

"The Italian Government will contribute some Euro funding for the work on the Monastery and possibly towards the new infrastructure, we should get some funding for Running Costs once we are open, also we will have Romans contribution, so we should be able to get there, especially as our final planning will be subject to many alterations inevitably."

"Mike that nearly always means an increase in budget not a reduction."

"Granted, but our team working with the Italian Project Team and Commune in Modena and Emilia Romagna, with the Vatican Accountants, should have a tight control set into the contracts. I spoke with Cardinal Benelli earlier today and he has approved the Conversion of the Monastery with the Project, for the clinic, subject to agreement on the final presentation of the Scheme meeting with his approval, which is a big step forward.

I have sent all the details from Max`s and my phone to the team in London, so they have an idea of what we hope to be working on."

"Well done Mike, good progress let`s have our supper, I need to see how Nikki got on with her driving today, she is having self-defence with her sister in the morning, also dont forget the concert in Lucca tomorrow night, to look forward to, with our guests vacating the morning after.

How did you get on today with the Markets, are we earning a crust?"

"Yes Dad, all good news, biggest earners are the Debt Purchase Divisions we are picking up very good deals across the Globe, with Companies and Banks wanting to offload debt to make their Balance Sheets healthier.

In the UK alone we have bought Debt worth £140Million for £2.6 Million pay out to date. The girls Algorithms are still turning up trumps for us in Commodities especially Oil and Gas prices, from Russia to South America, they predicted the collapse of Oil from $140 a barrel to $40 a barrel in 2009, which we cleaned up on even though it caused another Credit Crisis, so soon after the Banking collapse.

We could see the same thing happening again soon, we are watching the signs on a second by second basis."

8

After another outstanding meal from Maria and her team everybody went into the Cinema Lounge, where they watched a playback from Max and Mikes phones, of the proposed Valley area for the Clinic Site with the existing buildings, for conversion. The Americans all agreed it was an exciting Scheme, expressing a keen desire for full details of the Project and ongoing costs asap, to see if it could be one for them.

In the morning Able was on site at 10.00am. prompt, with Nikki all ready to go, Karena had dropped out as she had the morning booked for calls to the UK with the Hill Climb Association and Sirs Stirling Moss and Jackie Stewart, who had already expressed an interest in contributing to the scheme albeit in a an advisory capacity.

To have two such esteemed Motor Racing heroes on board would do wonders for backing from all the European and Worldwide Motoring Organizations, especially in Italy where they were both almost deified. Sir Jackie is the last surviving F1 Champion driver from the 1960`s he had his first win in Italy and the racing mad Italians love him for it. Sir Stirling to have set the fastest ever time for Italys Mille Miglia and to have raced against some of the all time greats, Ascari, Musso and Fangio is a stand alone iconic achievement, which can never be emulated again. It has to be remembered in Stirling`s day the drivers never knew how many of them would be alive for the next race, at one time they were losing a driver at every Grand Prix, it was a Man and his Machine against everyone else.

Today it is acknowledged every F1 car could race without a driver, the Teams have such control over everything that happens in the car, when it`s on the track, suspension, braking, steering it`s more like an XBOX Game, by comparison.

"Hi Nikki, how are you today? I want to give you a bit of background on the System we use in Krav Maga. It's a self-defence method that's been around since the `30`s, it was founded by an Israeli and it is a combination of different Martial Arts. I want to try to get some basics in your head, which as with the driving we did yesterday, need to be practised to become second nature, should the time come when you might need them for your safety.

One of the difficulties for women is that they are not naturally physically aggressive and Krav Maga uses fast aggressive attack positions, to finish a bad situation, as quickly as possible, with fast defensive positions.

The first principle is to get away from any confrontation as quickly as possible, this remains the main purpose, even after you have disabled an attacker. The idea is to quickly disable, an attacker temporarily or permanently should it happen, then remove yourself from the scene quickly, in case of other possible attackers joining in.

We use our hands a lot, in flat, closed, clenched, or open extended positions as weapons. A clenched fist is used as a hammer or a blunt instrument to smash into an attackers face, the heel of the palm brought up quickly to the underneath of the chin or brought up under the nose can be very effective, rigid fingers gouged into the eyes, forget about nails, if you leave one in an attackers eyeball that could well give you time to flee the scene, if necessary lose your heels. Knees elbows and feet similarly can be used with good effect.

There are specific moves when confronted by an attacker with a weapon, be it knife, bottle or gun which are worth learning and to extend your repertoire of safety for yourself. Just to point out there are Clubs all over the World and online tuition whereby you can get Certificates for Accreditation, also Personal Trainers who are accredited to the Worldwide Association.

OK enough chat, let`s see you do a few moves over here, it`s more realistic for you to be in street clothes, rather than Judo clothing as you will most likely be in street clothes when something occurs.

Having in mind what I just told you show me how you make a fist, not bad, but the thumb must lock over the clenched fingers to make the fist tight. Take a punch at my head as hard as you can, when you are ready, Able caught the punch a foot in front of his face with an open hand saying, way too weak, you need to practice with a punch bag for upper body strength, the power comes from moving your whole body behind the punch as you deliver it not just from your arm, remember you are out to disable your opponent not caress his sideboards.

Try some open handed strikes to head, face and neck as quickly as you can with aggression, key areas are below the eyebrows, mix and match your attacks. That's better, you will definitely benefit from punchbag workouts, fifteen minutes each day before your morning swim. Now try the hammer fist, lock fingers in as before but aim for nose, temples, side of face and if you get the chance the back of the head, if hit correctly it is possible to knock someone unconscious with a good strike to a low point on the back of the head.

Next time we will do some kicking. I have a meeting with your Grand Father in ten minutes so you could do fifteen minutes practising punches on the body bag, it may help if you shorten your nails a bit. See you tomorrow for half an hour at ten?"

"Definitely, it`s a good way to work off any aggravation, wait till I catch you with my hammer."

"Only if I am asleep."

"Is that a promise?"

"Time may tell."

"Time and I wait for no man."

"You mean you haven't yet found a man worth waiting for?"

"Absolutely, I was very young when I realised there is no Prince Charming, life is too short to live in hope one may be out there, see you in the morning, are you on duty tonight at the Concert?"

"Of course, I will see you then, we could go for a drink if you like, after we have dropped everyone back to the Villa, there is a bar I like in Viareggio open till three or four in the morning on the sea front, they have the most amazing home made ice cream and Granita, we could go on to a Club if you like, they are both strictly casual dress code"

The Concert was a huge success, completely sold out with a guest appearance of Mary J Blige, who was on top form, Georgia got standing ovations, Jessica Brando went down very well also, the Party headed back to the Villa just after 1.00am as they had an early start in the morning, for the guests returning to the States.

Able and Nikki went to the bar in Viareggio, where there were a couple of outside seats on the promenade.

"What would you like to drink?"

"Espresso martini will be fine thanks."

The waiter brought the drinks to the table "Yours looks interesting what is it?"

It's one I made up, the barmen love it when I order it, called a Capo di Tutti Capi, Boss of the Bosses, in homage to the Mafia, when in Rome and all that, half fill the glass with crushed ice then, Grey Goose Vodka, Aperol and San Pellegrino Blood Orange with a side shot of 60% proof Grappa, to sip with it, not for the faint hearted try?"

"Hmmm, see what you mean, maybe one for a chilly January evening? They have a good crowd in, good mix."

"Yep, they tend to meet up here, then go on to a Club, there's no place like Italy for people watching, always something going on, see if you can spot the Trans couples, it's always been popular in Italy, they are so stylish, hair, make up and clothes, sometimes you need to be careful with who is smiling at you."

"Next you will tell me you have been caught out, ha, ha."

"I never drink to let my guard down, so no, it has not happened to me, would you like another drink?"

"Thanks no, I don't intend to let my guard down either, but after sitting at the Concert a stretch along the sea front would be nice, it must still be twenty five degrees, let's take an ice cream, Fior Di Latte topped off with Baci for me Abs, I have been here before."

"Finest Vanilla with chocolate nut kisses on top, good choice, for me Frutti di Bosco with Custard based Crema ice cream on top, will do it."

They walked along the wide promenade for half an hour chatting, stepped down to the sand and went to the waters edge, taking their trainers off paddling along "Your Grandfather asked me to go to the States with you and your sister when you go later this month, are you ok with that?"

"Sure we are not going for long, we hope to have our project over here agreed and signed off by the powers that be by then, we have a separate Suite adjoining ours, where you could stay."

"Nik, dont look round, I think we have a couple of chancers following us along the shoreline, if anything kicks off you run like mad for the bar, stay there till I get back, if I'm not back in fifteen minutes get back to the Villa by one of the Taxis parked out front ok? we are going to stop and face each other, I will embrace you, pretend to kiss your neck, so I get a good look at them, if I say go run like hell, don't look back, I'm armed it will be fine, let's do it."

Able stopped, pulled Nikki gently towards him, one arm round her slender waist and nuzzled her neck tilting her head back so he could see the guys following, she felt him tense up as she heard the water splash, behind her, he kissed her on the mouth and shouted Go! Nikki sprinted for the bar as fast as she could go, as the two young boys ran past laughing, calling out "Ragazzo fortunato" lucky boy.

He got to the bar as Nikki was talking to a Taxi driver "It`s ok Nik, I sent them on their way, we had a face off, it's the only way I could think of to protect you and turn a bad situation to my advantage, it`s what we do in Krav Maga, the kissing move which was excellent by the way, you have practised before?"

They walked hand in hand back to the car in silence and drove back to the Villa, Able saw Nikki back inside, kissing her gently good night on both cheeks, saying "Thanks for a lovely evening, maybe a bit more planning next time on my part?"

"Can`t wait to see what you come up with, night Abs."

Next morning Yuri took the Americans to Pisa Airport for a lunch time departure while Able had a half hour in the gym with Nikki, going through more training moves in self-defence. He started the session by saying "Nik about last night, I like your company and I`ve wanted to kiss you for a long time anyway, but my first job is looking after you and the family, so forgive me but on duty around the family, I have to be detached from how I am feeling about you, otherwise I may miss something I should pick up on and you may all pay the price, that can not happen."

"I understand Abs, I would not expect anything less from you, last night was good for me too, let`s take it slowly and see where it goes, same time same bar tonight?"

"Only if you`re buying."

Max, Roman and Karena helicoptered up to Piandelagotti, with the Surveyor and Photographer at 9.00am. promising to be back by 7pm.

Karena wanted photos for a possible layout of the Hill Climb Area as the open meeting for all interested parties was due to occur in ten days time.

Michael had a conference call with Cardinal Benelli and the Mayor of Modena, which is the Region the village comes under, for all Planning and Property matters. The Mayor was very receptive to the basic idea of bringing the possibility of employment and additional tourist interest to the Region, in particular with the involvement of the Church, he assured Michael he would personally take control of the application, with proposals, as soon as they were ready.

A local election was due at the end of the year and his party was pledged to increase employment throughout the Region. Nikki contacted various Motoring Organizations in Europe and received several offers of assistance, in planning and logistics with invites to visit their venues.

Tommy had gone to the Clinic in Lucca for a check up with Physiotherapy, thankfully the Specialists were pleased with his progress to date.

Max, Karena and Roman made it back by early evening, having covered the required areas of interest with the Photographer, who promised to send all his photos to Max`s computer by the morning, once he had screened and collated them all.

By lunch time next day the photos had all been replicated with designated headings, dimensions and possible usage, with various options. Max spoke with the Cad Team at Canary Wharf to ensure they were up to speed with the family requirements. He asked for a draft completed Schematic on each part of the project by the week end, which Andrew the Team Leader said was achievable. In the meantime the Surveyor was appraising local Contractors, he had used on previous large projects, from Modena, Parma and Milan, who in turn were told to use any local sub Contractors, they knew to be reliable, for a prestigious project with Government and Vatican involvement.

They also had to understand it would involve the highest scrutiny and accountability on the quoted Contract Costings with severe penalties on any over runs to be borne by the Contractors. Max, Nikki and Karena spent the afternoon on the phones bringing the various Agencies up to speed assuring them that they anticipated having a basic plan ready for Second Planning Status by the following week.

They phoned Father Leo asking him to set up the Open Meeting at the village for the following Tuesday at 11am. in the morning, he mentioned there had been an avalanche of interest since he announced to the Parishioners that a meeting was forthcoming, about exciting development possibilities for the village.

Which was to open with everyone invited to attend. Father Leo had simply told the villagers the meeting was proposed by a wealthy International Company with Family ties to the village, which would all be revealed at the meeting. Tommy had asked Karena and Nikki to fly to London with Able for a couple of days as he had received a call from the IT Director for the European and American Divisions with concerns about possible hacking from Russia and China, breaking into the embedding of the new Algorithm Coding Systems.

Michael was going to the Banks in Panama and Cayman Islands with Yuri as company, they were only expected to be gone a couple of days. Max and Roman would field any calls coming in on the Village Project.

The Company Jet landed at Heathrow at 11.00am the girls were at Canary Wharf by 12.15pm and went straight into the Main Boardroom where Greg the International IT Director was in consultation with three of his Managers and half a dozen other suits with Visitor badges round their necks.

"Karena, Nikki glad you managed to get here, we have just started, these Tech guys are from GCHQ in Cheltenham, I think you know Steven Bligh the Team Leader, we got onto them as soon as we realized there was someone on our wavelengths messing with our data, they have been analysing it for 24 hours since we contacted them, they were just going through what they've found. As a first precaution when we realized something was up we suspended using the Algorithm Codes temporarily. If you guys would like to go through it from the top again. "

"Hi good to meet you both, we have spoken on the phone before, just to give you an idea of what's going on out there, at the beginning of 2010 you recall, China targeted Google and stole a variety of Intellectual Properties and in June, a Worm was found in just one Windows System which was used by Iran on its Nuclear Program. We believed it originated from Israel possibly with US help.

Nearer to home, last year a Turkish Hacker got into Bank of America and got details of 85 Million Credit Cards, one of five largest breaches ever. Just to remind you as soon as you have a Commercial advantage over competitors, there are armies of bad people out there working 24/7, to get past any Cyber Security, to climb on board with your new profitability.

They often contact the Companies and offer to tell them how to remove the virus for a massive sum, depending who the target is and whether the attack is for political reasons or financial gains. Many large companies will pay the ransom demanded as it is cheaper than the threat getting out, damaging their share price. In August last year Aramco, Saudi Arabia's Oil company, the wealthiest in the world was crippled for months by a Cyber Attack, thought to be the biggest most destructive attack in history. Finally, in the Financial world, in February this year the Bitcoin Exchange filed for Bankruptcy when they maintain 460 Million Dollars were stolen by hackers, with another 27 Million Dollars missing from their Bank Accounts.

We are currently assisting the US, as their White House Computer Systems have been hacked, by what they say is the most sophisticated attack ever against the US Government."

"So Steven, what can you tell us about our attackers now, who are they likely to be and where are they?"

"That is the 64 million dollar question Karena, as you know when you brought in your new Algorithm System we looked at it for you. We were concerned that the system software originated in Japan with parts of the electronics delivered from China, but time of activation was top priority for you both, which we complied with. We investigated as far as we could go in the time frame we were given, so we gave you the thumbs up with a caveat that there were no obvious hidden bits and pieces attached, or with any sinister false indicators in the kit.

So it may be that there was a Sleeper, which was activated by a particular sequence of entries on the system, we have identified two possible suspects and are running tests at HQ on them now, we will be in a position to let you know by tomorrow night latest. The good news is that you will be able to recover our costs if we find a fault, as you can sell the cure to the Company that provided it to you, as they must have the same problems you have found, unless, they are the installers of said Sleeper themselves. Once we have identified the items we may have the source as wel."

"More importantly Steven, how do we stop this type of Cyber Attack in future?"

"Good question Nikki, you must observe the basics which mean different levels of protection on your systems, not just complicated Passwords. You need different levels of Access to your Codes with each level and User to have separate Entry Codes with each level ring fenced with Security.

Any new software from an outside Company must be exhaustively tested by a Cyber Specialist Company, before being brought online in your business. It is a good start that you were pretty quick from the off when you spotted a possible problem, so by shutting down the Algorithm Systems you have stopped the problem in its tracks, when we have identified the source, we can repair and make fit for purpose your existing software.

My team are going round all your Computers and Laptops now using remote access, if the Hackers are professional, they will be really good at hiding their viruses, they can activate them before you even switch on and whatever anti Malware system you install, they can be extremely difficult to spot.

We do a monthly check on all your systems here and Internationally but the villains get more and more clever all the time. When one of them discovers a new method of covert installation, they sell it on to any takers and there are lots of buyers out there."

"Thanks for that Steven, can you give me a direct call when you have the answers maybe tomorrow afternoon? We have a meeting downstairs with Heads of Divisions in ten minutes, which will take up most of the rest of today, anything interesting call me direct please."

"Good afternoon gents, ok we are only here for today and tomorrow, so let's make it count, we will break for buffet lunch in two hours but I want meaningful results on my laptop from all of you by lunchtime tomorrow.

Where are you all with the China takeover of the London Stock Exchange, that will be announced at close of the market on this coming Friday? You all acknowledged my emails to you, on what our position will be, we are going Long on the Market on Futures to the max, the sale will never happen at will never happen, at £54 Billion it's way too low, you all have access to an extra £5Million each, to pick up as many Contracts as you can.

This goes across the board to all Brokers, our Banks and Investors. By Wednesday it will be clear it will be rejected and we can pick up some excellent Future Contracts at premium prices.

Nikki and Karena went round each of the Divisional Heads Portfolios and were satisfied they were ready for the week end moves.

Nikki and Karena stayed for some smoked salmon blinis, hot salt beef and rye bread bagels, reminding the Managers that the Company Summer Jolly was in a months time, 3 nights on a Superyacht in Sardinia with Luxury Cabins for 25 Senior Managers and Partners, its own Helipad, Gym, Sauna and Steam Room, Wine Cellar, Grand Piano, Cinema, over 100 metres in length and a Crew of 40.

Able was parked outside the building, in a Chevrolet High Security blacked out six seater vehicle, as the girls approached, he held the doors open "Where to Ladies? you are booked into the Dorchester for the night, just the one, we are scheduled to fly back to Forte tomorrow evening, unless you want to change the plans?"

"Jermyn Street, Mayfair for me Able, a friend of mine from New York has opened a Gallery with his brother, I'm staying with him, he has a flat in Chelsea, I will see you for breakfast at the Dorchester at 9.00am. ok sis?"

"Karena, you kept that quiet, how long has this friend been an item?"

"We met over a year ago, his name is Michelangelo Santini, Mikki is divorced, no children, wealthy family from Rome they have three galleries, Santini's in Chelsea, Harlem and Miami, he is the Director of Acquisitions for the business, flies all over, more than we do, that's all you're getting, the potted version.

He is a lovely guy, we hit it off immediately I want you to meet him, he is coming over to Pietrasanta next month to see some big Sculptures, he could be interested in. He can stay at the Villa now all the guests have gone, this is my stop, thanks Able see you at nine for breakfast, I'll get my bag from the boot don't bother getting out."

"Where to miss? the Dorchester?"

"Drop the Miss Abs now we are on our own please "

"Still on duty Nik sorry."

"What time do you get off duty?"

"Whenever you give me the word, but as you are on your own, I will stay in my room tonight in case you need me."

The rooms were all en-suite with interconnecting lockable doors inside, two doubles with a small lounge and a single.

Nikki poured a small Champagne from the mini bar and ran a full bath, checking out the news while she took her make up off. She washed her shoulder length naturally curly hair using the Molton Brown hair products and their excellent conditioner.

She sank below the surface of the water luxuriating in the soft bubble bath oils shutting out the world for a few minutes. Her thoughts went to Max and her Mum, her Grandfather and the project, reluctantly, she stood up slowly, thinking she should make a call allowing for them being an hour ahead.

Drying herself off she used her natural skin care moisturising oils and started drying her hair off in a soft wavy style, keeping it all off her face with hair combs behind her ears. She selected her favourite Red Cherry Balconette Bustier Bra by Italian Lingerie Brand Intimissimi with matching thong. She eased herself into her plain black knee length Cavalli Goat Leather dress, embossed with black metal beads. She picked up the phone and dialled Ables room number "I am going down to eat in half an hour, I've booked a table will you join me? As a companion not a minder?"

"No problem look forward to it Nikki."

Nikki was on the phone for half an hour going through the situation with the family about GCHQ, saying all being well they would be back by tomorrow night, they were seeing the Cad Team at 11.00am. in the morning, she resisted spilling the beans on Karena's new man.

The door knocked from outside and Able was there in an Armani slim fit electric blue suit, with a Cavalli pink snakeskin pattern tie, matching pocket handkerchief over a pure silk white shirt and Geox loafers,

"Nice tie Abs, love the look, suits you sir."

"You look stunning if I may say " Able said holding the door for Nikki.

"Do you prefer the lift or stairs, may I?" holding out his hand. They were led to their table "I'm starving Abs how about you?"

"Starter and main for me, or we could have separate starters and share a main?"

"It's a good call, mixed hot seafood starter and maybe share a Cote de Boeuf with sides will work for me, Tempura Soft Shell Crab with Slaw, its great here and Big Beef is always safe, shall we go straight to a bottle of wine? you choose."

"Red for me always, I don't pay homage to red with meat and white with fish, connoisseurs would say my palate is immature, I will try any wine, but I know what I always enjoy. So for me it is Brunello Di Montalcino, so called king of the reds 100%

Sangiovese grape, so it is reliably soft and the lingering after taste with soft tannins makes a really easy drinker, slightly chilled, here endeth the lesson for today."

"I like Brunello myself, were you a wine Salesman in another life?"

"No, but I had a job for a month in Milan, my cover was working in a top Restaurant in the centre, where my target was a big Industrialist who ate there every day, he loved his wines, so I needed to be able to recommend what was on our menu while recording as much of the conversations as possible."

"Are you happy working for the family, don't you miss all the cloak and dagger of different jobs all the time?"

"Sometimes, I am very fond of your Grandfather and your whole family, I have more stability in my life, not wondering what the next phone call will bring or where I will be told to fly off to at a moments notice. I do get calls from different sources from time to time, asking if I am available. The only other possibility that could interest me is starting my own company, Yuri and I have discussed it, maybe I would look at it if anything happens to your Grandfather how is your wine?"

"Perfectly chilled Mr.Bond, like yourself, ha,ha, try my Crab."

"You're right that's good, do you cook yourself?"

"I will if you will, or do you only do breakfast before leaving?"

"French toast, omelette, scrambled eggs with smoked salmon or just croissants."

"That covers all the bases, but do you do it a second time?"

"If I'm invited, how about you? cooking I mean."

"Of course, when I make the time, mainly Italian which takes a lot of preparation, it's one of those foods, like the Jewish recipes, that you only get out what you put into it. I make my own pasta sometimes as well, I love all the old recipes my Grandmother taught me, home made Ravioli where the pasta melts as you taste it, with Italian Pork, Salami with Fennel and Mortadella, it's to die for, next time I make some I'll do you a batch."

"I would prefer fresh, can I book an appointment?"

"It`s always by invitation only, it`s normally a close friend I have known a long time or family, someone who has done me an amazing favour, when I least expected it."

"I will have to see what I can come up with. Changing the subject have you had any more thoughts about changing your car?"

"I might go for a Ferrari, get it out of my system? I think the Ford GT40 is too tight, only for track days. I have had an invite to a track day at Maranello where they are launching their new Model the La Ferrari the first Hybrid car they have done, with two engines, one electric of course. It will be a real money spinner if you can get one, only 500 being produced, the stats are incredible, six and a quarter litre V12, the most powerful engine they have ever done, over 9250rpm, gull-wing doors for easy entry, under 3 seconds 0-100km/hr, 7 speed gearbox, racing steering wheel with paddles, carbon fibre brake discs, front and back, you could take the day off to take me?"

"Definitely wouldn`t want to miss that, could we be driving one back, exciting?"

"Nothing is ever that simple in Italy, I`ll have it delivered if it's a goer."

"Would you like another dink, wine or cocktail?"

"Espresso martini thanks, you?"

"Triple strength espresso with a teaspoon of double cream on top and a Grappa on the side it's a real caffeine injection, it means the coffee is dispensed into the ground coffee holder three times the normal amount, tamped down so it`s really compacted, then the hot water is filtered at high pressure through the holder giving it a real strong kick to the espresso, most places if you ask for a double don't put enough coffee in so it`s too watery, sorry but it is like you say you only get out what you put in."

"That's the second lesson I`ve had tonight, that is why I always use the old Moka machine, on the cooker top, it`s easy to make the strength you like every time"

"Do you have coffee or tea first thing in the morning?"

"Always cappuccino, with a manual frother, again because you get the density to the milk exactly how you like it."

"Can I book a live lesson?"

"You have to bring something special to the party."

"I promise I will, thanks for asking me to join you tonight, I`ll do the meal on my room tab."

"What do you look for in a girl friend Abs?"

"I don't look now, because she would have to be special to put up with my life style, she would need an independent life of her own, that would keep her fulfilled, while I am away on Contract and knowing she could get a call any time of the day or night, telling her I am critically ill in hospital or dead. It doesn't lend itself to a long term relationship, maybe someone in the same line of business?"

"But are you not lonely, do you not miss female companionship?"

"Sometimes, but then I never have to report in, I am a truly free agent, I have several girls I can call for a night out, when I am in their towns, how about you?"

"I am a bit of a solo artist myself, I find if I commit to someone they always end up disappointing me in the end. I go all in, but I also need my space and because of my family and life style, they need to be able to cope with the fact that I can always pay for and go my own way, whenever I want, most men find it unsettling."

"Easy to tease, but hard to please you could say."

"That's no way to get a breakfast, shall we have a stretch down Park Lane or take a bottle of wine up to my lounge?"

"You call it, we`ve got to be up early tomorrow, if we are down at 9.00am. for breakfast with your sister."

"You`re right, sign the bill off and I`ll order a bottle of Crystal for my room now, at the same time."

"As they got to the door a waiter was leaving, having put the ice bucket with Champagne and two flutes on the lounge table, open and ready to go.

"You pour Abs, I`m going to take these heels and dress off get more comfortable, you can lose your jacket and tie if you like, nice as they are, back in a minute"

"Abs went back into the lounge and poured two flutes, placing them on the coffee table in front of the two seater sofa, taking a seat on it as Nikki came back in with an amazing red and white zebra stripe, see through, flowing beach dress, at a glance Abs could see the balconette bustier bra and thong beneath the dress, with her slim, firm, form beneath, " I think we need the air con up a tad, I`m feeling a bit warm."

Nikki smiled as she put a couple of CD`s on Zucchero and Eros Ramazzotti, she took the flute and sipped gently, sitting beside him saying "You smell nice, Bulgari? one of my favourites, why didn`t you sit on the other single chair, it`s not a trick question?"

"Two reasons, one it`s your lounge and two you get to choose where to sit, on your own or beside me, I`m glad to see you chose wisely. You are absolutely stunning Nikki and thank you for a lovely evening."

"It`s not over yet, is it?"

"Not from me, but I like to give a lady a choice, you have an amazing tan, where do you get time?"

"It`s not natural, I apply it every other day, it's a soft tan colour, top the glasses up Abs" passing the bottle to him, at the same time twisting her back sideways on with her feet extended onto his lap.

"Be kind to me and massage my feet, tonight`s shoes are new and a bit tight."

Abs passed her wine back to her and admired her perfect legs, soft skin and defined muscles, as Nikki moved, her dress parted with one side dropping to the floor exposing her slim muscular thighs and hips, he massaged the soles, heels and arches of her feet "Have you got a moisturiser, you like, available, for a full body Swedish Massage, I am a fully certificated Masseur."

"I don't doubt it Abs, don't give me the Science, the ecstasy will do, my body oil is on my dressing table over there, help yourself."

She got up, slipped her dress off, reached behind her and undid her bustier bra allowing her ample but firm 36c breasts to perk upwards, as she bent down to remove her thong laying on her front, with her legs two feet apart. Abs went to the top of the bed, drizzled a cross of body oil along the back of Nik's shoulders and down to the base of her spine, he put a small amount onto his hands and gently massaged in small circular motions either side of her spine across her shoulders, moving slowly down each side, being firmer where there was muscle, easing off in between, he stopped the circular motions at the base of her spine coming half way up the bed.

Taking hold of her extended limp arm at her side, he applied more oil, with effleurage strokes up and down the length of her arm going over her hands and finger knuckles as well. After he had done the other arm he returned to the end of the bed saying "I am going to gently pull you down the bed, so I can reach your sternum more easily, its more difficult on a bed rather than using a proper massage table."

"No complaints from me sir."

"Using his thumbs and the heel of his palms, he gently massaged and probed in between the firm muscles of her buttocks, he found a few stress knots and warned her to hold on while he put a lot of weight onto pushing his thumbs carefully into each knot feeling them break up and dissipate into the surrounding area.

"God that feels much better, you do know what you're doing."

Abs oiled each leg individually, starting with the toes, the knuckles and in between each toe, moving from the arches up the calves to the thighs and hips her body was now warm to the touch, he gently drizzled some warm oil from his hands down the line of the sternum and either side of her inner butt cheeks, gently parting her legs to a foot wider than her shoulders.

His hands stroked the oil slowly down her smooth, silky butt area, as she moaned softly, coming back up to her tightly puckered starfish which he drizzled a few drops of oil on, tapping it gently with his forefinger before going down to the base of her vagina, which she raised slightly from the bed. He came round to her side and said she should turn over for him now.

She reached out and felt he was ready for her "You had better get out of your suit now, before it gets creased.

"Abs stripped off in double quick time, she had turned over, her arms down by her side her legs three feet apart with a pillow under her buttocks, he started to massage her shoulders, she took hold of his hands and cupped each breast with a warm oiled palm, using upward circular movements, then placing one of his hands over her vagina the other behind her neck. He kept the hand round her neck and went up to nuzzle the nape of her neck faintly licking her warm ear inside, exhaling hot air into it slowly.

He kissed her parted lips pushing his tongue slowly along the inside of her mouth licking her tongue, catching it with his tongue, lightly holding it with his teeth as she pushed it into his mouth. Her mouth was wet and warm they exchanged juices freely. He caressed each breast licking the aureola, tweaking each pert nipple, sucking them slowly and softly till they were nearly bursting.

Her nails dug into his shoulders as he got onto the bed beside her, his left hand moving swiftly down to her now hot vulva, which was wet with warm oil and her own juice. He stroked lightly up and down the extremities of either side of her lips coming to the top where his finger and thumb gently held the head of her wet clitoris stroking it and tweaking it, as a butterfly lands on a flowers stamen without even bending it.

Nikki was now moaning out loud, her nails scratching his back as she dug them in which spurred him on. He entered her with two digits easily, as she was ready but she pulled him directly over her removing his hand and putting both sets of nails hard into his muscly butt cheeks, forcing him into her as she wanted, holding him there with her legs wrapped round his waist, in a really strong judo hold.

She eased her hold and he moved strongly in and out with increasing pressure, she put his hands round her neck pulling his arms into her with her head angled back, she orgasmed, her whole body convulsing out of her control, Abs followed suit just after, staying inside her, till she and he subsided, then he laid by her side stroking her arms and neck as she turned onto her side.

He lightly stroked her back down to her spine for a few minutes, then with one digit went down inside her crevice to her rear entry point. He went round the starfish and her warm and undulating back to her vaginal opening, now warm and wet, he entered with two digits, to the inner upper front wall and with a rhythmic pulse massaged her G spot, till she orgasmed again, twice in quick succession.

He left her quivering quim and kissed her as he laid over her, stroking her head cuddling up to her, entwined together, neither one speaking. Eventually he asked "Is there anything I can get you? run you a bath, another massage even a cup of tea?"

"Don't move, stay beside me, till we have a bath together in the morning, wake me at 6.30am. please gorgeous, night my love."

Abs's phone went off at 6.30am sharp, he ran a bath, enough for two then ordered two double cappuccino's from the Concierge by phone, the waiter knocked as the bath finished filling. He woke Nikki with a soft lip kiss, then one on her forehead commenting how beautiful she smelt, from the warmth of her fit body, he propped her up with his pillows, giving her a coffee "I've run you a bath miss fit, I'm jumping under the wet room shower, it's quicker and we will never be down by 9.00am. if I get into a bath with you, so God help me for saying no."

"Ok babe, scrub my back though eh?"

"Only if you sit on your hands."

Nikki finished her coffee, went into the bathroom and slid into the roll top double bath, as Abs got out of the shower. He came over sponged off her back and went into his room and shaved and did his teeth, going back into the bathroom to make sure Nikki had not fallen asleep. She was leaning over the edge of the bath, naked, rinsing the soap suds with the shower head, her legs apart, he crept up on her holding her hands on the bath edge, going down on his knees in one move, his tongue going straight into her moist opening, she squealed with surprise "I missed out last night, I need your taste with me all day today, you're so good for me, you are super hot"

"I'll leave you now, I start work in an hour miss fit." he kissed her full on the mouth nearly taking her breath from her lungs.

"Another coffee? or will you wait till we go down. I can wait downstairs at our table for your sister to arrive if you prefer."

"No need, I'll have another coffee please, when you're dressed, if you are ready to let me get set for the day."

"Sure babes, see you shortly."

Karena and Nikki went straight to the Cad Dept. they had worked overnight to have a basic plan ready for the girls on their arrival.

While everyone knew it was a first draft, it was exciting for the girls to see the Monastery renovated in 3-D form, in compliance with all the traditional Timber and Stoneworks, the simple yet modern living quarters for the Monks and the additional buildings extended to encompass the work areas, all individually set out. The placement for the Guest Lodges accommodation in the grounds.

The Cross Country Ski Run was in place and Cycling routes laid out. The Hill Climb tracks had been set out in three separate possible layouts superimposed into the photos of the area provided.

All in all most impressive results, in a couple of days, they went through each of the plans in detail with the team over the next couple of hours, so they were both fluent in the details laid out.

"Guys you have really stepped up to the plate, I didn't think you would have achieved so much so quickly, now all we need to do our end is get the plans approved in principle, with the locals, the Vatican and the Planning Authority then we come back to you with all the alterations they require.

That's when the work really begins, you will be liaising with various departments in Italy not on your own, as we are on the ground over there and hopefully with our contacts we can get things expedited, reasonably quickly. We will be in touch next week to give you a heads up on progress, thank you again for your effort, much appreciated.

The girls went to see how the GCHQ investigation was going to check how close they were to identifying the enemy virus.

"Hello Steven, how far have we got with the virus problem?"

"It's as we suspected, without going into too much technical detail it is Chinese involvement.

We have seen this more recently in the States and Germany where the Chinese Tech firms invent these new viruses and get their manufacturing Companies which are basically all State controlled, if not directly owned, to put these devices into Mother Boards and Circuitry where they are disguised and difficult to trace, but we follow the previous leads and ultimately we find them. All their manufacturing Companies are signed up to give the State unlimited access to any projects they are working on, in whatever Country or capacity.

So the first step is to avoid all products with any parts manufactured in China, even though the base cost will be increased. Cheaper where the Chinese are involved does generally not save money in the end."

"We don't know if items we purchase from any Asian country will contain Chinese manufactured parts, from Taiwan especially, or even Japan Steven."

"I appreciate the difficulty Karena, but as a starting point I would say you should have written into all your purchase contracts a Clause Indemnifying you against any losses of material gain, or infringement of any Intellectual Property Rights, directly or indirectly attributable to any Chinese parts, used in your products purchased, that should make the Seller be more careful."

"We will take that on board Steven and where are we with cleaning all our computers down now?"

"Pleased to report we will be all clear by 4pm. today here, we are cleaning all your Subsidiaries by remote viewer access and that should be clear by mid-night tonight, I will confirm by email to you first thing in the morning Nikki."

"That's great, thank you for your help once again, we are visiting our Banks next week and the States, we will reiterate what we have agreed, about Purchasing Contracts today, with all of them and make sure they are up to speed."

They flew out of Heathrow in their allocated time slot of 5pm. and were back in the Villa by 7.45pm. where over one of Maria`s full on suppers, the family were brought up to speed with the events of the last two days.

Roman was excited to see the 3-D plans for the Project saying " now as you say, we have some meat on the bones, to work with.

"Nikki said she was going for a walk along the beach, to move the pasta along before going for an early night, they all agreed to be down by 9.00am. next day to get stuck into planning details, as the following Monday the presentation to the villagers was taking place. Abs accompanied her, the evening was beautifully calm and still warm enough, to just wear a top with jeans. They waited till they got round the corner and crossed the road onto the beach front, Abs reached out for her hand which she interlocked with his, they faced each other and kissed on each cheek Italian style.

"I`ve missed you through the day miss fit, it`s strange knowing you are near but I can`t come and touch you, it`s called being grown up, it's a pain."

"Same for me babes, it`s probably a bit easier for me because I am absorbed in whatever Project I`m on, meeting different people through most of the day, I have missed touching you today, after getting close to you for the last couple of days."

"We are both old enough and wise enough to know how we need to behave, if we want to change the dynamics we display, we need to be sure, yourself especially if we want to be known to be an item, we will soon see what your Mum and Dad think not to mention your Grandfather, I don't want to find a horses head in my bed one night."

"Come on Abs, I am old enough to live my life my way, I wouldn't want to upset any of my Family, but I expect and know they would realize it would be useless to try to interfere with any partner of my choice, if they or you felt you couldn`t continue working for the family we would move on together, in a way which suited us, you might set up your own Firm with Yuri and once you are established with some of your own people, you would not need to go out on every job that came in. I would still be involved with the family business presumably, though if that was not wanted I am financially independent and can live and work anywhere in the world,"

"Well I guess we carry on as we have before,when you think it`s right, we can tell them we are becoming involved to whatever degree you are happy with, I need to say now you tick all my boxes, so I`m in for the long run, until you say enough. I won`t put any pressure on you, we go at your pace, let`s seal it with a kiss beautiful."

"God, can`t you come to my room tonight?"

"Too soon, to close to everybody for comfort darling, I would be too up tight to perform."

"That I will believe if I ever see it."

"Let`s get an ice cream on the way back, a cone for me, come on last one to the Gelateria pays."

They got a couple of cones and sat on the beach close to the sea, listening to the water lapping in gently, there was no wind, they finished their cones and Abs got up took her hand and went to pull her to her feet, she yanked his arm taking him off balance, he landed beside her, as she put her leg over his lower body sitting upright on top of him. She leant down licking his lips with her warm moist tongue, pushing it into his willingly open mouth, she went down on him on the soft sand and forcefully continued to completion, wasting not a drop of Abs`s nectar.

"Would you like a coffee now Nik, or is it home James, time out?"

"I could go an espresso babe, first bar on the beach, yes I`m buying."

Next morning after an early breakfast, everybody gathered in the main lounge with the Cad Teams projected plans on all the TV Screens. Michael started the meeting by saying before we get into details, we need an agenda to decide on the best site and Schematic for the Hill Climb site, so we can eliminate the other two options, once we have done that I propose we discuss and hopefully agree on the format for the types of workshop and classrooms we want for Attendees.

Closely followed by an agreement on the girls Hotel Project.

"I think it sensible to split our time over two days as a target, so we have something concrete to present by Monday, anyone in disagreement now is the time to raise your hand. We need to all come together on both plans by tomorrow especially the Monastery, as this is the prime object for the Project Planning, everything else is an add on with the motive to drive interest in the whole site, making it appealing to different Social Sectors.

So that we brainstorm our ideas as quickly as possible, if we split into two teams for both Projects, with a stop time of four hours, when each team will present their ideas to everybody, we then agree any adjustments and get them back to the Cad Team, they will get the new details altered and back to us by tomorrow afternoon. We will then have a presentable detailed plan for display to the public on Monday coming.

Obviously we need to make any adjustments to the plans before we go to the Vatican, as well as the Planning Officials in Modena

"I suggest Max and Nikki join forces for the Monastery, as

Max has seen the actual site and myself with Karena will get into the Hill Climb, Cross Country Skiing and the new Hotel site, Roman will, if he is agreeable, float between us giving his input and acting as a Referee, if it gets heated, all in favour of that raise hands please, agreed let's get to it.

"Max and Nikki agreed the best option was to utilise any building materials from the existing buildings, as this would be essential to any approval for local planning applications. The entire flooring on the ground floor would be local quarry tiles in a dark red mottled finish all interior exposed timber, would be Chestnut, from the local Sawmills, the majority of all Italy's forests being in the Alpine region. The first floor would have terracotta floor tiles throughout, with all walls up and down smooth plastered, with artistic brickwork relief, to create interest, the entire interior to be painted in warm light vanilla, washable paint.

The central part of the building contained the Chapel, enough for 100 people, the individual rooms for the Monks and a large Commercial Kitchen with a Refectory seating 200, also the Admin Offices for the entire completed Project.

The new build to the left contained thirty adjustable large Rooms with movable interior walls, above would be the individual en-suite bedrooms with rooms for Attendees at the Clinic, fifty rooms in all.

The new build to the right of the Monastery would contain a Games Room, Cinema and Gymnasium with Indoor Pool and three Separate Lounges two with TV's.

Above would be the Medical Centre and Mini Hospital, Admission Rooms and Consultation Rooms with another fifty en-suite rooms for Attendees.

Power for the Project would come from the Hydro Electric Plants at Cuneo in the mountains above, with Solar Panels installed where possible and a separate emergency Generator Plant to the side. The gardens with vegetables, would all be laid out professionally as close as possible to the main buildings, while allowing for maximum daylight sun and adequate Irrigation supplied from the Natural Spring Water Well.

Included in the various Workshop Areas would be Pottery, Art, Painting and Sculpture, Woodwork, Computer and IT, Clothing Design and Fashion Jewellery, Languages, Cooking in the main Commercial Kitchen, Gardening and Animal Husbandry as the Clinic would have its own Cows, Pigs, Chickens and Sheep for self provisioning.

Marketing and Media Promotion, Photography to start with and two large Classrooms.

Michael and Karena in the meantime, had agreed on the site for the Hill Climb Course being a two kilometre S and Z featured style Track on Gravel and Scree on land owned by the Monastery, approaching the climb up the foothills with trees dotted in between what would be the track, starting from the edge of the lake, an S shape up to the halfway point then an acute Z at the top, dropping to the far edge of the lake and finish line.

The rise and fall of the terrain would enable areas to the side of the proposed Track to be levelled for Spectators, the whole Track to have crash barriers both sides of its entirety. It would be a Time Trial Circuit not an open race track. The Cross Country Skiing Course already went along the side of the lake furthest away from the proposed Hill Climb Track so the new Hotel would provide a half way stop and watering hole, for all the existing Sports people, young and elderly alike.

In relation to the Hotel, it was agreed to provide a Master Lodge, Alpine Style with Catering and Bar facilities. The accommodation to be individual Lodges, bought off plan and erectable in only two day, by the seller, included in the price, except for the required concrete base for each one, depending on overall size.

Full 3-D video plans in detail were available on line, from the various firms supplying the Lodges, so could be readily downloaded, with choice of finish.

Over lunch at the Villa it was agreed that the Monastery

additions could go back to the Cad Team for alteration and a draft plan in 3-D provided for the Hill Climb Circuit was ready to be actioned and was requested.

A decision on styles and numbers for the siting of the Lodges needed to be agreed, with layout for siting of Vegetable Gardens. The parameters for the Chickens and Livestock was pencilled in.

Actual activity of Wild Boar in the area would need to be monitored, to see if it was more feasible to employ a gamekeeper or fence in some large areas to enable the Chickens, Pigs and Sheep to wander and feed free range.

Also Roman thought the site was big enough to make available Archery and Clay Pigeon Shooting at low cost, as an additional attraction, he asked if anyone knew if the lake was or could be stocked with fish, for Fishing enthusiasts.

His idea of an indoor Rifle and Handgun Range was vetoed as it was felt it could be a possible hazard, given the possibility that some Attendees may not have been vetted sufficiently to make others feel secure.

The meeting was halted as Luigi, Tommy`s Cousin in the Carabinieri called in to see how they all were. Tommy took him into his main office after everybody had exchanged pleasantries and Able had assured him thanks to his prompt collaboration with the intruders, there had been no further interventions on the Family to report.

Luigi told Able that he had resolved the shoot out situation at the Motorway payment kiosk, there were no outstanding issues with it, he had brought back Able`s Glock as it was no longer needed. Tommy mentioned that he believed he had resolved any issues with his possible Adversaries and peace should reign for the foreseeable future. Luigi congratulated him, then continued.

"Tom, I hear you are looking at a possible project in the Modena Region the old family Village, I have had some contact from the local Police Chief warning that your interest may not be welcomed by everybody, he would not give any more details but advised you to either see him at his office in Modena, or send one of your sons if you cannot attend yourself, he is adamant it will be to your benefit, I have his number but he will not discuss it on the phone.

His advice is to make sure you have security at the Open Meeting, he cannot provide much cover himself, it is a bit Political as most things are in Italy in the end, I know you understand, just a heads up as you say, Ok?"

"Of course Luigi, I am always grateful for any information that smooths the way forward, I am sure it will be something we can sort out, with goodwill on both sides. I am speaking prematurely, but of course should we manage to finish the Project, your whole family will come to the opening as my Guests, for the week end and stay in a couple of the Ski Lodges."

"I look forward to the event Tom and good luck with everything, keep me informed if I can help with any situations Arrivederci."

"Able, a moment please."

"Sir."

"Able, Luigi has just told me about a possible situation which may give us some concerns for the open meeting on Monday coming up, in the Village, it`s the local Police Chief, he won`t discuss on the phone and will only speak to one of my sons, if I cannot attend, it could be a "Handshake" as they call it round here, a contribution to the local Cops Children Fund, there could be a few on the agenda once we get started, but from Luigi`s manner I think it`s more. I am contacting the guy in Modena in a minute and if we can get a meet tomorrow, we will know what`s likely to occur before Monday, if you can fly Michael up."

"Definitely sir, not a problem."

Tommy spoke with Commander Lodi who gave nothing away, but said he would gladly see Michael next day at 11.00am. in the morning. Able flew Mike up to Modena, where they were both ushered into the Police Chiefs private office, he introduced himself and stated it would be preferable if he spoke to Michael alone, at least in the first instance. Abs went out to get a coffee.

"This is all very intriguing Commander, my Father is sorry he could not come himself, but he is still getting over a large operation, I assure you I have his fullest confidence in Business matters and Private so feel free to give me all the details of the situation."

"He said as much to me yesterday, Mr. Beales so it is not a problem, in itself it is a delicate matter, which is private and not for public consumption, bear with me if l seem to wander in my story, but all will become clear at the finish. I need to start the story at the end of the Second World War, don't worry it is not a History lesson.

Briefly the Region where your Family village is was quite an isolated area at the time, with the locals very entrenched in their Political Allegiances. Unlike the UK where I believe you say two things we never discuss, are Religion and Politics, in Italy in every bar and café especially towards the end of the War, people spoke about nothing else, unless a pretty girl came in. The Village had and still has four distinct Groups in the Area encompassing, some ten or twelve villages, the Royalists not so much, The Fascists, the Communists and the Socialists. There was continuous violence between the youth groups at the time, all jostling for more influence locally and joining in with the ebb and flow of the continually changing National situation at the time. Now we come to the position we find ourselves in today.

At the end of the War, as I said the Communists in particular were searching out any Fascists and killing them on sight, in the hope that Russia's influence in Europe would enable them to rule in Italy.

Your family from what I gather were more middle Centrist Socialists, not wanting to be involved in the violence. Your Grandfather and his Brothers had emigrated from Italy around 1920, he went to England, his Brothers to the States, he had made an enemy of the local Communist, strong arm thugs in his Village, one in particular Dino Lucarotti, who was always trying to convince his family to join their movement, as the family was one of the oldest in the Village.

Your grandfather had done quite well for himself and came back to Italy at the end of the War to visit family, there was chaos all over, the Communists were everywhere with elections happening soon and Dino Lucarotti was an enforcer for a local Politician in Modena. He heard that your Grandfather was back in the Village and decided to pay him a visit with an accomplice. He found him in the one bar in the village with three Cousins having a quiet drink and approached him in a loud and swaggering manner intimating he was honoured, a now rich Foreigner had condescended to return to his original poor roots, to see the local peasants.

From the details of the incident at the time he insisted your Grandfather buy him a drink which he refused to do, turning his back on Dino who then pulled a revolver from inside his jacket pocket brandishing it and pushing your Grandfather onto the table with his Cousins, someone drew a knife, stabbing Dino in the arm with the gun, which he dropped. Dino`s accomplice grabbed him and they quickly left the bar together. Camillo and the Cousins followed them out, from here we only have mixed testimony, from a few Witnesses.

Dino had opened the boot of his car and turned to face the Cousins with a shotgun in one hand, the accomplice was loading his own as two shots rang out, someone had fired on both men in quick succession, he shot Dino in the chest who was on the ground bleeding profusely from his wound, his accomplice was hit in the leg and was writhing on the ground screaming.

The Cousins removed the shotguns put a tourniquet on the accomplices leg getting him back in the car, telling the driver to return him back to Modena and never to show up in the area again, if he valued his life. Dino in the meantime had expired from his wound. Here is where the records fail us as there is no record of what happened to Dino, at the time the Country was in total upheaval there were shootings and hangings all over the country as old scores were settled, hated local Turncoats and

Collaborators with the Nazi`s were shot by firing squads of Militia and Partisans who roamed the towns and villages, offending officials were dragged from their homes never to be seen again, a very different time to now it was the Wild West with no Sheriffs.

Within two days your Grandfather had returned to England and the flimsy statements from the four Cousins stated that all three Communists presumably went back to Modena, they were never seen in the area again. No further investigations were entered into and the case files closed."

"Well! Mr. Commissioner that is some story, from out of the blue, I have never heard anything in the Family history to point to such an event, I am amazed. My Grandfather is no longer with us he passed away, some years back. As far as I knew he never returned to the Village, but he did come back to Italy over the years buying various properties which he rented out or allowed family members to live in, he also sent sums of money over to help the family survive, but as far as I know that is it.

Even if I accept what you say, at this stage do you intend to reopen the case? what exactly are you proposing may I ask?"

"Scusami Signor Michael, you misunderstand my intentions, I would like to speak to your Father, only to add a current statement, to the File, when he is well enough, even if he can only confirm he has no knowledge to add, of what happened on that night, from conversations he may have had with Camillo, but there is possibly a more pressing situation to deal with."

"I think you have given me one big shock, for today, I hope the rest is more easily dealt with.

"The Commissioner went to the door and beckoned to Able to come in.

"Have a seat sir, I understand you are head of Security for the Family I have very good reports from Luigi Berti in Forte Dei Marmi, what I have to say now will be of interest to you, I am sure. We have had intelligence that a Contract has been put out on the open market, on the life of your Employer Mr. Tom Beales with a likely attack while he is in Piandelagotti, as the favoured designated point of the attempt."

"Where did this come from? have you any idea who the Principals are?

"Not exactly Mr. Able, our first thought was it may have come from the previous Principals who ordered the attack at the Villa in Forte, but as you say you have settled that connection, we have looked further afield. The word from our Intelligence people is that it is a private source, not organized crime at all.

We have no idea at this stage, we do not want to smother the Open Meeting with armed officers as the public may not then attend. I am happy to put three or four Carabinieri on the points of entry and exit, but I thought you may prefer to put your own people inside, I understand they are all experienced and Licensed Operatives who may carry firearms in Italy, Luigi has faxed me copies of their Licences. My men can provide hand held scanners for entry at the doors and the Military can do a Bomb Sweep in the morning, also we seal it off till you are ready to enter. Is also possible the whole thing is hoax."

"I think for the situation as it is, it sounds reasonable, I will need to get back to my Dad and we will call you later today with his decision to go ahead or scrap it, thank you for the call, we will talk later, if you get further intelligence please call day or night, he may simply decide not to attend himself at this stage."

Thank you Mr. Michael I await your response."

Tommy said he was shocked to hear about the War time exploits attributed to his Father in Law and maintained he found it hard to believe, he insisted he would attend the meeting on Monday come what may, he did agree to Ables insistence that he wear a bullet proof vest, on condition that Karena, Nikki, Tonia and Alexis agreed to stay at the Villa with Yuri and extra security.

Next morning Tommy, Max, Roman and Able and three of the security team arrived in Piandelagotti on the Helicopter, an hour before the meeting, the Bomb Squad were just leaving giving it an all clear.

Commissioner Lodi had ensured the doors were all covered with four Carabinieri all with machine pistols across their chests.

"Buon Giorno, Signor Able? I am Capitano Leone, we are at your disposal, my men have hand scanners in the cars and we are here until you have all left the Village, if that is good for you? The Commissioner asked me to tell you he has some more updated information, concerning the Protagonists involved in the threat, we have been notified about, he would like to speak with you when convenient."

"Thank you Captain, I will go inside and see to the disposition of my team then I will make the call. Father Leo turned up as they all entered. The large open hall had three doors to the outside Able told two men to cover them, the third to float inside. To the far end of the hall was a raised platform, with tables and chairs facing around 100 chairs in lines from the back to within six feet of the platform. To the left was a door through to male and female toilets. Tables down one side with display boards on the walls were being organized by Max.

They had brought metre high print outs of everything the Cad Team had finalised, the Centre Piece of the display was a 3-D model of the Monastery with a removable roof. Father Leo said "It all looks very impressive, you have worked a miracle getting it all done in a short time Mr. Beales, though having met your children I should not be surprised, I am pleased to see you are well today, this could be a most important day for our Village. I am expecting maybe 150 people, the notices we displayed stated voting was only allowed for people from the local areas, who must produce their Carta D`Identica, standing room only with the Press as well. The local Police notified me they would be here I thought for crowd control, I did not expect Carabinieri."

"A precaution I am sure Father, maybe an over reaction to some information they have, it is unlikely I will say anything to upset your tranquil Parish."

Tommy went over and showed him the model of the

Monastery which he could not believe, in conjunction with all the plans. Able said they were all set, as the Family and Father Leo moved to the tables and chairs on the platform, Tommy taking centre stage. In front of him were two boxes with slots in the top on the front in large letters SI and NO .

Doors opened and people came in singly and they were scanned for any weapons at the door outside, children and babies as well. The seats quickly filled up with both sides jammed with people, the Press were at the back, at least a dozen, no television crews thankfully, that would come later no doubt.

"Buon Giorno a Tutti" Tommy said loudly, can you all hear me at the back? Si, si came back to him. Roman was to his left, Max to his right, as he started "My Father Camillo, was born in this village and with his Brothers he emigrated many years ago to England and America, then came the Second World War, with all its horrors.

I fought in the War against Germany and made a very successful life for my family afterwards. I never forgot who I was and where my roots belonged. I always vowed that one day if I could, I would come back to the village and bring something back to it. Now is my time to do this, with your help and my family. My second son Massimo is here, his Brother Michael and my Grand Daughters could not be with us today but are all involved in our Project, my wife sadly is no longer with us.

My family who were related to the Bulgarelli`s lived in Frassinoro and emigrated to England when Camillo did. To my left, is Roman my best friend and old comrade, from the worst times of the War we both served in.

He is joining us in this project, we have brought the details of what we would like to create here, with your blessing and after we have finished our presentation, we will have a question and answer session, then we will ask you all to vote with verified slips into the boxes in front of me, we will give you the result before we leave today.

I ask please no mobile phones till after the vote, as we are so crowded, if anybody wishes to use the toilets please make your way to the door to my right now. Before we start the presentation which Massimo will do on my behalf, I will ask Father Leo to say a few words for your benefit."

After ten minutes, everybody had settled down again and Father Leo addressed his Parishoners.

"Good people of my Parish, as you know I was not born here, but was sent here by God and my Superiors to carry out my duties to counsel my flock and tend to your Spiritual needs, over the years I have become one of you, living in peace and tranquility. I believe in God who in his wisdom sends us all opportunities and also challenges.

We must decide that what is being proposed today, how we will vote on it, not just for ourselves but for the children and their future. It is an incredible opportunity, but if we do not see it as such we must not be frightened of it either, so I ask you all to consider your hearts and minds and pray for five minutes, for wisdom to guide your vote, thank you."

Everybody clapped loudly as he sat down. Max stood first, going through Tommy's original idea, expanding on the concept of the transformation of the Monastery with Vatican approval and the involvement from San Patrignano. He followed up with "We understand it is a lot to take in, from where the Village has been for the last 1000 years to what we now propose, there are many obstacles to overcome and the final scheme may be altered, from the way it looks now once the Regional Planning Department in Modena, have looked at it. But for it to be a success we need it to be self sufficient in costs and profitability to enable you all to enjoy its benefits. Your children as well. He went through the details of the Hill Climb Concept and the upgrading of the Cross Country involvement, with a group of the other villages in the area, also the Facilities with Lodges. He then threw the floor open to any questions, asking whoever had a question to state their name and which village they came from first.

"How many people do you believe will be brought into our

village from your plans?"

"We know how many we can accommodate, but the final figure will depend on planning, as well as the small amount of Monks at the Monastery we envisage possibly half of the Tutors will reside on site, others commuting from Parma or Modena, but overall anything between one hundred and fifty to two hundred and fifty."

"What about the increase in traffic, especially if you increase facilities with the car racing?"

"It is a fair point, there will be an increase, especially when as we hope we get to join in some National and International Competitions, but the roads will not be altered to affect the hinterland and the Village itself."

"How many new jobs will you create, will they be for outsiders only?"

"The reverse is true, Villagers will always have priority for any vacancies available which they are able to perform, they will also be able to use the Mentoring facilities in the Monastery, to learn new skills and improve job prospects, this will be enshrined and written into the Principals of the whole Scheme."

Before we break, please have a look at our displays of the project down the side of the wall to my left then if you have any further questions please approach one of us and we will answer your questions, then if you all care to sit for a while and talk among yourselves, also taking Father Leo's advice and pray for five minutes we will take the vote at the top table and should have your count supervised by Father Leo within ten minutes or so. My Family and I thank you all for coming today and hope this will be the start of a new way forward for all of us and our children, God bless you all."

One of Ables men came over to him, saying one of the toilet windows had the razor wire removed, that they had put in that morning.

"Give the others a red flag status, all of you on your game now, we need to get Tommy away, you cover my back."

Max now called everybody to come up to vote with their ID. "Please allow mothers with babies to get through."

Able pushed his way through, closely followed by his colleague. He got to the platform as the last woman in the queue thrust her vote into the slot at the same time as he climbed the three steps in one bound, whispering in Max`s ear to get outside immediately, as he reached out for Tommy`s arm pulling him in to himself "We need to evacuate you and the family NOW! sir."

In that same instant a shot rang out, followed by a second, Able was spattered with blood from Tommy`s shoulder, as he pulled him down the stairs and out of the side door, at the base of the steps.

Looking back he saw the shooter had been taken down by his back up, she was a young woman with a baby strapped to her chest her gun on the table, in front of Roman. The woman was under three or four bodies, but sustained no wounds the baby screeching it`s head off.

The Carabinieri had come in and were allowing people out one at a time. Tommy had sustained a glancing shot to his upper arm and Able had put a field dressing on the wound from the Carabinieri`s Command Vehicle, before driving him with Max to the helicopter, telling the pilot to go immediately to the A & E at Forte Dei Marmi where he would be able to land, saying he would call ahead to warn them.

He told him to return for Roman and himself as soon as he had dropped the family at A & E. Able phoned Commissioner Lodi and gave him the bare facts on the attempt, saying it was definitely not a professional Contract, only a light injury sustained and the Perpetrator with her baby, easily apprehended, both unharmed. His officers had been a tremendous help and they were heading back with the woman in custody, after she admitted she had removed the razor wire with pliers in the baby changing toilet, an accomplice had passed her the weapon, she would not disclose anything else to the Police at that stage. Able said he awaited with interest a call from the Commissioner as to what the reason was behind the theatrical attempt to kill Tommy.

Able went back inside the hall, which had completely emptied out now, with just Roman and Father Leo and fhe three bodyguards. They packed up all the display items. Roman had got the second bullet out of the wood panelling behind his head and slipped it into his pocket unseen.

"That took me back a few years Able, bullets flying around the place, luckily I had nothing to fire back with, how is Tommy?"

"He should be fine it was a glancing shot to his upper arm, he would be in the Hospital in fifteen minutes, the shock will hurt more than the wound, once he is patched up. Father I don't want to trivialise what has just passed but as the vote was concluded, we may as well complete the count while we wait for our lift back, as you are the Ajudicator anyway."

The boxes were opened on the table in the centre of the platform and duly put into piles. There were 189 votes in all with verified ID. There were 94 votes in favour 95 against with one of the NO's with no ID, on the second count.

"A draw exclaimed Father Leo."

"I think not Father, the last vote into the NO's was the Assassin girl, I don't think we count her vote as valid, it is here on the top of the pile."

"Gina Visconti, probably fake, still the Carabinieri will want it, we can leave it with the one they left in his car outside. We can head for the Church and leave in five minutes, the chopper will be waiting for us, on the clearing by the Church, Father you can lock up till the morning, the Forensics will be here early tomorrow."

"Of course Mr. Able, will you let me know how Mr. Tommy is getting on?"

"Without a doubt Father, thank you for all your help, could I impose on you and ask for confirmation of the vote, on Church letterheading, as I am sure Mr. Beales will want to know, I look forward to seeing you soon in the very near future."

Tommy had stabilised, by the time Able arrived at the

Hospital, they had sedated him and told the family he was fine, with only a flesh wound, nothing a good nights rest would not cure and advised them all to head home and pick Tommy up next day at mid day. The helicopter dropped the Team back to the villa in five minutes. They had encountered no unwanted situations at the Villa through the day, but Able had them all maintain high alert for the next 24 hours.

As Tommy came round in the middle of the night, he was drowsy and in pain, pressing his alarm to get a top up on pain relief from the night Nurse. As she left and the top up kicked in he became drowsy again, as the Priest came in on his night round.

"How are you my son? you had a bad incident today, but you are in a good place now I think?"

"Yes Father, have you come to give me the Last Rites of Mother Church?"

"That is one of my purposes, when I attend my parish here in the Hospital, is there anything I can offer you my son? I will sit with you a while."

"Father its years since I sat with a man of the cloth, is the content of the Confessional still a sacrosanct secret, between the Confessor and the Layman?"

"Yes my son, you, me and the good Lord only."

"I do not recall the exact way to start."

"Don't worry my son, just talk to me in your own way, in your own time."

"Father it is many many years since my last Confession, now may be a good time for me to commit to a cleansing of my soul. I don't think I will be able to come back and tell you if God is merciful or not. I have done many things in my past that I am not proud of, many of them if I could go back I would change. The saying is You can't make an omelette without breaking eggs, I must be one of the top Chefs in the world."

"Take your time my son, what is it that troubles you so much?"

"I have to tell you Father, but it is something I swore to take with me to my grave and I may not see the morning, we should always say that to ourselves before going to sleep, so we do not waste any of our next day, if we wake up.

It is a situation I found myself in just after the War here in Italy, I went to see my family in Piandelagotti with my Father in Law, I was involved in a bad situation that developed into a man being shot dead, by myself, after Camillo and my Cousins and I were attacked. One of my Cousins worked in the village bakery, I made him take me with the body to the bakery, where we forced it into the oven and stoked it up to over 1000 degrees Centigrade. My cousin was due to start baking the bread for the village at 4am. so we needed the body out by 3am. to get it ready for the bread.

Any blood and bits left we missed would not matter as he also used to cook pigs, beef and sheep in the same oven, so he was used to cleaning it down with stones to get it ready for baking. I had to wait for the charred remains to cool down, then I drove them to the woods in an old carpet and dug a hole three metres deep, put the remains in, with one metre of stones on top of them and two metres of heavy earth on that, covering the surface with dead wood, leaves and branches.

Even though we were never held to account for it, I see his face every night before I go to sleep. Camillo and I returned to England and we never came back to the Village. I had killed many men in the War, but this was different, can God forgive such a sin Father?"

"Is there anything else you need to tell me my son?"

"It is enough for me Father, it is the worst crime I have committed in my life, I have done many more, but I can face my maker with those, what penance can I get to reduce my crime in Gods eyes?"

"It does not work like that my son, remember Christ begged his Father to forgive the Jews and Romans who tortured and killed him in front of his Mother, his mercy is infinite, it is not a balance sheet, I cannot give you a penance for the crime you committed.

I can absolve you in Gods eyes as you put it, by absolving your soul from the Mortal Sin you have committed, so you will not automatically go to hell when you die, part of your penance is the on going guilt you will carry to your grave with you. If you were a younger man I would plead with you to give yourself up to the Police so that mans family can find peace, but which path you choose is between your Soul and God, you have a family of your own and you will consider your position with them, in the meantime we will recite the Lords Prayer, after these words in Latin and you will translate.

"Ego te absolvo a peccatis tuis, in nomine Patris, et Filii, et Spiritus Sancti."

"I absolve you of your Sins in the name of the Father, the Son and the Holy Ghost.

Thank you Father, I will now join you in the Lords Prayer, which I remember word for word still."

"My son it was a difficult thing for you to do, you are an important man in your world, with untold riches won by endeavour and untold and unspeakable business practices, Kings and Presidents dine at your table, you have power of life and death ultimately over many people when you take decisions, which affect their lives. You have now become one of the luckiest men alive by pure chance and talking to me."

"How has that come to pass Father? through your absolution?"

"No my son, maybe in part, you have now come to learn one of the great meanings of life "What Does It Profit A Man If He Gains The Whole World But Suffers The Loss Of His Own Soul?" many great and wealthy men have gone before you, who have not had the chance you have, to repent before they meet their maker."

"Food for thought Father indeed, as you say, I feel I will sleep more soundly tonight, God be with you and thank you so very much for your counsel."

Next day at mid day Able, Max and Nikki went to pick Tommy up from the Hospital, he was in high spirits, if contemplative, he was discharged in one hour.

"Guys, really strange last night, I was dozing half sedated, the local Priest came in, visiting the sick, he sat with me for ages talking, I don't remember what about, when I mentioned him to the sister this morning, she said no Priest visited last night, it's not the local Priests visiting night, weird."

Able had news from the Commissioner confirming details about the woman who had tried to shoot Tommy. It appears she was a relative of Dino Lucarotti who had vanished after a trip to Piandelagotti, after the War looking for a person who he had a grudge with, he had got into an altercation with some men in the only bar in the village, pulled a gun threatening some locals, when he was stabbed and his accomplice got him into their car and they drove off back to Modena he was never seen again.

Dino's family were convinced the Bulgarelli's particularly Camillo were involved, but as he went back to England where he had emigrated to there was nothing they could do to follow it up. After all these years when Camillo's son was holding an Open Meeting in the old homeland it was too good an opportunity to finish the Vendetta and clear the stain on their family honour.

The Lucarotti family put an open contract out on Tommy's life, but as it was so close to home his Grand Daughter decided to take on the shot for herself as there were no takers on the Contract. Part of the problem for them was the Fee was only 30,000 Euro's, no Professionals would be interested.

The risk and reward were not worthwhile, she got into the meeting with fake ID and a family member got the gun to her through the toilet window, she took her shot, it was lucky she was carrying the baby. It will be a long time before she sees her baby again, she has been charged with attempted murder and an act of terrorism against a Foreign National.

Tommy wanted to see what he could do to reduce the

sentencing, the woman would inevitably receive, while still being a strong advocate for due process of Italian Law.

"I am thinking of her child and if we can help to change their mindset on this Vendetta business, it will be a good thing."

"Grandad are you nuts, she tried to kill you, she should pay to the fullest extent of the Law and anyway it will take years to get to sentencing, you know how long things take here."

"Able I haven't thanked you properly for pulling me out in time, it all happened so quickly after that it was all a blur."

"All in a days work sir, we got lucky, it could have been a different story if the shooter had been a Pro, in all the excitement I forgot to mention Father Leo did the count on the votes and you won by a vote, but a close win is still a win as they say."

They pulled in to the Villa and Michael came out to greet them "Dad thank God you are ok."

"Michael we need to pull in some favours on this one maybe go with a press release saying the woman belonged to an extremist "Save the Planet Group" or something similar, speak to our Lawyers first, see what they come up with, I want it finished with asap.

Michael, Max, Girls all of you I have an announcement to make at breakfast tomorrow everyone in the lounge by 10.00am. I will need to speak with you Able in my office about 11.00am. if that's ok?"

"Of course sir, see you in the morning, good night all."

After the events of the previous day the lights were all out early at the Villa and everybody slept soundly. At 10.00 am. precisely all the family and Roman were gathered in the lounge with their coffees, as Tommy came in. He got a coffee and told them all to sit down comfortably as he had some news for them all.

"Everyone I love is in this room, except my wife, I have come to a decision and there is no dissuading to be done from any of you, I am retiring from the business, as of this week end. I want Michael and Max as joint CEO's to continue running the business, as they see fit, I will be around for advice if anybody needs it.

Karena and Nikki will be joint Vice Presidents, Nikki for UK, Europe, Karena the Americas. Michael and Max will share responsibility for Asia between them.

My lawyers will distribute my Shares in the Company between you all in the most Tax efficient manner, I need to survive at least five more years to ensure you get the best value from them as far as UK Tax is concerned.

I have decided to let the development in Piandelagotti lie, excellent though your proposals are. My heart is not in it anymore, we will keep faith with Father Leo and deliver on the Church refurbishment and Marble Commemoration Monument to the fallen in both Wars.

Max I will speak with you in a minute on our own, Girls you are now ready to fly as high as you want in whatever field you desire you are both a credit to your Parents and your Nonna has tears in her eyes in heaven looking down this morning. I am tired and it`s not just the last few days or the operation, I have lost the desire to wake up before everybody else and tear up some old rule books and write new ones, I want peace more than anything else, except to see all of you every day for the rest of my life, which is impossible as you must all lead your own lives. I want to go fishing with Roman, sea fishing of course and we can re-tell old stories to one another till we fall asleep over a good bottle of wine, or vodka in his case. That's it guys it`s enough for one day eh? let`s get some breakfast."

"As it`s time for announcements I have one to make, I am getting engaged, I have been seeing someone for over a year now, he is Italian American, Michaelangelo Santini from Roma his parents have an Art Gallery in London and two in America he is coming to Pietrasanta to view some Sculptures for clients, I have invited him to stay so you can all meet him."

"Shocks all round, Kareena no more please, Darling, I am so

happy for you and I can`t wait to see him, Alexis, Tonia, Max and Nikki grabbed Karena in a group hug and the tears flowed freely."

"Able come in get a coffee grab a chair. I wanted a word with you because I have just given the family some news, basically I am retiring from the business as of this coming week end, the business will be shared between Michael, Max, Karena and Nikki, I want you to know, I hope you will stay in your position if you wish to continue with the family, if you want to make a move you will have a generous severance offer and if you require a reference, with my recommendation you will have no problem in finding a position you would enjoy, what do you say? I`m handing out shocks all round this morning it seems."

"Well sir, I did not see that coming, I like working for your family and I have been happy here since joining. I have a special person coming into my life right now and my moves will be dictated by what she decides to do in the near future, that's the best I can say at the moment `sir, it has been an honour to look after you all, thank you. I have scheduled another defensive driving afternoon for Miss Nikki, if that still fits with her schedule today?"

"Check with her Able, I`m sure she will enjoy it, as it will give her something else to concentrate on, rather than worrying about me, good luck see you later on."

"Come in Max sit down, I wanted a word on the side with you, after the news this morning I hope you understand?"

"Of course Dad, I don`t know which shocked me more, you retiring, dropping the project or Mike and me getting hold of the controls."

"Max the project was too big and grandiose, the vote from the locals as expected was virtually 50/50, it was a long uphill sell, not that you wouldn`t have won in the end, but your brother needs your help, he needs to spend time with you to get you up to speed, the project would have been a diversion. You will spend time on your recuperation and you and Alexis seem to be getting on well again.

I am only joking now but you could always revisit the project in a few years when I'm gone, or do a simpler scheme between you all. Changing the subject I have decided I want to be buried between your Mamma and Camillo in England when the time comes, not here in Italy, I have no preference Cremation or Burial whatever you guys think best between you,"

"You sound as though you are planning on going next week Dad?"

"Just some overdue housekeeping son, go on and spend some time in the sun with your wife, take her out for a meal tonight, enjoy her we are not here for long, make it count." Max shut the office door behind him.

"God Mike, Dad is very strange this morning, talking about where he wants to be buried and how, where is Nik?"

"Gone for another defensive drive with Able, I think the shooting shook him up and made him realize he won't live forever after all."

"He is adamant the Project is dead, for the foreseeable anyway."

"With him off the scene, we will all have our hands full, we need to get you up and running as soon as you are 100%."

"I'm up for it Mike I've got a lot of catching up to do."

Able pulled up at the bar in Viareggio and they sat under an umbrella outside with two cappuccino's. "Well your Grandfather knows how to catch everyone off guard and get their attention."

"What did he say?Abs."

"He told me the four of you were taking over the Company and he is retiring, this coming week end, The Project in the Village is dead, for now at least, if I want to leave the Family, he would give me a generous severance offer and a high recommendation to any prospective employers, if I choose to leave, you don't think he suspects about us do you?"

"How could he? anyway if he did, he was certainly teasing you, it would not phase him to come right out and ask you in front of me, believe you me, without a shadow of a doubt."

"What happens now with us?"

"Nothing is changed, we wait until he has retired officially and sorted the Executive positions in the Company, when that is all completed, I will tell him and my Mum and Dad about us. If there are any problems we will be in a stronger position than ever as I will be a Main Board Executive and Major Shareholder.

We can go our own way if that is what we have to do, now kiss me James, before another Italian beauty takes your eye. We had better stay out for a few hours and say we had a good day on the course, last one to get a double room at the Principe Hotel pays, come on big boy."

Next morning Maria went quietly upstairs to Tommy's room with his first coffee of the day, tapped gently on his door and entered, he was still asleep in bed she placed the coffee on his bedside table and quietly opened the heavy curtains to let the sun in, she went over to straighten his bedclothes and plump up his pillows.

"Buon Giorno Signor Tom, una bella giornata oggi, sta bene Lei?"

He did not reply she looked closely to see if he was still asleep and realised he was not breathing, he had died during the night.

As the family gathered round Tom's bed it hit them all at the same instant, now they were on their own, as Max said to Michael, while hugging him and kissing him on both cheeks.

"The King is Dead Long Live The King"

The End

If you enjoyed this book please tell your friends and do not miss the next book encompassing how the Family lives move on after Tommy, up to present time entitled.

"Able Trumans Covenant"

to be published in January 2021.

Printed in Great Britain
by Amazon